#1

6/23

# RAIN
# DOGS

## Also by Baron R. Birtcher

*Angels Fall*
*Ruby Tuesday*
*Roadhouse Blues*

# BARON R. BIRTCHER

# RAIN DOGS

THE PERMANENT PRESS
*Sag Harbor, NY 11963*

For information, address:
  The Permanent Press
  4170 Noyac Road
  Sag Harbor, NY 11963
  www.thepermanentpress.com

*Library of Congress Cataloging-in-Publication Data*

Birtcher, Baron R. –
  Rain dogs / Baron R. Birtcher.
      pages cm
  ISBN 978-1-57962-318-0
      1. Marijuana industry—Fiction.  2. Human trafficking—
  Mexico—Fiction.  3. Mexican-American Border Region—Fiction.
  I. Title.

PS3552.I7573R35 2013
813'.54—dc23                                    2013010632

Printed in the United States of America

*For Christina*

# ACKNOWLEDGMENTS

This book would never have been written if not for my wife, Christina, and her unwavering encouragement. The same goes for my daughter Britton, and my daughter Allegra, who read the early drafts, and made it fun for both of us. Aloha pau ole.

Very special thanks to my publishers and editors at Permanent Press, Martin and Judith Shepard. To Lon Kirschner for the terrific cover art. And to Joslyn Pine for her copyediting prowess.

And to Daniel, Bridget, Ellie, Matthew, Fireman Bob and his better half, Cher, Haole-Boy Jim and Haole-Girl Julie, and of course, Nolan & Diane, and everybody else at Quinn's (Almost by the Sea) in Kona, Hawaii. Thanks for saving me a seat.

Grateful thanks to Karen Huff for introducing me to Manny Lopez; and thank you, Manny for your time and input.

And finally, to Scott Hartigan.

These men lie in wait for their own blood,
They set a trap for their own lives.

—Proverbs 1:18

# Beginnings

I've heard it a thousand times.

The war on drugs was a failure.

The war on drugs was a failure?

Bullshit.

Speaking purely for myself, the war on drugs kicked my ass. Changed everything and everybody I knew.

And I've had a lot of time to think about it, recall it in every miniscule little detail. It seems like a long time ago now, so much has changed.

It started in 1976. America was celebrating its bicentennial, people decked out in red, white and blue everywhere you looked. Unless you looked where I was. T-shirts said VOTE in big fat letters, and Abby Hoffman was still on the lam. Eight track tapes were on the way out, and cassettes were on the way in. But all my friends still bought vinyl.

*Godfather II* was on every movie screen in the country, and a few months later, it was *Herbie, the Love Bug*. Deep Purple was reaching the top of their game, Humble Pie couldn't get arrested, and the Bee Gees were just a few months away from unleashing a shitstorm of disco that would ruin music for a decade. This was before guys wore pastel linen blazers with the sleeves rolled up, and herpes was the *good* news.

But it was coming.

A couple years earlier, some clown from Colombia shared a Federal prison cell with a hardcore recidivist druggie from Mexico, and with the extra time they shared between shankings in the shower and race riots in the yard, they managed to figure out a way to make a fortune. Cocaine had all but disappeared from the narco-landscape back in the forties, but as the flower children of the sixties began to show an interest in smoking, shooting, swallowing and snorting anything that would get them high, the drug seemed ripe for a comeback. Little did any of us know that the era of bell-bottoms, tie-dye and fringe were about to give way to Angel Flights and hairspray and mirror balls. And coke. Lots and lots of coke.

For guys like me, it was the beginning of a brave new, scary fucking world. See, at heart I'm a pacifist. That's why I liked my quiet little life growing weed up under the redwoods in Humboldt County, in northern California. I'd make a few bucks, and head back down to the southern part of the state in the off-season for a little sailing, surfing and unprotected sex. All of it paid for in cash.

But the Colombians changed everything. Flooded the Florida coast with so much blow that they had to move a fat chunk of their operation into Mexico or risk losing the whole enchilada, no pun intended, to the U.S. Feds. It was war, and they brought it with them. Everywhere they went.

I've had a few years to think about it all. Time to remember, to dwell, before I get out of here. I mean, I didn't get here by myself, did I?

So here it is, the best I can put together from what I knew then, and what I found out later. Of course, there's no way for me to know exactly what some of the people in this story actually said, but I sure as hell know what they did, so I think my version is pretty damn close to the way it all went down.

This is how it happened, how they brought their war to me.

PART ONE:

# On the Border

SEPTEMBER, 1976

# Chapter 1

Sonny Limon squinted at the luminous dial of his watch, shook his head, and whispered into the darkness of the desert night. "He's not coming." His knees throbbed with the dull ache of squatting motionless in the cover he'd carved from a stand of stones and dry brush.

"Keep it down."

Steve Devlin felt, more than saw, his partner turn away. The kid was edgy, easy to be when you're out in the arroyo, nothing but black everywhere you looked. Except for the dim flicker of lights a half-mile away, on the other side of the feeble wire fence that marked the near-imaginary boundary between Mexico and southern California.

Limon mumbled something that drifted off into the shadows.

"You got something to say, say it," Devlin rasped. He checked the toggle on his radio for the third time. Still switched off. God, he could use a cigarette, he thought. And a drink. The waiting was making him as squirrelly as his partner.

"This is getting old fast. I don't find this shit amusing anymore."

"Take it up with King Mike."

Limon shifted uncomfortably on his haunches. "King Mike can either pay up, or kiss my *gringo* ass."

Devlin smiled, stared out across the emptiness of the canyon. "Yeah, okay, Sonny. I'll be sure and have Raul pass that along."

"If the sonofabitch shows."

Devlin slid off a few feet to his left, careful to keep his cover inside the thick copse of dry bloodweed. His patience was wearing thin and he wanted some extra distance between them. Sonny had been partnered with Devlin from the beginning, though he had proved more useful for his facility with the Spanish language than as an ass-kicker. Still, it was a partnership that was not without its advantages to Steve Devlin. It came in handy being teamed with the youngster on the detail.

The Border Area Patrol Group—BAPG—had been ranging along the U.S.-Mexico border for almost a year, a tenuous collection of about two dozen cops and Border Patrol officers collected from towns all over the south end of the state. They had been selected from the general pool of candidates based primarily on their ability to physically pass as Mexican nationals. As an afterthought, some bright bulb figured out that it would be useful if they could also speak the language. At first the unit had been called the Tactical Illegal Immigration Team, tasked to deal with the growing incidence of violent crime along the swath of rocky soil that had become the most popular crossing point for illegals to enter into California. The name lasted about five minutes, since that's about how long it took for everybody on the Job to start referring to the team as TITS.

Since their rechristening as BAPG—now simply the Bag—they'd earned a reputation as the baddest motherfuckers in the valley: king-hell, old-school knuckle-busters who were running up significant numbers of arrests for drug smuggling, rape and even murder. They might smell like dust and sweat and piss and dog shit by the end of a tour, but you did not fuck with a Bagger. It was no longer considered an Embarrassment Assignment—they had become rock stars.

The Bag's AO—Area of Operation—was relatively small in real estate terms, a mean and ugly stretch of desert waste that represented the DMZ between the overwhelming poverty of Mexico and the golden promise of southern California. Teams of two or three officers would lay among the soapweed and saltbush, jagged stones and sulphurous dust, ostensibly supervised by a command post at the top of the ridgeline. Realistically, though, they were alone. Radio signals were unreliable here.

Even Steve Devlin, who considered himself to be among the most swinging of the Bag's swinging dicks, found most nights in the arroyo to be a combination of hours of boredom interspersed with moments of sphincter-clenching terror. Strange noises would roil up from the dry stream bed below and bounce themselves in eerie echoes up along the crenellated canyon walls. Anything could happen. And did. It was not unusual to come across a *pollo*—an illegal immigrant—left for dead in the dust, stabbed, beaten or brutally raped.

"You hearing that?" It was Limon again.

There was a brittle sound of snapping sticks, only more rhythmic and persistent. Both Devlin and Limon had come to know that the Coyotes would often lead their ragged groups of *pollos* through the darkness by gently clacking stones together.

"I hear it. Keep quiet."

Goddamn, if there weren't a million ways to die in this fucking hellhole.

The clicks were coming closer, on a trajectory that would bring the *pollos* directly in line with where the two cops had hidden themselves.

"It's him," Limon murmured.

"Maybe."

Devlin slid the pistol from the holster strapped to his ankle, and from the corner of his eye saw Limon lay the sawed-off 12-gauge across his haunches, a High Standard model ten.

"Just hang tight," Devlin said, and thumbed off the safety of his automatic.

⌁

GLORIA LOPEZ stood at the edge of a pale circle of light looking out across the dry, rocky swale of land that marked the farthest northern reach of her country. The orange ball of the sun was only beginning to slip behind the low hills, throwing the canyon into its first wash of shadow. Her ten-year-old daughter, Marisol, was still holding tight to her mother's skirt and following Gloria's gaze.

A cold shiver washed over Gloria as she turned back to the crowd that had gathered at the field. There were hundreds of them, sitting beside open fires, whispering, weeping, waiting. These people had slaved and hoarded and scrounged for years to amass the money they used to pay the Coyotes.

*"Estoy incomodo,"* Marisol complained, looking more frightened than discomforted. Like her mother, she wore three layers of clothing. Once they were well to the north, they could peel off the outer layer or two, allowing at least one set that might be presentable enough to wear when looking for work in America.

*"Comienzo ahora, solo Ingles,"* Gloria told her. "Only English now, *mi querida.*"

The girl dropped her eyes to the parched grass at her feet, scuffed at a loose patch of dirt. "How much longer?"

Her mother looked up into slender strands of clouds that were stained the color of pomegranate in the dying sun. "When it is dark," she said softly. "For now, maybe something to eat?"

Marisol showed her a shallow smile and took hold of her mother's hand as they crossed the field.

They had only just arrived at the tamale cart when three young men, none more than sixteen or so, approached from the near side of the clearing. They were followed by a sorrowful, mange-ridden dog, who eyed a nearby campfire in hopes of a cast-off scrap or two. The taller of the boys wore a multicolored scarf tied around his head. The other two were short and thin, but all three had the feral, hungry eyes she had seen among so many such men.

*"Vengan,"* the tall one said, gesturing to Gloria in the Mexican way, waggling four downward-pointing fingers.

Mother and daughter kept their eyes to the ground, hoping the boys would go away, but they only laughed. *"No tenga cuidado, Senora,"* he said. Don't worry. "I think you need a guide. *Tiene dinero?"*

*"No, pero gracias, Senor."*

"It is very dangerous. There are American policemen out there," he said, gesturing broadly toward the darkness beyond the fence. "They dress as *pollos,* and will beat you just for walking across their border. They are bad and dangerous men."

She had heard the rumor before, around the campfires and food carts. Still, she hadn't the money for a proper guide, if there was such a thing, let alone these three who looked to be more dangerous than the American police. She had already selected the spot for their crossing.

*"No tengo dinero. Pero gracias,"* Gloria said again. *"Muchas gracias."*

The tall one with the headband stared at her for long, agonizing seconds, made worse by the way his friends appraised young Marisol. Finally, with a shrug, he turned and walked toward another group of *pollos*, throwing one last glance over his shoulder as he went, his steel-capped tooth glinting in the yellow light.

---

SHE COULD STILL hear the stray laughter of children playing in the distance, and the faint murmur of radios coming from the squalid shacks that lined the trickle of filthy water that was the river at this time of year. But Gloria knew they were getting close, knew by the far-off clicks that they were heading in the right direction.

They had been walking for nearly three hours, sharp stones and broken glass already beginning to tear her shoes to pieces. And it was dark. Darker than she had ever known. A sky without moon or stars, and an absence of wind that magnified every sound and filled her with a dread that felt like it might do to her mind what the stones and glass were doing to her shoes. But this was the price, she told herself. This was for Marisol and her future. Their future.

Minutes later, picking through a thick patch of wild artichoke, thorns lacerating her hands, Gloria found what she had been looking for: a shallow metal culvert, partially obstructed by rocks and old tires. She knew this would lead to the large concrete drainage pipe that ran beneath the border, and she clutched her daughter's hand tight, squeezing firmly, hoping to convey a renewed sense of hope.

All at once, like a wave from a rancid sea, a dense, nauseating stench assaulted their noses and brought tears to their eyes.

Instinctively, Marisol bridled, tried to wrench away from her mother, but Gloria Lopez held firm, pulled her daughter close and whispered in her ear. "We are close, Marisol. America is at the other end. Think only of that. Before long, we will laugh about this. We will forget all the rest."

Gloria felt her daughter's grip loosen, a brief nod against her breast, and knew the girl was with her as she lowered her head and entered the concrete tunnel. Long minutes of crouching in the confines of the pipe, pressing forward slowly, slipping in unseen patches of greasy waste and excrement, finally brought them to the end of the blackness and into the relatively fresh air of the arroyo.

A small group of *pollos* that had preceded them gathered at the mouth of the tunnel, some retching noisily among the stray piles of garbage and broken glass. Gloria fought the rise of her own gorge as she hugged Marisol close again, and felt a peculiar combination of revulsion and reprieve.

But what little relief she was able to grasp lasted only a few seconds, the time that it took for three young men to emerge from among the shadows and brush. Two were armed with machetes, and one held a small revolver. The one with the gun wore a colorful scarf around his head, a steel-capped tooth flashing in the meager light.

⊙══◆══⊙

IT WAS APPROACHING nine P.M. as the moon showed itself beneath the clouds, where its dim glow reflected only briefly off the ribs of the sky before it slid behind the canyon's edge.

Steve Devlin and Sonny Limon trained their weapons at a spot in the darkness where they had last heard the telltale clack of stones. Pale moonlight threw a hint of their shadows into the scrub.

The first hot pinpricks of sweat popped on Sonny's forehead, a dryness on his lips and in his mouth, a sensation he'd felt almost every goddamned night for the last year out here in the *sacahuista* and jackrabbit shit with Devlin. He shot a quick glance to his right where Devlin held his ground, the black-matte barrel of his weapon aimed into the brush. Sonny didn't know if he felt better or worse when he saw the slick shine of perspiration gathering in the lines of Devlin's face.

They were both stooped low, maintaining what cover they could among the weeds, waiting out a silence so heavy it felt like a physical presence. Sonny swiveled his head toward Devlin, his shotgun drawing a slow arc across the night, a question inside his eyes. Devlin

- 19 -

nodded, licked his lips and stared into the emptiness, senses primed for any motion, his knuckles white on the grip of his automatic.

A sound like shuffling feet just a few feet away brought the sights of both cops' barrels onto a point, and Devlin gave the sign.

"*Adelante*, motherfucker!" Devlin said. "Get up outta there. Now!"

Sonny Limon sidestepped left, sighted down his sawed-off, as a solitary figure rose slowly from the dark. He made no move toward them, only stood in momentary silence before thumbing a Zippo lighter to life, touching it to the cigarette pressed between his lips.

The face was unfamiliar to them, glowing briefly behind the flame before receding again into a blank silhouette.

Limon shot forward, blinking hard against the sudden light and pressed the cut-down shotgun into the face of the smoking man. "Down! Now!"

The man with the cigarette stood unflinching, snapping the lighter shut as he removed the cigarette from his mouth.

Steve Devlin came out of a two-handed stance, sighted the smoking man's heart over the barrel of his automatic. His hands were steady, but his breathing was shallow, his mouth as dry as the dust on which he stood. "*Bajada*, asshole! *Descenso!*"

The man placed the cigarette between his lips again, slowly stretched his arms outward, about waist-high.

"Senor Devlin," he said, smiling as though they knew one another.

Limon moved quickly, jamming his shotgun squarely into the center of the man's forehead. "On your face, fucknuts."

The dark man shifted only slightly, locking eyes with the younger cop. "And you must be Senor Limon."

Tight red slacks rode low on his narrow hips, cinched with a wide leather belt. His shirt flapped loosely over a strap undershirt. A grin cut his narrow face and formed deep hollows beneath high cheekbones that spoke of the *Indio* blood he carried in his veins.

Devlin held his aim. "Where is Raul?"

"My brother thought it best that I meet you personally this time," he said, tobacco smoke rolling out over his heavily accented English. "I am Marco Zamora, the brother of Miguel."

Devlin lowered his gun. "You have any idea how close you were to having your *frijoles* blown away, *pendejo*?"

Limon took a step back, but kept the shotgun trained on the point of Marco Zamora's nose.

Zamora shrugged.

"Where's Raul?"

"As I said, Miguel thought it better that I meet you myself." He turned to face Sonny over the twin barrels of the sawed-off and smiled. "Do you mind putting that away?"

"Blow me," Limon spat, feeling the rush of adrenaline turn into a sour ball in his stomach.

"You're late, *amigo*," Devlin said. "Another few minutes, you'd be staring into the headlights of a Border Patrol Jeep."

"We need to talk," Zamora said.

He pursed his lips and whistled, like the trill of a night bird, and the darkness came alive. No fewer than two dozen *pollos* moved in from the bushes, gathering submissively behind Zamora, their faces betraying their fear of both Marco and the American police. Marco Zamora took another pull at his smoke, pointed to one of the men, gestured him closer and rattled off something to him in Spanish. "This one has something to show you."

Zamora turned to the others. "*Marcharse!* Go on, now," he ordered. Without a backward look, they disappeared into the night as though they had never been there at all.

The sole remaining *pollo* lowered his head, work-roughened fingers kneading the fabric of his tattered shirt. Zamora spoke to the man again, gruffly kicked his buttocks with the toe of his pointed boot.

"For God's sake—" Limon said, turning his eyes toward the rim of the canyon.

Zamora smiled patiently.

Devlin eyed him. "Just give us the money and go."

"It is not so simple, Senor Devlin. Miguel wishes me to show you—"

Devlin didn't let him finish. "Shut up."

"—the way we intend to bring—"

"I said shut the fuck up."

A sharp cry split the distance. Devlin's eyes caught Limon's. "You hearing that, Sonny?"

"Yeah. What was it?"

"Sounds like somebody screaming."

It came again, the reverberation of cold panic rising up from the dry wash, maybe fifty yards away.

"God*damn* it," Limon said. "Get our fucking money, Steve."

"Where the hell are you going?"

"All that racket . . . we're about to have two more teams up our asses, and this whole thing is gonna turn to smoke."

Devlin locked eyes with Marco Zamora, drawing comfort from the automatic at his side, squeezing the grip inside his damp fist. "This is bad for you, *cabron*," Devlin said. "Time's running out on this bullshit."

⊙══╪══⊙

SONNY LIMON took off in a half-run in the direction the screaming had come from, feeling his way through the night, zigzagging through the *chuparosa*, loose rocks and soil. He knew he had precious few minutes before he would be forced to try the radio, call in a sit-rep that would either bring the choppers or signal an all-clear. If the radio failed, as it so often did inside the canyon, he was screwed. The support team would be right on top of them all, Devlin and Zamora included. And *that* would be a very bad scene.

Cold sweat ran down between his shoulder blades and he felt his pulse quicken.

The screaming continued, female shrieks of animal panic and the more muted sounds of physical struggle. It came from the direction of the drainpipe down by the service road. He knew the place well, having spent interminable hours waiting at the dirty end for the streams of miserable bastards to pour out into the night. The team had staked it out so often the *pollos* had all but abandoned it to try their crossings out in the open. But tonight, of all nights, it had apparently come back to life.

He slowed to a crawl as he approached, the fetid odor of sewage reaching his nostrils as he moved through the dense underbrush. The last of the moonlight slid off the lip of the canyon, low clouds pressing down heavily as he pulled to the edge of the clearing. A young-looking Mexican held a group of *pollos* at the point of a machete. The group lay prone before him, bellies pressed into the hard ground. Their belongings lay in a pitiful heap beside them: church medals bearing the images of saints, large oval belt buckles, and an assortment of watches and coins that shone in the dim moonlight. A second man, his machete hanging loose at his side, had his hand cupped roughly over the face of a woman, watching with interest as a third forced himself between the legs of a young girl.

One of the bandits cried out as the woman bit into the meat of his hand, freeing her just enough to scream again, calling out a name. He slapped her face with his bloody palm. Then, upon seeing the mark he had left on her, went at her again, harder this time, excited by his own violence.

"You have to wait your turn, *vieja*." He laughed and pushed her face into the dirt.

Limon stepped into the clearing, his shotgun aimed squarely at the heart of the bandit who now hovered over the fallen woman, rearing back for a vicious kick to her ribs. "*No mas*," Limon shouted, his eyes flat.

The young man watching the *pollos* took off at a dead run, but the other two, either from shock or bravado, held their ground.

"Drop 'em *now*, goddamnit."

Sonny Limon could see the thoughts working fast behind their eyes. He could see they knew their advantage, separated as they were by several yards. The one with the young girl rolled quickly off her, a movement Limon caught in his peripheral vision, enough to notice the shine of the revolver being swung around on him. Instinctively, he squeezed the shotgun's trigger and opened a hole in the rapist's chest that knocked him into the dirt. Machete took one step toward Sonny, then gave it a second thought; he turned and ducked into the filthy opening of the concrete pipe. Limon started after the runaway thief, but didn't get far. The woman on the ground grabbed him suddenly, clutching his hand with such strength that Sonny knew he'd lost his shot at the last of the escaping bandits.

The *pollos* who had been spread-eagled on the ground disappeared in a cloud of dust, ready to take their chances with the American authorities, while the woman continued to kneel at Limon's feet. She was holding his free hand in both of hers, pulling it to her face and whispering something in a wet, mewling moan. A few feet away, the rapist was pulling himself in bloody circles, a viscous pink stream of saliva trailing across his cheek. His young victim wept quietly, three pairs of tangled pants still wrapped around her ankles, her face marbled with bruises.

◦━━✦━━◦

NO SOUND CARRIES so easily through the canyon as gunfire. Limon knew it was now only a matter of minutes before the choppers and support teams would work their way down into the arroyo only to discover his partner holding a fistful of dirty cash and Limon himself standing with three Mexican citizens, only one of whom hadn't been either raped or shot. This was rapidly becoming the monumental circle-jerk of all time. Sonny Limon knew the world was about to collapse around his head, and felt himself go numb.

Devlin broke into the clearing a few seconds later, the sound of rotor blades floating down from the hills to the north, but one look at his partner's face told Limon that things had already gone from bad to worse.

"The money?"

Steve Devlin answered with a vacant stare. He hadn't yet registered the man bleeding to death ten feet away.

"Did . . . you . . . get . . . the fucking . . . money?" Sonny asked slowly, his skin clammy with adrenaline burn-off.

The heavy thrum of rotor blades was growing nearer, probably no more than a minute before the harsh glare of the searchlight would pick them out and illuminate the scene like blue noon.

"I'm gonna fire my weapon," Devlin said.

Limon stood stock-still, his eyes empty and spooked.

"Sonny! I've got to fire my weapon. They're coming. This's gonna look ratshit you putting that guy down without me ever taking a shot."

Sonny shook his head slowly, inching further from reality. Devlin racked the action on his pistol and blew three quick rounds into the dust beside the dying rapist.

"We gotta get this square, Sonny. We were down here together—"

"Where's the bread, Devlin?"

"—there were three of them, two with machetes, and this piece of shit on the ground here has a pistol. He drew down on you and you shot him—"

"The money, Steve. Where's the money?" His voice was calm, nearly disembodied. The chopper's rotors were beginning to kick dust and tiny stones into the air.

"—the other two came at you, and you shot at them, but they took off."

"Yeah, I get it." Limon's tone was dead. "Where's the money?"

Steve Devlin pinned his partner with a look crowded with rage and fear. "There is no money, alright?"

The bandit on the ground was groaning, drowning in his own fluids, his lips smeared black with discharge from his lungs.

"You got blood on your hands," Limon said.

"I know."

Limon grabbed Steve Devlin's free hand, held it in front of Devlin's face. "I mean, you got *blood* on your fucking *hands*."

Devlin stared, as though seeing it for the first time. He moved to wipe the blood on his shirt, but Limon grabbed his wrist.

The helicopter passed overhead, white light cutting back and forth through the darkness not far from where they stood. They were almost out of time.

"Wipe it on *him*," Limon said, pointing to the dying Mexican whose chest was heaving in ragged spasms.

When the chopper finally found them, Steve Devlin was on his knees, heavy smudges of blood staining his forearms and face.

The woman named Gloria Lopez cradled her daughter to her bosom, whispering, crying, kissing the top of the girl's head.

"*Dios mio, me siento tanto,*" she repeated, over and over, until her voice was lost in a cloud of flying debris.

# Chapter 2

I was sitting in a metal lawn chair, grooving on the purple desert sky, and the spray of white stars that floated there. Frampton's new album was cranking on the eight-track, reverberating inside the silver, croaking, vibrating box that was my Airstream trailer, and I was thinking to myself how nicely things were working out for old Peter since he'd left The Pie.

I had flown down the day before. More accurately, I had been flown down by my friend, business partner and pilot, Colt Freeland on a mission of mercy that would bring a few keys of Mexican weed back to California where things had, predictably, gone somewhat dry. It seemed that every year, just before the late October Humboldt harvest, the local supply chain completely broke down. So I took the opportunity to make a quick downhill run from northern Cal to the tiny dirt runway not far from the private smuggler's cove here at Punta San Ramon, about four hundred klicks south of the border.

Technically, the Airstream belonged to my mother, but that's only because it would be hard to explain to the Feds how someone with no visible means of support could afford her. I'd learned some nifty ways to launder my money through the Christmas tree lots, firework stands, and Halloween pumpkin patches I had set up in my mom's name.

For years, she had been a housekeeper and seamstress for the local gentry in the Orange County beach town where I was raised. But when Dad finally took off for good, I kind of ran amok, selling pot to the kids whose parents my mom worked for. It was a lucrative business, a little too lucrative, and eventually I was forced to cop to the truth with my mother. Of course, that was *after* she found the fifteen grand I had stashed in the old typewriter case that sat on the floor beside the desk in my bedroom, as it had for I don't know how long. If my goddamn cousin hadn't come to borrow it during one of my trips up to Humboldt, she likely still wouldn't know. Well, that's probably bullshit, but it would have taken her a hell of a lot longer to find me out.

After the obligatory shouting, threatening, and tears, I managed to convince her that we could sort of work together. To her credit, it didn't take long for her to embrace the notion that working a few days a year in the holiday-tradition racket beat the hell out of waxing floors six days a week. Suffice it to say that it's nice to have a partner I can trust. Other than my buddy Colt Freeland, I mean, who is also totally cool.

But my trailer here in the middle of Nowhere, Mexico was a kind of busman's retreat for me. It was a bitchen little corner of a couple hundred acres of scrub that my Mexican connection and landlord, Eduardo Chacon, ran cattle on, among other things. As it turned out, I had no idea how many other things. But I'm getting ahead of myself.

So, like I said, I was grooving mightily on Frampton and the night sky when Eddie snuck up on me, like he always does. The locals call him El Brujo, but I called him Eddie, which he seemed to get a kick out of.

Early in our association he had scolded me when I had referred to him by his nickname.

"Do not call me by that name," he said. There was a sternness in his tone that, at the time, made me think that that was the last deal we would ever do.

"Everyone calls you that," I said, kind of defensively.

"I am aware of this, but I do not wish for you to do so."

"Okay."

His expression turned inward. "Do you know what it means? *Brujo*?"

"Like a wise man, right?"

"No. A *brujo* is a sorcerer, a witch." He shook his head and turned his eyes back on me. "A *brujo* is a man who should be feared."

"I meant no disrespect."

"I know," he smiled. "You are a polite and honorable young man."

"Thank you," I said, and stood silently; then, "What would you rather I call you?"

"Call me by my name: Eduardo."

"Eduardo," I said, testing it.

"Eduardo," he repeated. He smiled and extended his hand. We shook in the American way.

He was slight and sinewy, but solid as granite wrapped in dried leather. His brown eyes still danced behind the heavy folds of his eyelids, an effect that was sometimes enhanced by tequila or a hand-rolled smoke. He dressed in simple work clothes, but always neat to a point that hinted at his meticulousness. His hair was mostly black, only beginning to show his age at the temples, but the goatee he wore was gray and smartly trimmed.

Eduardo had lived his entire life alone, though it was the way he had chosen for himself. The people of the region held him in awe, and more than a little fear. The truth was, Eduardo Chacon was a very heavy cat, but from that moment on, he was always cool with me and treated me with honesty and respect. As time went on, he ceased to be Eduardo. For me, and me alone, his name was Eddie.

"You're stoned," he said from out of the dark, startling the hell out of me. It was the first I had seen of him since I had arrived the day before, which wasn't altogether unusual.

"I am."

The old man drew a bottle of cloudy liquid from the rough-hewn cotton knapsack he carried across his shoulder and offered it to me. I knew it was *sotol*, his homemade cactus moonshine, a nasty imitation of tequila.

"Hard liquor has never been my drug of choice, Eddie," I said, and lifted the smoldering roach to my lips. "But thanks."

He shrugged eloquently, uncorked the bottle and helped himself.

"How'd you know I was here?" I asked. His hacienda was at the far end of the ranch, near the cove, so I knew it wasn't the music blaring from the trailer that had sold me out.

Eduardo smiled, brushed a hand across the gray stubble of his beard. "You walk across a beach, no matter how briefly, you leave prints, no?"

"Right on," I said, took a final toke off the bone, snuffed it, and stuck the bitter end in my shirt pocket.

He nodded, silently mouthing the words I had just said. Eddie had a fascination for American slang. He looked up at the cloudless sky, and had another pull of *sotol.* "You are hiding this time, or here on business?" he asked me finally.

"A little of both."

"Ah," he said. "*Policia?*"

"No. A woman."

"Right on." The way he said it made me laugh. Eddie took no offense.

"Here's a head-trip for you, Eddie: the more you ignore a woman, the more she seems to want you."

"This is quite true."

"All my friends are strangers, man. That's the way I like it, you know, that's the way it needs to be. So I tried to be cool with her. I mean tried to mind my own business. But the more I minded it, the more she did, too. Goddamn, you just can't win sometimes."

"This is often the way with women."

"You know what I say? If it flies, floats or fucks: rent it."

Eddie tipped back another hit of his moonshine and wiped his wet lips with the back of his hand. "But you have a boat *and* a plane."

"Even so, it's a good saying."

"You are right, my friend. It is a good saying," he smiled. "Tell me about the business. Buying or selling?"

"It's still September, Eddie," I reminded him. "I'm buying."

He pursed his lips, then nodded sagely.

"I need a hundred pounds."

"You have run out?" he joked.

"It's another month 'til harvest time and things are running a little dry. You know. It's like this every year." My growing season ran from early April to the end of October—Fools to Ghouls, we called it. Eddie's season was the opposite. It worked out well for both of us, kept us in business all year long when we wanted to be.

"*Si,*" he said. "But I am afraid it will be more expensive than the last time. Things are changing down here."

"You're harshing my mellow, Eddie."

"I'm sorry, but it is true. La Plaza is getting hungrier now."

Drug trafficking in Mexico is controlled from the top, operated by key government agencies and important officials among the elite. When you got right down to it, the drug lords themselves, in spite of their wealth and violence, were really only pawns, the front men and the fall guys when things turned to shit.

And it's not just the work of a few bad-apple politicians and cops, but a time-honored system of organized corruption that runs from Mexico City all the way through the state capitals—from *El Presidente* to the local police. The concessions are granted along administrative and jurisdictional lines, and are generally known as La Plaza.

A Plaza holder not only had the obligation to generate money for his protectors, but to use his intelligence-gathering abilities to finger independent players who tried to avoid paying the necessary tribute. It was a no-fucking-around arrangement.

"How much more?" I asked.

"Twenty dollars per pound."

"That's an extra two grand, Eddie."

"I think Miguel has something new going on."

I don't know how much I was really supposed to know, but I knew who he was talking about. Miguel Zamora. 'El Rey Miguel.' King Mike, the Plaza holder in the region. I'd never met him, and never wanted to. But in my business, it's a good idea to keep track of who's who.

"I guess I've got no choice, *amigo*. There's about fifty people waiting for this load back home."

"Business," he sighed. "It is not simple, like the old days."

I laughed. "The old days didn't sound so simple, either."

Eduardo pulled the other lawn chair up beside me, sat down and pulled a pack of Marlboros from his pocket and shook one out. "Perhaps not, but the guns are bigger now. And the men are more impulsive."

Eduardo was born around 1915, he had told me once. When Prohibition began in the States, his father, Andres, found it profitable to sell jugs of his moonshine *sotol* to bootleggers in the mountains of Aldama and smuggle them on the backs of mules all the way down to Nogales on the Mexican side, where Americans could cross the border to make their purchases. The trip took more than a week, moving only at night, through dark canyons and deep valleys to avoid detection. It was always a difficult trek, but Eduardo had learned from an early age the nature of the smuggler's trade.

The Americans across the border in Arizona would pay generously, so Eduardo's father eventually found a way to sell directly to them, bypassing the Sonoran Plaza and the Mexican rangers—*Forestales*—that roamed the hills.

Eduardo told me once of being with his father and Macario Vazquez, one of the most famous of the *sotol* smugglers, when they shot it out with *Forstales* in the mountains outside Carichic. No one was killed, and the men got through with their cargo, but the Mexican rangers learned to fear the two men. It was there that Eduardo learned that violence could be used to his advantage.

His story always ended there and I never pressed him on it. We had built our relationship as much on what we told one another as what we withheld.

Now, in the warm desert night, Eddie lit his cigarette. He sucked down a lungful and exhaled a blue cloud as he continued.

"These men are different, my *amigo*, and I fear that King Mike is changing with the times."

That didn't sound good.

"Colombians?" I asked.

"*Sí*," the old man nodded. "*Coca.*"

"Shit."

I'd heard that the cocaine cartels had begun to make moves on some of the other growers up in my neck of the woods, too. They were bringing a previously unheard-of level of violence with them into the pot business, which had always been pretty damned benign. Up in Humboldt we growers were fighting tooth-and-nail to keep them the hell out, but it was beginning to get hairy out there.

"You're full of bright news tonight, Eddie."

He took another drag of his smoke and chased it with a mouthful of his moonshine. "Bad news does not get better with age," he said.

"No," I agreed. "This world turns to shit in a hell of a hurry, once it starts turning."

# CHAPTER 3

Three miles inland from the ranch of Eduardo Chacon stood a two-story hacienda, built in the traditional style, surrounding a central courtyard complete with swimming pool and swim-up bar, and enough lush landscape and open space to host the region's most lavish fiestas. The hacienda and its grounds occupied less than four acres of the ten thousand that Miguel Zamora had named "Rancho Tronada"—Thunderstorm Ranch—for this is how he truly saw himself: a terrible and unpredictable force of nature in this, that is to say *his*, corner of Mexico. And it truly was his now, he had earned it. He was El Rey Miguel in this part of the country. King Michael.

Miguel stood before the enormous picture window in his study, gazing out across the garden. He was lost in thought, watching the last of the purple twilight blanch from the sky, when he heard the knock at the heavy wooden door.

"Come," he ordered.

It swung open slowly.

"Senor Zamora?" the girl said, as Miguel turned away from the sunset. "Your guests are here."

"Thank you, Susana," he said. "Please give me a moment, then see them in."

She nodded deferentially and began to back away.

"And Susana? Please tell my wife to be ready by ten. We'll sit for dinner in an hour."

*"Si, Senor."*

He withdrew the tiny brown vial from the pocket of his vest and unscrewed the lid in a practiced, one-handed manner. Miguel was well-tailored and elegantly dressed, taller than the average Mexican and broad across the shoulders. He always enjoyed dressing well in the evenings after a hard day on the *rancho*. Fortunately, this was one of the many traits people had come to expect of El Rey. Tonight he had adopted the style of a cattle baron: dark blue western shirt, black vest, large oval belt buckle, black slacks and ostrich-skin boots. He tilted his face to the tiny spoon he held between his fingers and felt the pinpoints of sweet tingling behind his eyes. He checked his reflection in the mirror above the bar and brushed away any stray white crystals with the back of his hand. He drew a deep, satisfied breath and examined his image one last time before turning away.

A moment later, Susana returned. She held the ornately carved wood door for three men as they entered Miguel's study. As the last of them passed through, she pulled it silently shut and proceeded upstairs to deliver Miguel's message to the Senora.

As much as Miguel liked to believe his success was his own, there was no way he could deny that these men were the gatekeepers. These were the representatives of La Plaza, and this meeting part of a monthly ritual. A ritual he had come to despise.

"Good evening, General," Miguel said. He offered a callused hand to the heavyset, balding General Diego Acosta. This was the man who oversaw the Directorate of Federal Security—the DFS—in this part of Mexico. As was the general's custom, he arrived for the meeting in full-dress uniform: gleaming black boots and matching Sam Browne, epaulettes resplendent with brass stars, and row upon row of colorful ribbons pinned above the pocket of his tunic.

"Senor Zamora." The General nodded, his tone curt enough to instantly rekindle the pique Miguel always felt in the man's presence. Miguel's annoyance was made all the worse when the General casually tossed his uniform cap on Miguel's long leather sofa, as though it were his own.

"You are well?" Miguel inquired.

The General's lips twitched involuntarily beneath his heavy mustache. "Well enough, considering the troubles since Tlatelolco."

The DFS was the internal political police force that had been assembled at the end of World War II, and was part of the powerful Interior Government Ministry. For decades, the agency had kept a close eye on anyone holding political views that might be at odds with Mexico's one-party system. More recently, the Directorate had put down a number of makeshift guerrilla movements that had sprung up all over the country, resulting in the "disappearance" of nearly two thousand villagers. The General had the ear of *El Presidente*'s brother, and it was a near certainty that some percentage of the bribe money Miguel passed to General Acosta found its way into the hands of the President himself.

"Please make yourself at home, General," Miguel said with just the right dash of sarcasm, he thought, and turned toward the other two. "Comandante Rivera, Senor Cruz, welcome to you both, as well. A drink?"

Miguel went to the bar at the far corner of his office and prepared a snifter of brandy for each of his three guests. He watched Rivera and Cruz settle into the plush club chairs that faced the sofa on which the General now reclined. When he returned with their aperitifs, Miguel Zamora took a seat at the far end of the table, casually crossed his legs and raised his crystal glass in a toast. "Continued success, gentlemen."

"Continued success," Rivera echoed. "By the way, where is your brother tonight?"

"Marco is up north in Tijuana, Comandante, working on a new bit of business."

Comandante Rivera was the regional head of the Federal Judicial Police. He was a man of medium build, dark skin, and heavy-lidded vulpine eyes. Unlike the General, Rivera was not in uniform, but dressed casually in a powder blue leisure suit, a white shirt open at the collar, with a heavy gold chain about his neck. Also unlike the General, he was a man accustomed to independent action, rarely troubling himself with the bothersome details of chains-of-command.

"Tijuana?"

"Attending to the *pollos*, Comandante."

"Ah, *si*," he said, shifting slightly in his seat. "Let me begin by saying that you have been very generous to the people of this town. The soccer field, the new school—"

"A successful man is wise to share with the people who help to make him so," Miguel cut in, believing he knew what was troubling the Comandante. He was reminding him with as much subtlety as possible that not only were they all in this business together, but of the importance of Miguel's own hand in the growing prosperity of La Plaza.

The third man in the room, Dario Cruz, nodded knowingly. As always, he was falling comfortably into the role of the Governor's proxy, toady and possible spy. As the regional Governor's First Assistant, Dario Cruz had had a great deal of practice at it. His manner was solicitous and overly formal, his gestures often betraying an effeminacy that he tried hard to keep at bay. Cruz was dressed in a business suit, his pencil-thin mustache trimmed immaculately, and his hair swept back and held in place with pungent pomade, parted on one side with the precision of a razor.

The General made no attempt to disguise his distaste for the Governor's aide, nor did Comandante Rivera so much as cast a glance in his direction.

"Nevertheless," Rivera continued, his small-caliber eyes roaming Miguel's face as he spoke. "I believe we need to address the complaints of the local police."

Miguel shrugged. "They stole three of my trucks."

"So you march them at gunpoint all the way to Las Posas, and leave them tied up to the trees?"

"It is important to maintain proper authority," Miguel smiled. "As you yourself know, Comandante."

They shared a brief laugh at the irony in his statement. Miguel Zamora not only ran the marijuana in the region, but was responsible for at least one-third of the four-by-four and pickup truck thefts reported at the Tijuana border. Miguel often traded the stolen vehicles for small quantities of cocaine—outside the purview of La Plaza—which he skimmed for himself. These men had never inquired as to the disposition of the vehicles, and he, of course, never mentioned them either.

Comandante Rivera sipped at his brandy and eyed Miguel over the rim. "In this situation, we will need to allow the police to save face."

"And how much will this cost me?"

"It is not only that, Miguel," Dario Cruz cut in. "The Americans are beginning to bring pressure on the Governor. Their DEA desires to constrict the flow of narcotics that come in from our country."

Miguel waved it away. "I am already in the process of strengthening my contacts with the American police, Senor Cruz."

Miguel despised Cruz and his vaguely effeminate manner. He looked again at the clothing the younger man wore: a creamy leather jacket, slightly belled mocha slacks, and cowboy boots with stitching that matched the jacket. This 'man' was most surely a *maricon*.

"What else would the Governor suggest I do? I assume the money I give you each month finds its way to his pockets."

It was the General's turn to speak. "We think we need to make a show—to 'capture' a shipment of *coca* on this side of the border. Or, perhaps, take down one of your fields of marijuana."

Miguel Zamora tried not to allow his astonishment to reach his eyes. "The *coca* is out of the question. The Colombians pay almost fifteen hundred a kilo for its protection."

"It is only money, Miguel," the General said.

"Our relationship with them is new, and probably more profitable than the *pollos* and marijuana combined. But it is about more than money. It is a relationship that requires trust," Miguel answered. "Things could begin to go very badly if they were to suspect what you are suggesting. Very badly for everyone involved."

The room was dense with silence for a long moment. It was the Governor's man who finally broke it. "I take your point."

"That leaves a field of marijuana as our only remaining solution," Comandante Rivera offered. "We can give you a little notice, and you will be able to harvest what you can. The rest we will need to capture and burn."

"And make a show of it for the news cameras," Cruz added. "An elegant solution, actually. For all of us."

"I beg to disagree," Miguel Zamora said, pointedly. "The *mota* belongs to me."

General Acosta raised his eyebrows, deep furrows reached all the way to the point where his baldness began. "A cost of doing business, no?"

Miguel looked at his watch, allowing his fury at their collective arrogance to subside before he spoke. "My wife will be down for dinner shortly," he said, and went to a locked drawer in his desk. He returned to the table with three small velvet bags and handed one to each man.

Predictably, Miguel thought, the *maricon* was the first to examine the contents. He upended the bag into his palm and arched his brow. "I don't think I understand," Cruz said.

"What would you say if I told you I have a new way of washing the cash that comes from our business?"

Comandante Rivera and the General leaned toward him, their sudden interest undisguised in their eyes.

"Go on," Rivera said.

"I believe that the demand for cocaine moving into the United States will be so great that we will have trouble moving the cash and distributing it among La Plaza without drawing notice. If that happens, even the American DEA will be able to discover and follow the flow of our money." Miguel let that sink in for a moment before he went on. "What you are holding in your hands are uncut diamonds. I admit they are not beautiful to the eye in their raw state, but they are absolutely untraceable, and their value is not limited as currency can be."

Miguel could read in the General's expression that he clearly liked the idea of receiving their *mordida* in the form of raw stones; so much easier to skim a little extra for himself before passing it up the line. And impossible to trace.

"We'll need details, of course," Dario Cruz said.

Fool, General Acosta thought. You overstepped again. How does the Governor tolerate you? As a negotiator, Senor Cruz, you are nothing more than an impatient child.

"I can't do that, for reasons that I am sure are obvious," Miguel smiled slyly. "But I will tell you this: for the past several years there has been a bloody civil war in the Belgian Congo. One of that country's most important resources is diamonds. The diamond trade is very strictly regulated there, but the ones you hold in your hands have been smuggled out undetected and unaccounted for. I have a relationship with a trusted friend who, in turn, has contacts with Irish mercenaries fighting in the Belgian conflict. These Irishmen have problems in their own country, as you know. So, they exchange these diamonds for the currency we have collected from the sale of our product and use it to acquire guns for their own Irish war. We receive a modestly discounted value in stones, and the flow of the transaction remains invisible to outsiders."

Comandante Rivera nodded his understanding. "And much easier to transport than large quantities of cash."

"Exactly," Miguel said. He dearly wished he could simply reach into his pocket for another small dose of the *blanca*. This needed to come to a swift conclusion. "Any final questions?"

"How can we be sure that we will be able to liquidate the stones?"

Miguel Zamora absently rubbed his nose with the back of his hand. "These are diamonds," he smiled. "They do not diminish in value. By comparison with the fluctuating value of currency, you may find that you will prefer to keep them intact."

Comandante Rivera was already a step ahead, his imagination dancing with the notion of numbered accounts in Switzerland, Antwerp, or the Canary Islands.

The General, too, was lost in thought. Such a plan would indeed make Miguel very popular with the Colombians. Not to mention with the other men in this room. He had had his concerns about Zamora's recent unpredictability, but El Rey Miguel, despite his obviously growing fondness for the *coca*, the General conceded, could be a very clever man.

⌐━━━◦

YOLANDA ZAMORA regarded her reflected image as she removed the earrings she had worn for dinner, for the first time seeing both of her parents in the face that looked back from the mirror. Her father was there in the regret and disillusionment that haunted her deep brown eyes; her mother in the proud, patrician set of her jaw line. Yolanda had always been a beautiful woman, petite yet powerful; but tonight she felt every one of her thirty-three years staring back at her unkindly.

Dinner had been another unpleasant affair, as they increasingly were when the men came to meet with her husband. Lately, nearly every occasion was made all the worse by his use of cocaine. Without thinking, Yolanda crossed her arms, covering her naked breasts as she recalled sitting across from the General, with his slippery eyes. The Pig. That's how she thought of him. In fact, she had nicknames for all three of the visitors: the Pig, the Peacock, and the Fairy. It almost made her smile. Almost.

"Come to bed," Miguel called to her from the bedroom.

"*Momentito*," she answered softly, not yet willing to break away from the solitude she enjoyed in her private dressing room. She believed Miguel still loved her, she wanted to believe it, anyway; that he still appreciated her soft caramel-colored skin, the deep amber of her eyes, and the firmness of breasts not yet having given in to their battle against gravity. But to all things belonged a beginning and an end. Of all things, her parents had taught her that.

Turning away from the mirror, Yolanda removed a gauzy night-gown from the closet hook and slid it on. She gently smoothed the fabric as she switched off the light and entered the bedroom.

Miguel was lying in bed, arms folded behind his head and staring past the open window into the night. The weather was beginning to change. A cool desert breeze pushed gently at the draperies and cast ghostlike shadows upon the wall.

She slid beneath the sheets beside him, but he continued staring as if he hadn't noticed.

"Miguel?" she whispered.

He shook his head slowly. "They're going to kill me."

"Nobody's going to kill El Rey Miguel."

She turned onto her side and watched his fingers twitch with un-spent energy on the comforter. "They are killing me already. *Vampiros*. They like to watch me bleed."

Yolanda reached out, intending to stroke him softly, as she used to, but he pulled away as if scalded by her touch. He tossed the linens aside, rose naked from the bed and paced like a cat. Even in the dim light of the room, she could see that his eyes shone restlessly, vibrating with liquor and white powder.

"I don't understand, Miguel. Those men are bound to you by the money you give them."

He brushed his fingers through the thick black hair that now hung loose across his forehead. "You're right," he said bitterly. "You don't understand."

Yolanda watched him pace, perspiration shining on his bare skin. She swore that she could feel the heat of his growing rage. This was no longer the Miguel she had fallen in love with. This was his shadow, made empty and cruel by the demands of the business he had built, and the *coca* that stole him from her bed more and more often. He had changed with the coming of the Colombians, had taken up an unhealthy interest in guns, even arming himself when he was inside their own hacienda.

Yolanda had met him while attending college in Mexico City. She was the refined and beautiful daughter of a successful banker, Miguel the favorite son of a struggling cattle rancher. She had thought Miguel handsome in the way of a man who is raised outdoors and works long hours with his hands. He thought she was strong and stunningly attractive.

Before they were married, Miguel petitioned her father in the traditional way and won his respect in spite of a father's natural concerns about Miguel's family and financial condition. It was a loan from Yolanda's father that started Miguel's roofing business. It didn't take long to see that he was a natural businessman. Two years later, he had repaid Yolanda's father in full, and convinced him to finance a new venture: raising cattle on the Baja peninsula. With those funds, Miguel purchased the first thousand acres of Rancho Tronada.

As the cattle operation grew, Miguel acquired more acreage and continued to prosper. Though his success multiplied, stories began to filter back to Yolanda about the nature of her husband's business dealings. It was then that she discovered that Miguel had repaid her father's first business loan with money he had made by selling marijuana, shrewdly exploiting the privacy and excellent surveillance points that his empty rooftops provided.

Now, the cattle were just a front for the hundreds of acres of *mota* Miguel planted and grew, and her father had become an unwitting participant in laundering his money. Shortly after that discovery, there had been an ugly confrontation between the two men.

There would never be another.

Her father had never been the same afterward.

The man had been trapped, inextricably and irreversibly entwined with Miguel as a result of a father's love for his daughter. It was no longer possible to discern who bore more shame, Yolanda or her father.

Back in their room, Miguel had finally stopped pacing. He stared out across the balcony into the starlit sky.

"I'm going out," he announced.

"It's nearly one o'clock in the morning. I want you to stay."

He spun away from the window and faced her.

"You want," he spat. "You *want*? Those three errand boys from La Plaza—they *want* too. Everyone *wants* from El Rey Miguel. Nothing is ever enough. I build a school for the village; I dig wells for their fresh water; I build a bridge across the river . . ."

He stalled for a moment, saw her clutching a pillow tight to her breasts. He could see she was afraid, but he couldn't gain control of himself. He found himself disgusted by her display of weakness.

"I pay those pigs a hundred thousand dollars a month—a hundred thousand dollars a *month*—for La Plaza, so that you can live like a princess. And still you *want*."

Yolanda turned on her side, rolling away from his rage. She heard his heavy footfalls as he approached the closet and dressed.

There was nothing to be done now. She was a prisoner of his life, of his increasingly erratic hours, late nights—and the nights when he wouldn't come home at all. And when finally he did, he would be wearing the same clothes he had worn when he left the house, stinking of liquor and smoke, the smell of strange women on his fingers.

For Miguel, this was his right, what he risked everything for. It did not matter how big the castle, as long as he was king of it. Here he was lord.

He slammed the bedroom door behind him as he left.

Yolanda lay in silence, her throat dry and aching from tears that wouldn't come. This was what her life had become. A life at the edge of the thunderstorm.

# CHAPTER 4

Sonny Limon was trying to pinpoint just exactly when his life had turned to shit.

Eight years as a cop, and all he had to show for it was maybe half the pension he might get to keep when his soon-to-be ex-wife was finished eviscerating him. Assuming, of course, that he didn't get bounced before he reached retirement in another twenty-two years (the bad news), or end up stacking time in a Federal pen for going on the pad for the Mexicans (the worse news). The scheme had sounded so solid at first. Doing business the old-fashioned way with a veteran like Devlin seemed like a no-brainer, which it pretty much was. A fistful of cash a couple times a week for looking the other way while a sorry batch of wetbacks walked into San Diego without harassment. What the hell, right? They were coming in by the thousands every week, through a border crossing that was more like a kitchen strainer than a barrier.

But the flow of King Mike's *pollos* kept growing while his cash seemed to have stopped coming altogether. Which created a big problem for Sonny Limon. Once you're in, you're in. Like he had once read somewhere: Culpability isn't currency, and sharing it doesn't reduce a person's portion. In fact, it seemed just the opposite. Culpability grew like a tumor and Sonny Limon had begun to feel it consuming him.

Steve Devlin was another story entirely. Sonny could only guess at the graft a balls-to-the-wall player like Devlin had immersed himself in during his twenty-odd years on the Job. Nothing seemed to get to him. Not much, anyway. But even Devlin would have to admit that it felt like the wheels were coming off this thing with Miguel Zamora. Last night had been off the rails.

He tipped back the watery remnants of his first Jack and Coke of the day and tried to wrap his head around the trajectory of his life.

At first, he and Maddie had been in love. Animal, passionate, sex-on-the-kitchen-counter love. Maddie was pretty and petite, and she thought Sonny was both charming and manly in that dark-eyed, quiet, cop kind of way he had. He wasn't all that big, but he was muscular. She liked that he was compact, strong without being intimidating. But his assignment with BAPG—the Bag—had changed him. The silences grew longer, his absences more frequent, until they finally became a nightly thing.

Maddie came from a family who knew how to argue, knew how to yell, and expected the same in return. But Sonny was cut from a different cloth. He would wait her out silently, watching her with his innocent eyes, which only ended up making her so angry she had to throw something. Which she did, barely missing his head with a leaded-glass vase.

He slapped her.

And that was it.

At the end, he hadn't even attempted an excuse when she came down to the dive bar the Baggers used as a clubhouse at the end of a tour, and found him pressed into a corner with his hands full of another woman's tits.

"Jesus Christ," he said to no one as he took his empty glass to the bar.

Vern the bartender caught Sonny's eye in the clouded mirror. "Must be a hell of a leak in your glass there, Sonny."

Sonny's smile didn't reach his eyes. "Big hole in the top."

He slid back into the booth he shared with no one.

THERE'S A REASON cops keep to themselves.

Most of their careers are spent trying to defend the invisible border that separates regular, hard-working human beings from the army of recidivists and meltdowns who daily roam the streets acting on their most sadistic and self-destructive fantasies. Cops see only the worst of people, and over time, only the worst in people. Their silence is born as much from self-preservation as from an inability to put their everyday experiences into words that even a normal civilian could comprehend.

Steve Devlin pushed through the swinging doors of the Bison Room, a dingy, red Naugahyde cop joint at the edge of the old Gaslamp district that smelled indistinctly of a combination of mold, stale smoke and spilled beer. Sonny Limon was still there, having moved to a stool at the far end of the rail, trying to avoid his own reflection in the mirror behind the bar. The empties lined up in front of him looked like a glassware display.

Homicide dicks from the PD and the Sheriff's office had taken nearly three hours investigating the scene out on the arroyo, which of course had been blown to smithereens by the chopper. So, in the end, the only things that were going to carry any weight were the statements Devlin, Limon, and Gloria Lopez gave them. That had taken the better part of the day. Now, the remains of the evening were theirs to waste as they saw fit. The Department would take some time, as they always did, dotting i's and crossing t's on the shooting.

Sonny finally looked up and saw Devlin strut in with his clean white bell-bottom slacks and matching jacket, a gold medallion hanging in the V of his open-neck sport shirt. He had gone home to shower and shave, before coming in to regale the regular constellation of cop groupies with another heroic tale from the Mexican DMZ. Sonny had washed off in the Department locker room. He had thrown on a pair of his least ratty jeans, a T-shirt and windbreaker, and looked like he'd come out on the losing end of an all-night card game at the Moose Lodge. Sonny wanted no part of the groupie bullshit. Not after last night. Maybe not ever again. Back when he was a rookie, he had bought into the whole trip, but he'd come home once too often to a sleeping wife, with his head full of spiders and smelling like strange pussy. Now he lived in the back of a camper in the station house parking lot.

"Jesus," he said again to nobody.

Steve Devlin worked his way through the growing crowd, waving casually when he made eye contact with a fellow cop. He swung a leg over the stool beside his partner and waited until he finally raised his head.

"You got that look, Sonny."

Limon went back to staring into his glass. "What look?"

"Like you got one foot out the door."

He caught a blast of Devlin's cologne and shook his head. "Just another fucked-up night in Crap Central."

"Feeling sorry for yourself?"

"This is no kind of job for a real person."

Devlin waved down the bartender, ordered a Jim Beam, rocks, like always. Twenty-some years on, three ex-wives, alimony, and he still drank his cocktails off the top shelf.

"It's alright to feel sorry for the *pollos*, Sonny. Just don't feel sorry for anybody else. Their whole system is fucked. Ours isn't." Devlin sucked down a mouthful of Beam. His face was deeply lined, tired and showing his age, but something else glowed behind his eyes. "Let's get a table. We gotta talk."

Sonny didn't argue, just picked up his glass and followed his partner to a booth at the back. Devlin waited until Sonny took a seat, leaned across the table, and spoke in a voice barely audible over the ball game on the TV above the bar.

"History Lesson, son: these people are coming across whether we collect a little vig or not, and it's never gonna stop. You want to know why?"

"No." Sonny couldn't bring himself to give a shit when his partner went into speech-making mode. Devlin was talking to himself anyway. "Why?"

"'Cause there ain't an Anglo kid in this whole damned state who knows how a lawnmower works."

"I don't give a rat's ass about that." Sonny lifted his glassy eyes. "We're getting hosed here, Steve. Fucking Miguel is hanging us out."

"Don't count on it."

"What are you talking about?"

"Leverage."

Sonny laughed. "I'd like a hit of whatever you've been smoking."

"He needs us."

"Really." Sonny's voice dripped with sarcasm.

Devlin shrugged, his eyes narrowing with the hint of a smile.

"What the hell happened out there, Steve?"

"Marco was trying to get the little *pollo* to show me something. Show *us* something before you had to take off."

"If it wasn't a big wad of cash money, I don't think I care."

"It wasn't. And you do."

"Stop fucking around, Steve. I'm in this up to my nuts, here. What happened? How'd you get blood all over your hands?"

Devlin took a furtive look around the room, smiled casually. "The *pollo* was carrying contraband. Inside him. It wasn't coming out and we were running out of time."

"*Inside* him?"

"He couldn't seem to puke it up, so Marco gutted him."

"Fuck. Me."

Devlin tossed back what was left of his drink and settled back into his seat. "He gets these poor bastards to swallow balloon loads of shit before he sends them across. They get caught, we just send 'em back home in an Immigration Service van."

"No harm, no foul. And Miguel hasn't lost a cent," Sonny nodded.

"That's why we're making the big bucks, son." Devlin pulled a pack of Tareytons from his shirt pocket, lit one and blew twin flumes of smoke from his nostrils. "Clever bastard," he said. He tilted the Jim Beam to his lips, savoring the warm sting on his tongue.

Sonny wasn't sure if his partner was talking about himself or King Mike.

"This is fucked up," Sonny said. "It isn't just about looking the other way while a few *pollos* move across the border anymore."

"Game's changing," Devlin said. "There's something new in the air. It's 1976, the Bi-fucking-Centennial. Seems like five minutes ago it was the Summer of Love. No love out there anymore, though, is there?"

Sonny watched Devlin sweep the room again with his heavily lidded eyes, but said nothing.

"You have any idea what these guys pull down? Guys like King Mike?" Devlin asked.

"I don't give a shit about—"

"Six, seven million a year, I figure. Maybe more. That's just for running *pollos*. King Mike ups the ante with this balloon shit, there's something serious going down. It's score time, son. Time to find you a real estate agent and start looking for a beach house."

"It's a deal-changer, man," he said. "I don't know."

"In for a penny, in for a pound, Sonny."

"That's the voice of experience? That's your twenty years talking?"

"That's reality, *amigo*."

"It seems like murder to me."

"That's not something you want to be saying again. Get it out of your head." Devlin looked up as three women came through the door. He'd banged one of them a week ago. She was a little on the meaty side, but she had a fantastic rack and was a grateful lay. He started sliding out of the booth to make for the women as they approached the bar.

Sonny grabbed his elbow. "Listen, Steve—"

"Get it outta your head," Devlin said again. "Everybody dies."

He turned and headed toward the bar, leaving Sonny to pick at the scratches in the tabletop with his thumbnail.

⊶⊷

SONNY LIMON was sitting on the curb, pulling at the neck of a pint bottle wrapped in a paper bag, when Devlin came outside an hour later. He leaned against the base of one of the old-fashioned gas lamps that still lined the street, bathed in a pool of flickering yellow light.

"Pull up a sidewalk," Sonny said.

"I don't think so."

"Right. The white suit."

Devlin shook another cigarette from the pack, lit it, pulled the smoke deep in his lungs. He could feel the end of Indian summer in the night air, the first hint of the coming chill, and looked across the street into the dark, empty storefronts that had, one by one, shuttered their doors and moved uptown. He didn't like change, but the atmosphere was full of it. The Beam hadn't done its job tonight, either. There was no warm glow, only a fatigue deep in his marrow that made him feel like an anachronism.

Sonny Limon set the bottle on the curb beside him, startling Devlin as it tipped into the gutter and rolled its glassy echo up the empty street.

"It wasn't always like this," Sonny said, his tone formless and indistinct.

"Was that a question?"

"I don't know."

Devlin looked at his partner's face, at the hair that fell across his eyes, the heavy shadow on his unshaven face. "Go home, Sonny."

"What for?"

"You need to snap out of it," Devlin said. He cast a glance up the sidewalk and exhaled a stream of blue smoke. "I can't have you getting spooky on me."

"Don't worry about it."

"You are beginning to seriously piss me off, kid. I need you to pull your shit together, and pull it together *now*. There's something I didn't tell you: Miguel wants a meet. That means both of us."

"I don't know if I want to do this."

A hot flush ran up the back of Devlin's neck. "Okay, Sonny, here's History Lesson Part Two. You listening?"

Sonny stared at an empty place between his feet.

"Here it is. You wanna know why I'm with the Bag? They sent me over from the Intelligence Unit after my cover got burned working a bust. I thought it was fucked at the time, but then I figured I wasn't gonna get rich in IU anyway. Let me tell you something. My first patrol unit? I watched my training officer palm more cash than a televangelist. He was shaking down anybody with a pulse. He was taking kickbacks from an ambulance company for dispatching them to car accidents, from funeral homes for referring DOAs. I never saw anything like it, but I never said a word. I wasn't in it, but it opened my eyes. Wide. I got three ex-wives, you follow me?"

Limon picked up the empty bottle from the gutter, turned it over in his hands. Devlin didn't wait for an answer.

"So, what's your story, Sonny? I'll tell you: at first it was a little extra cash. And you liked it. Then a little more. And you liked that even better. So did your old lady. Shit, she liked it so much, she walked off with it. And your house. And your car. You like living in a camper? Taking a shower at the Squad every day, walking across the parking lot in your bathrobe and skivvies with your little toothbrush in your hand?"

"Fuck you."

Devlin hawked a bitter laugh. "Nobody's innocent here. Look around. That dead *pollo* isn't on you. I watched that poor asshole get filleted like a tuna last night. Thing is, I don't have time to cry about it."

"It isn't the same. And my shoot was a fucking public service."

"And Marco Zamora is the loose-cannon brother of a Mexican *padrino*. This shit's gonna keep going on whether you're in it or not."

Sonny felt like he was going to puke, leaned his face into his open hands and sighed.

"IA's going to make you take some downtime while they process the shoot," Devlin said. "I'll do the same."

"It wasn't your shoot, Steve."

"I'll take a Stress Leave—I was right there with you, right? We won't have to burn any vacation time. Nice and clean. We'll truck on down to Mexi, see what King Mike's got on his mind. We don't like what we hear, we boogie. End of discussion. What's he gonna do, shoot us? Nobody's gonna take down a pair of American cops."

Devlin held his gaze.

Limon looked away. "I'm already feeling like I got eyeballs drilling holes in my back," he said. The booze was making everything worse, making him paranoid and sick, popping beads of sticky sweat on his lip. He had nowhere to go, and all he wanted was to remain in the darkness of the street. He had come to hate daylight. Light was discovery. Light was accusation. He wanted to be in the dark.

"Fuck 'em, *amigo*. Everybody skims. Everybody."

"I don't like it," Sonny said.

"You don't like what?"

"The meet. The Mexico thing. I don't like it."

"It's too late for that, son. These fuckers don't bluff."

Sonny felt his stomach turn over.

Devlin tossed his cigarette butt into the street, launching a shower of glowing ash. He crouched down, put his hand on his partner's shoulder and made Sonny look him in the eye. "I want you to be clear on one thing."

"Let's hear it."

"In a world full of poseurs, the fearless will rule. And I am the most fearless motherfucker in the valley."

# CHAPTER 5

The afternoon was hot and clear, a pale wind blowing down the *bajada*. Eddie and I waited at a spot not far from my trailer, in a dusty clearing cut into the scrub that served as his runway.

Eduardo leaned against the bed of his beaten-down Ford pickup, digging in his ear with his ignition key. He watched me wrap duct tape around the last of the two-pound bricks of marijuana I'd bought from him, then helped me stuff them inside a pair of old Army duffel bags. It was nicely dried, red-haired *mota*, and would fetch a pretty good profit in spite of the extra dough being soaked from me by La Plaza. At nearly three thousand bucks a pound, my partner Colt Freeland and I would clear nearly a hundred-K. And we hadn't even brought in our own crop yet.

Like I said, it was a good business.

But it was nothing compared to what those Colombian fuckers were beginning to pull down with their goddamn coke. Pot had been a nice quiet little thing for a long time. Now those South American assholes were stirring up interest among the Feds that was going to get unhealthy for everybody. Nobody I knew was happy about it.

Colt was flying the old Cessna down from northern California and I wasn't expecting him for another half-hour, so Eduardo and I cracked a couple cold cans of Tecate and enjoyed the afternoon sunshine. We had the barrels of avgas, filters, and pumps ready for refueling, and there was nothing else to be done before Colt and I motored out of there for the run back to the bootlegged dirt strip we used up in Humboldt County, a few miles outside Garberville.

I turned the conversation to the subject of Miguel Zamora. "You okay with King Mike?"

"I'm an old man. I have no interest in cocaine. I pay La Plaza what it asks for the *mota*, and they leave me alone."

I could tell by the way he answered that there was more to it than that, but if Eduardo wanted to tell me about it, he would. Outside of that, it was none of my business. Still, I cared for the guy and didn't want to see things change.

"This is a fine ranch, Eddie," I told him. "You have everything squared away? You know, legally?"

"I do not know what you mean."

"I'm talking about official paperwork," I said. "Title. To prove this place is yours."

He made a sour face, waved the thought away like a bad smell. "No man owns his property. Those kinds of rights are a fiction."

"What's that supposed to mean?"

"They have always been nothing more than a figment of the imagination. This land belonged to my father, and now it belongs to me. Why would anyone be put off by a little scrap of paper that says somebody owns something."

"It's what separates us from the dogs," I said.

"I'm afraid you are mistaken. A man owns something only until someone else takes it away from him."

I smiled. "What, you're a communist now, Eddie?"

A shrug. "A realist."

"A Mexican."

"You say that like an insult," he said.

"I say it like I think you're full of shit. Look around you. Look at this spread. You're telling me you wouldn't fight someone who came to take it from you?"

"I did not say that. I would cut the balls off someone who tried to take it away from me. I was only saying that it is arrogant and naïve to believe that a piece of paper can substitute for the fire in the belly that makes one protect one's property."

I had to admit he was trying my patience, which he often did intentionally, for his own amusement.

"*Sí*," he answered. "I have the papers."

"You're giving me a headache, Eddie."

"Because you know I am saying the truth."

⊙━✠━⊙

COLT FREELAND landed the twin-engine Cessna 337 on the short strip of dry-packed clay, turned and taxied close to where Eduardo and I waited with the fuel. He revved one final time, let the engines flame out and climbed down from the cockpit.

As always, he wore aviator shades, a crumpled straw cowboy hat, faded jeans and a snap-button western shirt. Colt is a big guy for a pilot, a couple inches taller than me, maybe six-three, and solidly built. He grew up in a small town out in east Texas whose name I never remember, but he generally keeps his drawl under control most of the time—except when he's drunk, or stoned, or trying to charm some unsuspecting filly out of her Dittos jeans.

Colt grinned around the well-chewed swizzle stick he always had pressed between his teeth, and tossed the old man and me a quick salute as he headed toward the tumbleweeds to take a leak. When he had finished his business, I pulled a Tecate from the ice chest, tossed it to him, then went to work hand-cranking the fuel pumps while Eduardo manned the nozzle. The quality of the fuel was sometimes an issue, so it had become our routine to take our time and slowly filter it through several layers of cheesecloth as it went into the tank.

"I swear to God, I think my bladder's getting smaller," Colt said to me as I worked the lever at the top of the drum.

"But you can still land that sonofabitch in a parking stall."

Colt smiled. "Fuckin' A, hoss."

Eduardo and I finished refueling and checked the engine fluids while Colt stretched his legs. When we were finished, I walked back to the pickup, grabbed the two duffels we'd stuffed with weed, and tossed them inside the plane.

The heat shimmer on the valley floor reflected the nacreous glow of the late afternoon sky. The light was thickening into brilliant hues of ochre and crimson, the peaks in the distance fading and growing dim and as blue as smoke.

"Better roll before it gets any darker," I said at last.

Eduardo nodded. "You take care, my friend."

He came to me then, took me in his arms for an *embrazo* and kissed both of my cheeks, in the Mexican way. He inclined his head toward the east, in the direction of Miguel Zamora's neighboring ranch and spoke quietly in my ear. "These things that are happening here could become much worse before they get better. Do not be careless, and I will see you again in a few months."

"Don't worry about me, Eddie. I've been trying pretty hard to get through the rest of my life without being any more of an asshole than I've already been."

❦

WHEN I FIRST got home from 'Nam in '72, I'll admit it took a while to pull my shit back together. But after a few months of nothing but drinking and smoking, fucking and fighting, I decided to get back in the game and restart my business in earnest. The real money, I figured, depended on moving myself up the food chain. Dealing weed had been fine, but I needed to be my own supplier. Besides, I'd spent enough time in the jungle to learn all I needed about plants. Marijuana in particular. The way I looked at it was, there are two kinds of dudes in this business: the ones who need a forklift and the ones who don't.

My first partner was a guy named Python, a name that had nothing to do with snakes. He didn't last long. This business isn't too forgiving, and you've got to keep your act together at all times. Flakes and fortune hunters are as common as a beer belly at a tractor pull, and the ones who don't get their asses blown away end up in jail. That was not going to be me. Life's too short to watch the sun set through cyclone fence and razor wire. Long story short, Python's dead now. Died of excessive nymphettes on one of his many trips to Tlatepango.

Colt Freeland is something else entirely.

I had first met him while we were both on a few days' R&R in Bangkok, Thailand. I was tossing dice at a table at the rear of the sweltering, smoke-filled back room of the Singha Bar in the seedy Patpong district. I'd thrown a hard eight three times in a row, my stack of chips growing heavy along the rail. The crowd was three deep along the box, squeezing in to get their bets down as I palmed the dice for another pass.

Somebody pushed a drink my way as I caught the eye of a thick-set Air Force second-louie who had laid heavy on eight, the hard way, and taken his winnings off the table. I was shaking the bones, trying to ignore all the eyeballs boring into my skull, when the big Air Force sonofabitch came at me across the green felt and planted a memorable right cross on my cheekbone. Hot white lights were popping inside my head and my knees were beginning to go weak when the pair of scary looking Thai pit bosses rushed in to break up the scuffle. They grabbed the pair of us, and dragged us roughly out the door. But not before I scooped up a handful of my chips and stuffed them in my pocket.

I landed hard in the dirty street, my ears still ringing and my face on fire. The Air Force dude was not far behind me. The Thai meatheads yelled something at us in a language neither of us spoke, but we understood the message clearly enough. They slammed the door behind them and left us sitting on the pavement in an alley rank with the odors of rotting garbage and all manner of kitchen midden and bodily waste.

"You're a hell of a good cheater," the big pilot smiled. "For regular Army."

"How's that?" I said, a bad imitation of puzzlement moving across my throbbing face.

We stood and brushed the crap off ourselves as best we could. My uniform trousers had torn at the knee, but I didn't really give a damn. We walked toward the flashing lights and noise coming in from the boulevard.

"I never saw anybody palm dice like that in my life. Very nice. You made me about five hundred bucks."

"So what's with the sucker-punch?"

"I saw the bosses watching you. You were about two rolls away from getting yourself beaten into coma."

I looked back down the alley, at the door we'd been tossed out of. Red and blue neon throbbed against the storefront windows and the filthy pools of water that had collected in the street.

I lifted myself up on unsteady legs and gingerly touched my face.

"Buy you a beer?" he offered.

We dodged street beggars, hustlers and pickpockets through late-night crowds of wanderers until we located the cowboy-themed dive that Colt had been looking for. We wound up drinking the sun back into the smoky, gray Bangkok sky.

So after my first partner, Python, slabbed-out, I called Colt. And that was that. We've been partners ever since.

❦

WE WERE ABOUT an hour outside of McKinleyville, at the heart of the Emerald Triangle where the northern California counties of Humboldt, Mendocino and Trinity meet, when I turned away from the window. We were flying low and fast, just over the treeline, and just under the radar. Colt was staring at me out of the corner of his eye.

"Where the hell'd you wander off to?"

"Memory Lane," I said, and changed the subject. "How's the new kid working out?"

We had just lost one of the guys that helped us out with the farming, and had to replace him on short notice. I like to run a lean operation, but the last month of the growing season is not the time to come up shorthanded. I've always had a rule that you don't work with anybody you haven't known for at least five years—cuts down on the risk of Porcine Infiltration, if you know what I mean—and Colt had enlisted an acquaintance of his from back in the old neighborhood. Actually, it was a friend of Colt's younger brother, but they'd all gone to the same high school. I hadn't met the guy yet.

"So, the new kid?" I asked again.

Colt lingered a few seconds longer before answering. "He's okay."

"'Okay'? That's inspiring."

"Young. Short attention span. Prone to boredom."

Not good when you're sharing a tent in the middle of the freaking redwoods thirty miles from the nearest town.

"Plays guitar, though," he said. "You'll love this: he spent the last year giving the rich kiddies lessons—forty dollars an hour; he'd spend about twenty minutes with them, then split the bread fifty-fifty with

- 56 -

the students as long as they wouldn't rat him out to Mommy. Now he says he wants to be an actor."

"Took the parents a year to figure out it was taking three times as long as it should for the little bastards to learn guitar?"

"The guy's not the brightest dude I ever met, man. You tell him to go dig a hole, you better go out later and tell him to stop."

Terrific.

PART TWO:

# Too Many Hands

# CHAPTER 6

Yolanda awoke to a cacophony of heavy trucks and men shouting orders to one another in the driveway beneath her window.

She had finally fallen asleep only a few hours earlier, exhausted and angry, Miguel still absent from their bed. The smell of her husband's cologne still lingered on his pillow, and she felt a renewed flush of self-disgust when she realized that she had drifted to his side of the bed during her fitful sleep. The night had been torpid and hot; now the air that slithered across the balcony and into her open window promised a day even more unpleasant than the last.

Yolanda pulled the sheets to one side and arose, the dim throb of a headache developing behind her eyes. She plucked a dressing gown from the footboard, tied its waistband around her as she pushed aside the curtain and gazed below. A gang of men was loading picks, shovels and other hand tools into the beds of a half-dozen pickup trucks. She watched as they hurriedly completed their tasks, then drove off. Before long, the small convoy was lost inside the fine white cloud of a tractor as it led them through the open gate and onto the *caliche* road that cut its way through the low mesquite and greasewood bushes beyond the wire fence. When the last of them was out of view, she turned away from the window, padding barefooted to her bathroom to perform her morning rituals. Never once would she allow her eyes to stray across the cold glare of the vanity mirror.

When she had finally finished dressing, Yolanda called for lunch on the intercom—the only device that remotely resembled a telephone in the entire hacienda. In Miguel's deepening paranoia, he refused to allow a permanent line to be installed, placing and receiving his calls, instead, from the payphones affixed to the walls of the telephone exchange office in the village of El Salto, miles away. She sat alone at the small table on her terrace, waiting in the arid heat of midmorning for the passage of another day, watching far-off clouds of dust from the trucks of her husband's *pistoleros* dissipating into the sun-bleached dome of sky.

⊂━┿━⊃

MIGUEL RETURNED TO Rancho Tronada sometime after lunch, parking his truck in the middle of the narrow gravel turnaround between the main house and the two-story outbuilding that served as garage, service shed, and living quarters for Miguel's brother, Marco, and some of the other men.

Yolanda listened, following the echoed stutter of boot heels on ceramic tile as he passed through the kitchen and into the foyer. He stared at her wordlessly when he finally found her, seated beside a window in the enormous living room. She made no attempt to look up from the book she held in her lap, watching him instead in her peripheral vision. He was wearing the same dark jeans and western shirt he had thrown on before he stormed out the night before, only now they were as deeply wrinkled as the lines that had lately begun to form at the corners of his eyes.

"I am back," Miguel said at last.

His choice of words cut her. He had not said he was 'home.' Yolanda couldn't remember when she had last heard him use that word, and a familiar, uninvited thought passed through her again. *Perhaps if there would have been children.*

She nodded, turning another unread page of her book. "I see."

He moved into the living room, making no attempt to touch or kiss his wife. Instead he sat heavily on the sofa and watched as she pretended to read. There would be no apology, there never was. But she found herself grateful, at least, for the distance between them: where she couldn't pick up his scent, where he had been, who he had been with, and what they had been doing together.

Miguel had known from the beginning that he never wanted a family. Everything he had ever seen told him that children were at the heart of disappointment and regret. Besides, in his line of work,

- 61 -

they could be used as leverage against him. He never told her of his vasectomy, secretly relishing the irony of the early years of their marriage, when Yolanda had wanted continually to try to conceive. He loved that she arranged for sex with him at all hours of the day and night, while he knew full well that none of their efforts would ever be rewarded with a child. There was another thing, too. He loved the knowledge that if she were ever unfaithful to him, he would know instantly, doubtlessly, if she were ever to become pregnant.

Yolanda felt the weight of his eyes on her, but refused to satisfy him with her attention. She heard the rhythmic tick of his fingers tapping the leather of his boots as he examined her, the slow intake of breath as he prepared to speak.

"Do you remember when I first met you, Yolanda?" His tone was uncharacteristically low, emotionless.

She gave no answer, only looked across at him, at his sleep-deprived face, the glaze of his red-rimmed eyes.

"You were dancing," he continued. "You used to love to dance . . ."

Yolanda watched him brush a tremorous hand through a thick tuft of disheveled hair, sighing deeply. He uncrossed his legs and turned his attention to the floor between his boots.

". . . *salsa, merengue, la cumbia.*"

"Yes," she said. "I did."

"I took you to the fiestas and the nightclubs." Miguel gazed past her, or through her, and into the broad, white light of the afternoon. "Do you remember how the men would watch you when you danced?"

The silence was long, but she said nothing. Outside, a clutch of small gray birds landed in the shade and cried softly to one another.

"I watched you, also," he said at last. "But the others, they watched for different reasons. And the dancing, it became something else, too. It changed. In a way, it began as only dancing to you, but I saw it become something different."

"I would still love to dance."

"No." Miguel's eyes were empty, focused on whatever it was he saw beyond the panes of glass. "It has been damaged by what others made it seem."

"I don't understand why you're saying these things."

His mind came back from wherever it had been, and his eyes found her face. She watched him slip a pack of Winstons from his shirt pocket, tap one out, and reach for the lighter on the table—a short-barreled pistol that emitted flames instead of bullets. Miguel kept his eyes locked on hers as he turned it over in his palms, passing it from one hand to the other, then slowly trained it on a place between her breasts and pulled the trigger. It snapped to life with a click that made Yolanda start. A teardrop of pale yellow fire licked out from the barrel.

"You lied to me from the very beginning. You were never who you pretended to be," she told him.

"You saw and heard what you chose to."

"The sin is yours alone, Miguel. I trusted you." She turned toward the window and watched the tiny gray birds flit away, disappearing into the distance. "My father trusted you."

"It is the nature of things that they change, whether we like it or not," he said. He lit his cigarette. "And sometimes they take our plans along with them."

She brought her fingers to her throat, stroking the smooth string of pearls Miguel had given her so long ago. Pearls, he had told her then, are the only precious gems born of pain, suffering and death. She had been a fool then, and had found it romantic. All the nights they had spent tangled up in one another like rain inside the clouds. Gone.

A vague haze of cigarette smoke hovered high among the rafters, trapped in thin shafts of light that filtered through the gaps in the room's heavy drapes. She watched it float there, blue-gray and motionless, as she listened to Miguel cross the foyer and close the door softly behind him.

"YOU'LL BE FINISHED on time?"

"It is a very big hole, Senor Zamora."

Miguel stood beside Esteban, his burly ranch foreman. Miguel put a hand on his shoulder and squeezed. "But you will be finished by morning, yes?"

The big man tossed a sidelong glance into the widening cavity the others were carving from the crusty soil. "*Si*," he answered. A brown swirl of dust roiled away on the blistering wind as the tractor dumped another load.

Miguel watched him closely, recognized something behind the man's eyes. "I know what you are thinking, Esteban."

The foreman was startled. "I am thinking nothing, *Padrino*."

"I don't believe you." Miguel Zamora's lips parted in a sanguine smile. "I believe you are thinking, 'What is to go into such a large hole?'"

"It is not my business, Senor."

"This is true," Miguel agreed. "But I promise you will find out soon. Just be certain it is ready by morning."

"It will be ready."

"*Esta bien*, Esteban." Miguel tucked an American twenty dollar bill into the man's pocket. "I will be back in the morning to see it."

The foreman watched El Rey Miguel climb into his truck and rev the engine. Esteban gave a tentative wave as his boss accelerated in a tight half-circle, throwing a tail of sand and stone into the air.

⌀━✦━⌀

MIGUEL PUSHED HIS way down the rutted road that followed a line of low foothills, skidding, and honking impatiently when one of his cattle grazed into his path. He rolled up the window, cranked the AC on full, and turned up the volume on the *Norteno* music—the Mexican country and western—he liked so much.

From his window, he watched the shapes of *ocotillo* and desert thorn blur by, only to disappear again in the white cloud that filled his rearview mirror. He pushed the truck hard, across wide arroyos and dry washes, past deadly looking bayonet plants and tumbles of fallen rock. Miguel lost himself in the sensation of speed and the jangle of music that blared from his speakers until he finally arrived at his destination. He slammed on his brakes and waited for the dust to blow away before he got out.

This was where it had happened, already a year ago.

Miguel had been driving back from a drop one night—one of the first deliveries from the Colombians—when he had been ambushed by three gunmen. They had been standing in the back of a stake-bed truck, lying in wait for the yellow slashes of headlights from the Bronco that carried Miguel and his cousin Lucas.

The night was so dark that Lucas never even saw a shadow of the vehicle in which his killers stood, only the muzzle flashes as they opened fire on the Bronco. They cut loose with a spray of automatic weapons fire that first blew out one of the Bronco's front tires, then worked their way up along its grill. The radiator exploded in a gush of steam as the bullets pelted the hood and into the windshield. Shattered glass and brass shell casings flew into the night, disappearing into the blackness.

Miguel ducked below the dash and waited for the Bronco to skid to a halt. When it did, he looked over to see that his cousin Lucas had been hit twice: once in the throat, and once in the head. The bullet had torn a gaping chunk from Lucas' skull, leaving a splatter of blood and greasy ooze on the window behind him.

Miguel snaked out of the side door. In one hand he held an assault rifle, and a .45 pistol was tucked into the small of his back. He took up a position behind the ruined vehicle, and waited them out.

When the *judiciales* arrived the next day, they found only Miguel's shot-up Bronco and the bodies of three dead men: Agustin Moreno and his two sons, who, not long before, had held La Plaza. It was rumored that a set of tire tracks had been found near the body of Agustin Moreno. A heavy truck had driven over his body again and again before finally crushing his head like an oversized grapefruit. Someone had also used a sharpened machete on Agustin's son, cleanly severing his skull just above his brow. The second son was found several yards away, shot point blank through the eye.

Miguel had the shot-up Bronco placed on concrete blocks at the intersection where he had just parked his pickup truck. He smiled, now, at the monument he had erected to memorialize his rise to supremacy. To Miguel, however, it was also a reminder that the Pig, the Peacock and the *Maricon* were never, ever, to be trusted. La Plaza belonged to him only as long as he held the power, the money, and the will to kill for it. Most importantly, the money.

He made a hasty sign of the cross out of respect for his cousin Lucas, and turned onto the road that led back to the hacienda.

ROLANDO, THE HOUSEMAN, was loading the last of her suitcases into the rear of the station wagon when Miguel returned. Yolanda watched from the kitchen window as her husband slammed the door of his truck and strode across the gravel drive to confront the man. She couldn't hear what was being said, but didn't need to when she saw the look on the old man's face. Her hands began to tremble as Rolando began removing the suitcases and brought them back into the house.

Yolanda crossed to the butler's pantry, removed a bottle of rum from the cabinet and returned to the kitchen. She was standing over the chopping block, macerating a sprig of mint with a heavy cleaver when Miguel pushed through the door.

"If I had come back a half-hour later, you would have been gone," he said. "You would leave without saying goodbye?"

She gripped the knife with both hands, willing them to stop shaking, not wanting to reward him with her fear. "I am going to Mexico City."

"Ah," he nodded, a thin smile on his lips. "Mexico City." He took a step toward the kitchen counter and picked up the glass Yolanda had filled. Miguel sniffed at it. "*Mojitos,*" he said dryly. "I thought we agreed you would quit."

Yolanda looked up into his face, both terror and rage glowing behind her eyes. "I need to leave, Miguel."

"Our house, or our marriage?"

"Does it matter?"

"I suppose not."

Her heart skipped a beat, and she was immediately ashamed of her body's betrayal. "Then let me go."

"This is not the time, Yolanda," he said. "I need you here."

"You don't need me, you need my father."

Miguel shrugged, leaned casually against the counter and crossed his arms. The eyes that had once so admired her now appraised her with empty contempt.

"So you were going to Mexico City, and then coming back?"

"Of course," she lied. "This is my home."

He showed her the same thin smile as before. "I don't think this is true, Yolanda. I think that if you're no longer here, your father would lose interest in his business arrangement with me."

She had never heard him utter the words so plainly. It chilled her blood. "Then I'm a prisoner."

"You are my wife. *Hasta le muerte, mi vida.*" Until death.

"I'm not your wife. I am a hostage."

Miguel considered her for long seconds. "You are a reminder," he said finally, with a candor that unnerved her more than any of his lies. "You are leverage."

<hr />

YOLANDA STOOD AT the kitchen window, drinking deeply of the rum she had poured herself. Her hands had ceased their quaking, but her face was flushed with the heat of debasement. She watched Miguel lean against the bed of his truck as he stared out across the sunbaked earth, at the skunkbrush and manzanita that grew beyond the gate. She heard the door open behind her and turned to see Susana, her housemaid, there.

"You heard all of that," Yolanda said softly.

"Yes, Senora. I am sorry."

Yolanda waved it away, ice ringing gently in the crystal tumbler she held. "Do you have a cigarette, Susana?"

The girl's eyes darted sideways, looking for escape.

Yolanda smiled. "It's okay, Susana."

She searched her mistress' face for duplicity and saw none. "I can get one from my bag."

"Bring two."

"Of course, Senora," she said, and returned a moment later, two cigarettes on an outstretched palm.

Yolanda lit both with a wooden kitchen match, passed one to Susana with unspoken understanding. "Just this once."

The girl showed her a shy smile, sharing a secret with the lady of the house.

# CHAPTER 7

The new kid was there when Colt and I landed.

He had driven down in the old International Scout four-by-four that I called the Bushmonster, a beat-down looking beast roughly the color of Silly Putty, and a body designed by the same guy who invented the shoebox. But she ran like a Sherman tank, and you gotta love that when you're way up here on the other side of nowhere.

The new guy had, at least, arrived prepared. He had spread out a faded green canvas tarp in the Bushmonster's cargo area, a bottle of Jack Daniels and a pair of Coleman lanterns resting on the hood. Truth is, as good a pilot as I know Colt Freeland to be, I never got used to landing in the dark, in the middle of the forest, on a dirt strip marked only by a handful of flashlights. It always leaves me a little irritable, so you'll understand if the first thing I did was grab the fat spliff the kid handed to me and light up.

"Thanks," I rasped and handed it back.

The kid was tall and rangy, with lank brown hair that fell past his shoulders. He stood with that hunched kind of loose-limbed stoop that too-tall kids and dopers always seem to adopt somewhere along the line, and he was gaping at me like I was a potted plant.

"Say something or stop staring at me," I said.

I reached my hand out and the kid slapped me five. "Name's Ricky," he said. "Ricky Montrose."

'Ricky.' Fuck.

"Is that with a 'y' or an 'ie' at the end?" I asked.

He gazed at me blankly, my sarcasm sailing by him like a paper plane.

"How old are you, Rick?" I tried again.

"Ricky," he corrected me.

"Do I look like I enjoy asking questions twice?" I said.

He shot a glance at Colt, who was busy letting loose another heavy stream into a clump of wild twinberry at the edge of the airstrip. Maybe his bladder was getting smaller. Colt just zipped his fly and shrugged in the kid's general direction.

"Twenty-two," Montrose answered finally. He pulled his long dark hair into a ponytail and tied it in place with a leather strap.

"Twenty-two," I repeated. "Then your name's Rick. I won't call anybody over the age of twelve 'Ricky.' I don't do diminutives." I mean, how can you trust anybody past the age of puberty with a handle like Billy or Bobby or Timmy? Hell, I can't deal with chicks with names like Bambi, for that matter.

"You call Eduardo 'Eddie,'" Colt offered as he strolled back from the bushes.

"Stop helping," I said to Colt. "Besides, that's the exception that proves the rule."

The kid looked dazed. "Who's Eddie?"

"None of your business," I said.

"Oooh-kay," Rick sighed, kind of exasperated. "So what's your name?"

"Who wants to know?"

"Me. What am I supposed to call you?"

"Boss."

"Seriously," he smiled. "What do you want me to call you?"

"Boss," I said again.

"Are you shitting me?"

"Not even one little turd's worth, Rick."

"You don't have a name?"

"Of course I have a name. I just don't know why you'd need to know what it is."

He snuffed the smoldering joint he had pinched between his fingers and slipped it into the breast pocket of a faded military fatigue jacket, then wiped his sweaty palms on his jeans.

I felt a little poorly at getting off on the wrong foot with Rick Montrose, so I pointed at his jacket and made an attempt at civil conversation. "You were in the Army?"

"Uh," he said. His eyes slid away from mine. "No."

"You're twenty-two, right? Draft ended three years ago. So, what branch were you in?"

Montrose shot another glance Colt's way and didn't answer me. Which was a pattern that was beginning to piss me off. Like I said, treetop flying is not my bag and makes me cranky.

"Don't look at him, Rick. What's he, your lawyer?"

"I Four-F'd out," he said. "Braces."

"Braces?" I said. "On your *teeth*?"

"His dad's an orthodontist," Colt added.

"Fuckin' perfect," I said. "A post-pubescent, draft-dodging, pseudo-guitar teacher named 'Ricky' who wants to be an actor." I shook my head and went back to the plane to grab the stash.

While I humped the ditty bag of dope over to the Bushmonster, Colt and Montrose peeled the fake tail numbers off the plane. There was a private airport—a real one—about forty miles away, where Colt ran his rental and charter business. With the major exception of the flying he did for our little enterprise, he worked hard to keep the rest of his activities legit. To that end, he had to get the plane back before daylight, spray it down with Lysol to get rid of the smell, and get back here before his man came in to open up the shop. Colt only had four planes, but he got visited by the Feds about twice a year. Somebody wise once said, *Keep your friends close, and your enemies closer*. Well, the frequency of Colt Freeland's contact with the authorities kept him very much in the loop as far as their attention to the Humboldt community was concerned. Worked out nicely for everybody in our circle of acquaintance, as long as they remained on our good side.

Fifteen minutes later Colt was airborne again and I drove back to camp with the new kid.

⌒⊱━⊰⌒

THE NEXT MORNING I woke early, ate breakfast, had a quick cup of coffee and headed out on my Yamaha dirt bike.

It had only taken about four hours for me to move the smoke we'd brought up from Mexico. Suffice it to say that with the harvest still a few weeks away, there were some folks who were damned glad to see me. It also gave me the chance to make the rounds, visit some of the other growers and catch up on things. I had saved the last half-key for the final stop on my route—Junior Stavro's makeshift farm.

I pulled up to Junior's tent just before noon. He was standing out back, poking at something on his gas-fired grill with a long fork. Bud, his ratty-looking retriever, was snoozing at his feet. Limpid feathers of smoke trailed up into shafts of yellow light that filtered down between the redwoods that camouflaged his operation. The crisp autumn air was laced with the aromas of forest loam and broiling meat. I'd done a bit of social imbibing along the way, so by the time I got to Junior's I was toting a fairly significant case of the munchies.

"Brother, my brother." He said it like *bru-thuh*, which sounded funny coming from a short, stocky white guy wearing nothing but sun-faded overalls and flip-flop sandals. His beard was thick, growing high on his cheekbones. His hair came down to the middle of his back, parted in the center and held in place with a tie-dye bandana. For the past two years, every time I heard McCartney's "Junior's Farm" on the radio, Stavro's image came into my head.

"The candyman cometh," I told him.

"Nice timing, dude. Beverage or a bite?"

My stomach growled on cue. "I could do with a little feast."

He aimed his fork at a Coleman cooler that sat beside a camp chair. "Beer yourself and saddle up," he said, glancing at his watch. "Gonna be a few more ticks."

Like most of us, Junior was a seasonal resident. He'd been using this corner of some rancher's land for as long as I'd been around, growing his crop in the shelter of the old-growth pines that blanketed the hills, and poaching his irrigation water from a weir that fed about a hundred plants. His operation was pretty small, so he could run the whole thing with just himself and his Old Lady of the moment.

"Where's Jill?"

"Town." He flipped the burgers, and plopped down in the chair beside mine. "So'd'ja bring back any souvenirs?"

I hauled a brick out of my backpack. "What would you say to a pound of *sinsemilla*?"

"I'd say, 'Hello, Sinsie,'" he leered. Junior hauled a pocketknife out of his overalls, slit open the package and buried his nose in it. His face lit up like he'd just been paroled. "Nice," he said, taking his new little bundle into the trailer. "Same deal?"

"Sorry, man," I said. "I gotta nick you an extra hunny."

Junior shrugged. "Beggars and choosers, right, man?"

"Naw," I said, feeling a little guilty passing along Eduardo's price increase. But only a little. "My friends down south are beginning to embrace capitalism with more enthusiasm than they used to."

We ate in silence under the Douglas fir and tan oak, grooving on the natural sounds inside the forest. The weather had begun to change with the approach of autumn, the breeze growing noticeably cooler, the daylight hazy and thin. When we finished eating, Junior took the metal plate I had in my lap and put it in an oversized bucket of water beside the tent. He ducked inside for a second, then came back with a joint between his fingers.

"Anybody tell you about Buddy?" His words rolled out on a blanket of blue smoke as he passed it to me.

"No," I said. "What about him?"

"Rippers, man. They had guns, too."

"Shit." Rip-off artists were the bane of our existence, but the fact that they were arming themselves was even worse news. As if we didn't have enough problems.

"Fuckin' bummer's what it is."

Junior took another drag and extended it back to me. I passed. I prefer to take my bad news as straight as possible, though it was already a little late for that.

"Anybody get hurt?" I asked.

"No, but they were lucky. Buddy said they had assault rifles. Like the fuckin' Army, man."

"From around here?" Junior knew what I was asking.

"Who knows," he said. "But you might want to think about wiring your trees."

"If I wanted to live my life laying Claymores in the bush, I woulda stayed in 'Nam," I said with a bitterness that surprised even me.

"I'm just sayin', brother." *Bru-thuh.* "Hey, how's your new boy working out?"

Word traveled fast. "You met him?"

"Just for a minute. Seems okay," Junior said. "A little young. But seems alright."

I felt a sudden, pressing need to get back to my camp. A prickly bastard of a premonition was crawling up from my shoes.

"The fun's starting to seep out of this business, Junior." I made my way to the Yamaha.

"Don't be a stranger," he said as I kick-started the bike.

"Thanks for lunch, man."

⊙━━━━⊙

OUR CAMP CONSISTED of a pair of oversized surplus tents strung up military-style beneath the heavy canopy of conifers. One served as our sleeping quarters, the other our mess and supply tent. When I pulled in, Colt and Montrose were working on the old El Camino I'd bought for making the long hauls of stash down to southern Cal.

I had looked all over for that particular model because of an odd engineering quirk it possessed. The car had originally been designed to have a station-wagon-style rumble seat in the rear cargo area. But some government regulation or another snafu'd that, and the seat was scrapped. But the half-barrel shaped hollow spot in the truck bed still remained, covered over by the manufacturer with nothing more than a thin sheet of metal. It was the perfect hiding place for the transport of weed.

"That was quick," Colt said.

"Timing's everything," I said, stuffing the duffel full of cash into my footlocker. "What are you doing to my car?"

"The kid came up with a good idea."

"Yeah?"

"Take a look."

Rick Montrose's skinny, sweaty body was wedged between the El Camino's cab and the propane tank I had installed a couple of years earlier, just after the Saudi Oil Crisis rationing had begun to put a serious crimp in my travel arrangements. The prospect of waiting in long lines at the gas pump with a hundred pounds of extremely aromatic weed stashed in the back of my car seemed like a very bad business move. The propane tank solved a big part of that problem and extended the car's range enough so that we could make it all the way to southern Cal without a stop.

I came around behind Rick Montrose and peered over his shoulder.

"Hope you're not too attached to the propane, dude," Montrose said.

"Why?"

"Check it out."

He had taken the empty tank and built a dummy tank inside of it, leaving about two inches of space all the way around.

"The way I rigged it," he told me, "the gauge inside the car'll still work, still look real if anybody checks. And I figure we can stuff another, say, hundred pounds inside the dummy."

When I looked up, Colt was grinning like a chimp. "Kid just doubled our load capacity."

"And shortened our reach," I said.

It had always been the hairiest part for me, the driving back down south. Even when you wrapped the dope in plastic bags and taped it all up, it reeked like a trunk full of pine-scented skunks. This new idea was a double-edged sword. If Colt was right, we just shaved our travel exposure by half; getting caught with two hundred pounds landed you in jail just the same as a hundred pounds would. On the other hand, we'd have to pull off somewhere along the way and top off the tanks in order to make the distance.

"We're going to have to use jerry cans to refuel," I said.

I was still getting used to the idea, thinking through the new procedure necessitated by Rick Montrose's ingenuity. Montrose looked a little hangdog that I hadn't jumped up and down with praise for him.

The kid skulked off to clean up in the makeshift sailor's shower we'd rigged behind the tent, while I rolled a fattie for the three of us to share. I figured you might as well celebrate the good news if you're gonna freak out about the bad.

The sun had dropped behind the mountains by the time the kid came back to where Colt and I stood beside the camp stove. I torched the joint and we watched the sky go from blue to purple, another night coming down.

Montrose was brooding and distant as the silence settled in around us.

"It was a clever thing you did there, kid," I offered.

He was seated on the forest floor, leaning his back against the trunk of a blue spruce and staring at his feet. "Stop calling me 'kid,'" he said.

I didn't appreciate the copping of attitude. "Now, why would I do that?" I asked.

"'Cause I'm not a kid."

Colt's face was marbled in firelight as he whittled a stick with a hunting knife, an amused smile in his eyes as he listened to our exchange.

"How old are you?" I asked.

"I already told you. Twenty-two."

"How old do you think you were when I was twenty-two?"

He waited a long moment, still exploring the space between his shoes. "How the hell should I know?" he said finally.

I did some quick math in my head. "When I was twenty-two, you were about thirteen. What do you think I would have called you back then?"

"I don't know."

"I would have called you 'kid.' You know what my dad used to say? He used to say that a man isn't worth a damn until he's thirty."

Montrose took a deep toke off the joint he held between his fingers. "Well, your dad sounds like a dumbshit."

"Really? You know my dad?"

"How could I?"

"That's right," I nodded. "So how about you leave calling my dad a dumbshit to people who actually knew if he was one or not."

Colt Freeland chuckled and watched Rick Montrose sink back into his funk.

Montrose heard Colt laugh and turned his eyes in Colt's direction, hooking a thumb at me. "What's his problem?"

"Well, Rick," Colt smiled as he unscrewed the cap on a pint bottle of Jack Daniels. "I'd say his problem appears to be *you.*"

# CHAPTER 8

The soldiers swept in at ten o'clock that morning.

Comandante Rivera had sent word through Marco the night before, and Miguel's men had spent the night hastily trimming what buds of *mota* they could, carting it off in the backs of trucks, laying it out on the floor of the drying shed at the far side of the ranch. Now the military convoy had come, followed by three civilian vehicles that Miguel knew carried a cadre of the Peacock's hand-selected news reporters.

Miguel and Marco stood near the top of a rise, some distance away, watching the commotion through binoculars, careful to shield themselves from view. Comandante Rivera had exited the lead car and positioned himself in front of a sizable field of marijuana. He paced imperially as the reporters and, more importantly, their cameramen began to assemble around him.

Miguel lowered his binoculars and looked away from the scene. "Such a waste."

"We got what we could."

"Not even by half. Those *viboras* enjoy doing this to me."

Comandante Rivera was gesturing widely as he spoke to the reporters. His words were lost to the distance, but Miguel knew that whatever it was would be lapped up by the *Norteamericanos* in time for their nightly news. Assholes. This was costing him a fucking fortune, every cent of it coming from his own pocket.

"There it goes," Marco said, and Miguel lifted the field glasses to his bloodshot eyes.

The soldiers had entered the field, placing a half-dozen old tires at various points inside. The tires had been soaked in gasoline and ignited, the black smoke and roiling flames making for great television as Rivera's men slashed and burned the marijuana—the Mexican government's tireless efforts against *Los Narcos*.

"A fucking circus," Marco said.

"*No tenga cuidado.*" Don't worry. "Tonight we make up for it."

"You should let me kill him."

"Rivera? The Peacock? It would feel nice, but do no good. They are like a shark's teeth. You rip one out, another comes up in its place."

"Still . . ."

Miguel gestured toward the burning field, at the black columns of smoke rising into a washed-out sky. "Keep an eye out, Marco. Be sure they stay well away from the airstrip."

"What time?"

"Between seven and eight o'clock, I expect."

"I'll be there." Marco turned away and started down the sandy slope.

"You heard what I said, Marco?"

"I heard you. Between seven and eight."

Miguel shook his head. "You keep them away from the hole."

# CHAPTER 9

Steve Devlin passed the holding cell on his way to the locker room one floor below.

Some perp, an otherwise relatively normal looking Hispanic, was screaming and banging his hands against the cage.

"Pig!" The guy yelled at Devlin as he went by. "Nazi!"

Devlin stopped in his tracks. "Do I know you?"

"Fuck you!"

A uniform was finger-pecking a typewriter at a desk a few feet away. Devlin caught his eye, hooked a thumb at the man in the pen. "What's with this guy?"

"From what I understand so far," the officer said, barely raising his eyes from the machine, "every white cop is a Nazi and every black cop is an Oreo."

"Latinos?"

"Jury's still out."

"I see."

The uniform nodded and continued typing his report.

The perp started banging his head against the chain link. "Come on, pig, bust me up!"

"Shut up, shithead, I'm talking here," Devlin said, pinning him with his eyes. He turned back to the typing cop. "What'd he do?"

"Started out as an altercation over a seat in a movie theatre."

Devlin nodded and said, "Musta been a hell of a good seat." He smiled and pushed his way through the door to the stairwell.

It was late afternoon, the locker room filled with cops coming off their day tour, showering and changing back into civvies. At the far end of the room a couple of cops from the BAPG were getting into their field gear: filthy jeans, hiking boots, and heavy shirts. The weather had started to change from Indian summer to an all-out autumn chill.

The one named Torres caught Devlin's eye. "IA done with you yet?"

Devlin shook his head. "I'm not back on the schedule 'til next week."

"Making you see the shrink?"

"Yeah," he lied. "Where's Limon?"

Torres and the other Bagger exchanged a look. "Out in the trailer park. He's in a ball."

It was their own cynical shorthand that covered anything from a hangover to a nervous breakdown.

Devlin stopped off at his locker on his way out to the parking lot where Sonny kept his camper. Some smartass had put a yellow happy-face sticker on its dented metal door, and added a bloody bullet hole between the eyes with a felt tip marker. Underneath, it read 'Bag Team says Have A Nice Day.'

⊙═══╪═══⊙

SONNY LIMON was sitting alone in his camper, lost inside his thoughts as the newscast spewed from a cheap portable television on the counter in what passed as the kitchen.

Here he was, not even thirty years old, half a continent away from the yes-sir/no-sir life he'd spent as a kid living with his dad back in Albuquerque, only to end up falling into the same passive backseat patterns of his childhood. Only now it was his partner, Steve Devlin, in place of the Old Man.

Sonny used to rock the street pretty hard when he'd been a beat cop, before his language skills earned him a transfer to the Bag. What the hell was he now? What had he become?

He wasn't a dirty cop. He didn't think of himself that way. Devlin was right about that, at least. Everybody had their hands in something, right? Even if it's a free lunch at the sandwich joint you dropped into every day, or the freebies from the dry cleaner, maybe a blow job from the hookers down in the district. But this shit with

- 81 -

King Mike had become something else. It had gotten to the point where he was afraid to look in the mirror for fear he'd see nobody there at all.

He'd been an asshole to think that a little extra cash could hold his marriage together. He should have seen that Maddie wasn't cut out to be the wife of a cop. She wanted too much. It was like there was something in the water supply up in San Marino that drove that kind of girl to be Queen of the Rose Parade, then load the kiddies into the Mercedes wagon and slip off to the summer house in Newport Beach. He should have known better. Maddie should have known better.

But your options become simple and few when you're in sewage all the way to your chin. Like it or not, it was time to sack up. Either go with the program, or go under the boots.

STEVE DEVLIN walked out the locker room door and into the fading afternoon light, to the far end of the lot. He pounded his fist on the door of Sonny's camper.

"I know you're in there. Your bike's parked right here."

When Sonny cracked it open, he was wearing only a pair of striped boxers and a white T-shirt. He briefly scanned Devlin's face and turned back to the darkness inside.

The space was cramped, stale and close, thick with the smell of bacon grease and burned coffee. Devlin slid past Sonny and stepped into the confines of the galley.

"How about a drink?"

"Help yourself."

Devlin began rifling about, opening cabinets, searching their meager contents. Cereal, a box of stale saltines, Rice-A-Roni.

"Glasses are on the right, above the sink," Sonny said.

"Jim Beam?"

"Early Times," Sonny answered. He slipped a quart bottle out of a rack beneath the dining table.

"Good Lord."

"Yes or no?"

Devlin reached into his shirt pocket, withdrew a crumpled pack of Tareytons. "What do you think?"

"Don't smoke in here."

Devlin shook his head, cast his eyes toward the weak gray light that shone behind cheap window blinds. "I ran into Torres and Franks inside. They said you're in a ball."

"I am in a ball." He handed the drink to his partner, then turned toward the local news, coming in fuzzy and blue on the little set. Absently, he adjusted the rabbit-ear antenna, then gave up when the reception only got worse.

"Well, get the hell out of it."

The younger cop's face remained impassive. "I'm off the schedule for the next four days."

"Good. You're cleared with the lieutenant?"

"At the afternoon briefing. It was his idea."

Devlin's eyebrows shot upward, an expression Limon didn't fully comprehend. "It's on with Miguel for tomorrow, Sonny. Be at my house at eight in the morning. I don't wanna be driving that road in the dark."

"Fine."

Devlin put down his glass and turned to leave. He took hold of the door handle, then thought better of it. "This only works one way, now, Sonny," he said over his shoulder.

"And what way is that?"

"Both of us together, or one of us dead."

"I'll see you at eight."

"Eight o'clock," Devlin repeated. "And take a goddamn shower."

# Chapter 10

It was late afternoon by the time Colt and I finished checking the plants.

The late September sun floated low on the horizon, diffused and indistinct behind the heavy shelf of rain clouds bringing the change of seasons in from the northwest. The camp was washed in pale silver light as I finished my evening routine, toweling off lukewarm water in the chill breeze and digging inside my footlocker for a fresh set of clothes.

Rick Montrose had taken the Bushmonster into town for a fresh supply of canned food, bottled water, propane and beer. Colt was in the mess tent, trying to light the Coleman stove, cursing the wind between pulls at the bottle of Jack Daniels in his hand.

Once dressed, I took the last warm can of Olympia from the cooler, shut the hinged lid and took a seat on a stump outside the tent. The sweet smell of conifers and wild cascara mingled with the scent of coming rain. The pine canopy was alive with the clatter of redwings and scrub jay as I closed my eyes and turned my face to the dimming blush of the sun.

I was lost inside my own head, wrapped in fantasies of Mexico and sailing down the coast to Manzanillo after the harvest came in. But somewhere in the back corner of my brain Junior Stavro's comment about the rippers seeped in like smoke from a grease fire.

In the old days, there weren't so many of us up here. The operations were small and the business fragmented. It used to be, you'd see a car you didn't recognize, you'd take a potshot at it with a .22 and that was the end of it. It wasn't like that anymore. Now the rip-off artists were beginning to come in armed to the teeth, knowing full well some of the growers had their places wired tight, strung with modified Claymores and Bettys, and protected with a full-bore military-issue arsenal. There was a lot of money being made now, and there was a war getting ready to start. Right here in the damn redwoods.

I heard Colt come out of the tent, his boots landing heavily on the dirt and stones and pine needles, pulling me back from my darkening thoughts.

"Feels like rain," he said, tipping his head toward the sky.

I nodded and lifted the beer to my lips, taking in the coming twilight. "I talked to Junior Stavro. You hear about Buddy Ray?"

"What about him?"

"Rippers took him off a few nights ago. They were packing automatic rifles."

Colt adjusted his cowboy hat and spat a stream of Copenhagen snuff onto the forest floor. "I mighta heard something on that."

"I'm thinking we ought to reflect real hard on hauling ours in early."

"How early?"

"Like, now."

"We'll lose a good three weeks of growth, hoss. That's serious weight."

"There's worse things can happen."

He took another swig from the bottle in his hand and looked into the clouds. His eyes were rimmed in pink, glazed with the first hint of whiskey shine. Long moments passed as he pulled the hunting knife from his boot and began tossing it underhand into the trunk of a nearby pine.

"You know what your problem is?" he asked me finally.

"Which one?"

"The one that's got you all bunched up."

"Tell me."

He took a step back, gestured broadly into the thick stand of trees that surrounded us. "You think all this belongs in a time capsule. Like it's supposed to be 1970 forever. Things change."

I tossed off the rest of my beer, crushed the can under the heel of my muddy hiking boot and watched him walk in slow circles as he spoke.

"You make money," he went on. "People smell it. They'll crawl out from under every rock from Mexico to the Canadian border and burn this world right down to the roots just to get a piece of it."

"Not on my watch," I said.

He looked away from me, the smile on his face like a slash in a fresh brick of clay. "Someday, they're gonna go ahead and legalize this shit, that's what I think. They're gonna have to, just to stop the bleeding."

I picked the crushed beer can out of the dirt, stood and tossed it in the rubbish heap. "Then we'd better make our roll before they do."

He sighed, and spat another wad of tobacco juice into the undergrowth. "Maybe you're right."

I shrugged, pulled a J from my jacket pocket and torched it. "Pigs get fat, and hogs get slaughtered, Colt."

"It's your show. You think we oughta hare out early, we hare out early."

"That's what I'm talking about," I said. "Full throttle, and fuck the rest of 'em."

THE SETTING SUN bathed the camp in copper light and caught that first curtain of drizzle like a shower of shattered crystal.

Rick Montrose pulled the Bushmonster to a jarring halt beside a copse of maple whose leaves had begun their transformation from deep green and sage to the amber spectrum of fall. He stepped down from the truck and reached across the seat for a box of groceries. The rest of his load was in the back, tucked inside coolers of ice and covered with a worn canvas tarp.

"Where the hell have you been?" I asked.

He smelled of beer and cooking grease. His eyes slid off my face before he answered. "Stopped off at the diner."

"He's got a thing for Gina," Colt announced as he pulled the cover off the back of the Bushmonster and lowered the tailgate.

"Good for you, Rick," I said. "She's real . . . decorative. Now, forget about her."

"Forget her? What are you, nuts?" Montrose went around to the back of the truck to haul another carton of supplies off the bed, a look of incredulity on his face. "That chick has an ass that makes me want to eat her skirt."

"I gotta agree with you there," Colt smiled. "The only thing might make her any sweeter'd be fold-away tonsils and tuck-away teeth."

I knew the girl. She was the kind that dots her i's with little flowers. I took the last of the coolers into the mess tent and came back out with a cold six-pack.

"I need you to start thinking with your big head, Rick. We're considering bugging out early. This is not the time to be fucking around."

Montrose looked surprised, disappointed maybe. He took a can from the six-pack I'd placed on the table beside me, pulled the ring-tab and tossed it out into the ferns. "How come?"

"Lotta reasons. And stop throwing shit into the bushes. The trash barrel is right there."

"She's outta your league anyway," Colt said.

Montrose threw an angry look in his direction. "Screw you."

"Seriously, Rick," Colt drawled. "That girl's a big ol' helping of Good God with a side order of Lord Have Mercy."

Montrose tried to ignore him and looked at me instead. "Well, what's any of that got to do with me and Gina?"

Even Colt had heard enough. He slammed the Bushmonster's tailgate shut, came over to where I sat and fixed Montrose with a stare. "There isn't any 'you and Gina.' There's just Gina. Whatever wet dream you're living in exists only between your ears. This bullshit stops now. Conversation concluded. You'd best be hearing me."

Montrose took a hit off his beer and looked from Colt to me. "What fucking difference does it make?"

The kid hadn't been with us long enough to know the rule. No pussy when you're in the field. Especially not local pussy.

"Horny men talk too much," Colt said.

"You want to know how a fish gets caught?" I asked.

Rick Montrose flashed me a petulant glare. "How?"

"He opens his mouth."

<hr/>

THE RAIN HAD waned to a light sprinkle by the time we hit the rack that night. Montrose was quietly strumming his guitar at the rear of the tent, while Colt sat at the foot of his own cot, whittling silently. A gas-fired lantern hung from a nail hammered into the center post. It was turned low and dappled the canvas in pale yellow light and deep shadow. I was lying on top of my sleeping bag with a thousand details running loose in my brain, but the kid wasn't one to suffer silence too easily.

"I had a band back home," he offered for no reason. "Prodigal Frogskin."

"Yeah?" Colt said. "What happened?"

"Nothing. We just kinda went nowhere."

"Wow. What a shock," I said. "With such a good name and all." I wasn't in the mood for small talk, or any kind of talk at all, truth be told.

Montrose had had enough of me, too. "Are you always such a prick?"

"Yeah," I answered without turning around. "Why do you ask?"

The kid shook his head, sighed, and settled back on his cot.

"I'll drive into town first thing in the morning," I said, thinking out loud. "I'll call San Diego and let 'em know we're coming down ahead of schedule."

"Works for me," Colt said. "Me and Rick'll start hauling while you're gone."

The terrain where we grew our weed was steep and shot through with moss-covered stones and loose soil, unsuited for any legitimate form of agriculture. But it was perfect for our purpose. The hardest part, with the rain preparing to come in earnest, was going to be the cutting of those eight-foot plants—heavy with moisture—and bringing them back to camp. We'd devised a system where we carried them down three or four at a time, laid out on Army surplus stretchers, but the going could be slippery and treacherous. Once I had the drop arranged with my contact down south, I'd come back, working as long as it took to trim the buds and wrap the bricks in heavy plastic.

"You're sure about this?" Colt asked me.

"Yeah. I wanna move fast. Three, four days, tops."

I rolled onto my side, watched Colt snuff out his smoke and zip himself into his bedroll. "You gonna reach out to El Brujo?"

I thought Colt might have been hitting the hooch a little hard that night, and there was my proof. "Shut up, man," I said.

"What?" Colt was squinting at me in the dark.

I shot a glance toward the back of the tent, toward Rick Montrose, who was all ears by now.

"Gimme a break," Colt said. He rolled onto his back and stared moodily at the wind as it ruffled the crown of the tent. "Kid don't know nothing about El Brujo."

"Just go to sleep. And stop saying that name."

I drifted in and out of an uneasy slumber, surrounded by the sounds of the night. Screech owls. Crickets. The drone and churr of wildlife inside the forest. Maybe an hour later, I was awakened by a sense of something crawling across my chest, a manic flurry of tiny feet. I opened my eyes in time to see a forest rat scratching at the heavy cloth of my sleeping bag. I rolled instinctively, abruptly enough to upend my cot and send both Colt and Montrose reaching for the pistols they kept stashed beneath their pillows.

I stood quickly and flicked on a flashlight. I caught the startled creature in the beam of light, cowering in a corner of the tent.

"Relax," Montrose laughed. "It's just a fuckin' mouse."

"Fuck you, it's a *rat*," I said, my heart beating hard. "I don't like rodents."

Montrose walked over, lifted the edge of the canvas and let it out. "What, are you kidding? We're living in the middle of a god-damn forest."

I switched off the flashlight, stepped through the door flap and into the cool of the night. I could still feel the damn thing crawling across my chest. Montrose and Colt followed me outside.

But the kid couldn't get that shit-eating grin off his face. "You don't like hamsters even? Guinea pigs?"

"Are they fucking rodents?"

"Yeah."

"Then no, I don't."

Montrose just shook his head. "Jesus," he sighed, and went back inside the tent.

⊙━◆━⊙

THE RIPPERS HIT us just after midnight.

I was still outside, calming myself with a joint. I had an automatic rifle slung across my shoulder on a heavy strap as I stared out into the tree line, wanting to pop the next little furry bastard that tried to make a run for my cot.

Out of the silence I heard heavy rustling inside the shrubs not far away. It seemed to be coming from several directions at once, and I could tell right away that it wasn't a bunch of broke-dick hippies out to score a couple of buds. This was a coordinated strike like I hadn't been involved in since I'd left Indian Country. This was about to become a bona fide fuckaree.

The first shot whistled like an incoming mortar, and brought Colt and Montrose out of the tent at a dead run. I had no idea where that shot had been aimed, but the motherfucker was loud.

Then everything started happening at once.

Off to my left, maybe twenty yards away, Montrose starts yelling. He sees the guys. Three of them, armed like they're raiding Entebbe. Colt opens up on them with his AR-15, short burst, and one of the rippers goes down. I hear him screaming out in the dark. Next thing I know, tree bark is flying off the big redwood beside me, pelting me like shrapnel across the face. Tracers are coming at me in long, red streaks. More automatic fire rains down from the berm behind me, where Colt had been only moments before. I lock down and pivot, squeeze the trigger on full-tilt rock-and-roll straight back in the direction of the tracers. I've got sweat pouring down my back, sweat stinging my eyes, gun smoke and cordite heavy in the air. It smells sweet, metallic and pungent all at once.

The rippers break contact suddenly, and everything goes completely still for a few seconds. Long seconds. Unnaturally quiet. I can hear one of the rippers drag the guy Colt had shot and pull him down behind a rise. Colt comes from his position behind me, eyes as wild as mine, searching the field of fire out in front of us. I hear Montrose coming up from below, his feet making this soft hiss on the pine needles that blanket the forest floor. He has a ten-gauge pump shotgun gripped tight in his white-knuckled hands.

The seconds stretch into minutes as we wait, adrenaline leaching through our bloodstreams, the familiar leading edge of anxious exhaustion. We're all looking at each other, a sort of combat shock binding the three of us in the exaggerated hush. I lean against the big tree behind which I'd taken cover, relieved, and gaze upward into the forest canopy. Gray smoke from our firefight drifts away on the breeze that riffles through the high limbs. I look over at Colt and begin to say something. I feel like I'll maybe start laughing, but I see his face turn ashen.

He starts to bring the AR-15 to his shoulder as a parting burst of three sharp cracks splits the air, hammers into the tree trunk less than three inches above my head. It's so close I feel the air displacement against my ear. I hear the rippers take off for the main road, where they must have parked their truck. I turn and look at the gaping hole where three smoldering, misshapen rounds had buried themselves. Rounds that had been meant for *my* fucking head. The blood turns to ice beneath my skin, and I feel like I am being pierced by a million tiny pins. I try to maintain an outward calm, but inside I am redlining: heart rate up over 130, BP busting 170.

"Seems like we've done that before," I say to Colt and try to smile.

"We spent time In-Country, hoss," he says. "We've done everything before."

⊶⧫⊷

SWEAT TIME.

Adrenaline burned through my veins like battery acid. I felt something hot and wet at the corner of my eye. Goddamn. Back in Vietnam, fear and killing-venom often rushed through my blood-stream in tandem, like I couldn't even tell if I was more terrified or pissed off. I don't imagine it matters much in the end, as long as you stay vertical. Still. Shit.

"The choice isn't ours anymore, Colt. They know where we are."

Rick Montrose was badly shaken—his entire body was racked with involuntary spasms and he appeared as though he was about to vomit.

I stepped off into a small clearing and waved Colt over with a nod. I spoke in a low whisper, my eyes still roving the dark beyond the redwoods. "We gotta move."

"We're not even half ready."

"This is turning to crap in a handbag, Colt."

"We can hold on."

I tossed a glance at Montrose. He was doubled over, puking in the ferns. "Not in a free-fire zone, we can't."

"So, what are you saying, man?"

"We've gotta start the load-out first thing in the morning. Send what we can down south while we try to harvest the rest."

Colt turned his head and eyed Rick Montrose. "And who's gonna stand watch on the weed? Me and the kid?"

Like that would do any good. "You and me. We're going to have to send Montrose down with the stash."

I watched Colt turn it over in his head as he slipped the AR-15 off his shoulder. He planted the stock in the dirt beside his boot and heaved a sigh. I felt exactly the same way.

Montrose had reached the dry-heave stage, balanced on unsteady legs and using his shotgun as a cane. His eyes shone in the reflected moonlight, red-rimmed and glassy. He stared blankly as Colt and I crossed the clearing and came back to where he stood.

"Change of plans, Rick," I said. "You're driving the first load down south. Tomorrow. As soon as we can get it together."

"Me?" He swallowed dryly and looked like he was going to puke again.

"Colt and I need to stick around and guard the plants."

"You think they're coming back, those guys?"

I looked at Colt from the corner of my eye, saw the sweat beading on his forehead, the rise and fall of his chest as he breathed. "Probably."

"God*damn*."

Amen.

# CHAPTER 11

The plane came into view at about eight forty-five that night. Almost two hours late by Miguel Zamora's reckoning.

Marco looked across at his brother, who was armed only with the .45 revolver tucked into his belt at the hollow of his back, always the cowboy. Still, Miguel looked calmer than he'd appeared at any time during the past several days: shades of the old Miguel, the one who always had the moves, the answers, the one who kept his head when order turned to chaos.

The sky was clear and black, flushed clean, and sprinkled with flickering stars. The dim line of the horizon shimmered with the vestiges of desert heat still emanating from the arid soil.

"Get Carlos on the radio," Miguel said, his binoculars locked onto the incoming plane. "Tell him to have everyone ready."

The brothers were standing on a low rise at the far end of the airstrip, its boundaries marked by makeshift kerosene torches. A transient breeze carried ribbons of pungent smoke and the aromas of creosote and grazing cattle.

Marco shifted the Kalashnikov to his other hand, letting it hang freely as he depressed the talk switch on the walkie-talkie. He clicked twice, then whispered the foreman's name. "Esteban."

Two clicks in return, then, "*Si*."

"It is coming."

"*Esta bien*."

Miguel felt his fatigue melting away, supplanted by a heady sense of anticipation. Lately, it seemed that everyone had his hand out for a taste of Miguel's money—money he had to work hard to make for himself. He'd built a bridge over a deep gully on the road to La Purisima; he built a home for senior citizens in the heart of the village; he added rooms to the school and paid for its furnishings; he provided uniforms and equipment to the soccer and baseball teams. To local officials he gave dozens of the automobiles and trucks he'd stolen in the U.S. to be sold for cash or traded for drugs. All of this was, of course, on top of the hundreds of thousands of dollars he paid every month to the Pig, the Peacock and the *Maricon*. It was almost like La Plaza was little more than a system of taxation. A system that was threatening to break him.

Miguel had had to keep moving for days on end just to keep everything running properly: the product coming in, the dealers supplied, authorities pacified, and his army of *pistoleros*, packagers, farm hands and intelligence sources paid off. Of course, he had his girlfriends, too, lodged at hotels and cantinas in town. It was exhausting work being the King. But with cocaine, at least, he could get by on an hour or two of sleep a night. He could see more clearly, respond more quickly, when the white lady was simmering in his blood. It was becoming more difficult every day to imagine how he could get along without her.

This, however, was his great bold move. The one that would help right the scales. All it would take is a bit of smooth talking with the Colombians when it was over. There may be some threats, perhaps even some violence, but in the end he believed that the Colombians needed him badly.

"Here it comes," Miguel said.

The plane, an odd-looking twin-engine OV-10 Bronco, banked hard and came in low over the runway, leveling off at no more than thirty feet, then made a final pass to clear the field of livestock.

"Beautiful," Miguel whispered as it came in for its final approach.

The Bronco kicked plumes of dust and scattered stones as the wheels made contact and taxied to the end of the runway. Engine noise split the night as the pilot revved the engine and pivoted the plane to face the oncoming breeze.

"Stay here," he said to Marco. "I may need you."

Miguel stepped out into the runway, flicked his flashlight three times—his signal to the pilot—and walked slowly toward the plane.

Marco watched through the field glasses his brother had left behind. He saw Miguel speak briefly with the pilot as he slid open the cockpit window, explaining the procedure. Miguel pointed into the brush, where his men waited to unload the cargo, careful not to alarm *el piloto* with the sudden appearance of a dozen men from out of the darkness.

Marco's heart raced as the pilot left his seat and disappeared into the cargo area. If things were going to turn bad, it would be now. He kept his eyes glued to the binoculars as long seconds ticked by. Marco nearly laughed with relief when, a few moments later, the pilot unlocked and released the rear door.

Miguel's head disappeared into the hold as he took in the sight of two thousand pounds of cocaine. It had been divided into one-kilo bricks, wrapped in wax paper, and gave the appearance of nothing more sinister than blocks of imported cheese.

The pilot, who had disembarked from his plane, allowed the engines to run, remaining prepared for a quick departure. Miguel's men formed a bucket brigade to unload the cocaine, between the rear of the aircraft and a deep hole that had been dug beside a livestock watering cistern near the runway. A rusted metal hatchway lay at the bottom of the hole—the entrance to a cylindrical metal tank sunk deep beneath the desert floor. One of the men squeezed down into the storage tank and stacked the packages inside, while the others passed them down, one by one. When the last of the bricks was laid in, the hatch was slammed shut and locked, and the hole refilled. No one but Miguel, his brother Marco, and a dozen of Miguel's most trusted men would ever know what was buried there.

When Miguel's men finally filed away, back into the brush, Miguel leaned close to the pilot, who was still standing near his plane, and spoke to him one last time.

It was supposed to go much more smoothly.

The pilot panicked when he saw Miguel slip the .45 from his waistband, and instead of throwing his hands into the air and taking a merciful shot to the temple, he took several steps backwards, dying badly as he backed into one of his own propellers. Blood splattered the engine cowling and windscreen as the blade sliced through the pilot's head, cleaving him all the way down to his chest, throwing ropes of wet gristle and viscera into the air before he slumped into the dirt at Miguel's feet.

⊙═╤═⊙

MIGUEL AND HIS brother looked on as his men rolled the plane into the deep trench they had excavated only the day before, the pilot's mangled body secured inside the cargo hold. Esteban, the ranch foreman, was guiding the tractor as the aircraft slowly disappeared under the tons of loose soil that had been mounded, waiting, beside the gaping hole.

Marco smiled and hefted his Kalashnikov horizontally at chest level. The deep grooves of the gun's ammo clip were filled with freshly stolen Colombian coke, and Miguel stood before his brother, snorting the lines directly from the clip. It was a style considered *muy macho* by Miguel's *pistoleros*.

"Congratulations," Marco said. "Almost exactly as you planned."

Miguel straightened, sniffed the powder deep into his sinuses and wiped his numbed face with the back of a blood-spattered hand. "Except for the pilot."

"A bullet or a propeller," Marco shrugged. "Either way."

"We'll celebrate tomorrow. *Una fiesta grande.*"

"You think that's wise?"

Miguel traded places with Marco, holding the gun for his brother as he took his turn with the coke. "I am El Rey Miguel. A king displays his power, or he loses it."

Marco snorted the last long rail off the clip. "The Colombians?"

Miguel ran his tongue across dry lips, gazing down into the pit that now completely entombed the plane. "The shipment never arrived."

Marco's expression was shot through with doubt. For the first time he thought perhaps some plans were better when they remained as plans.

Miguel laid a hand on his brother's shoulder. "You never heard the story? A year or so ago, when a pilot miscalculated his fuel? Before he leaped from the plane, he put the drugs inside a tractor tire and dropped it out, high over the mountains. Men looked for months, but never found it."

"And your point is?"

"My point is that these things happen from time to time. The cocaine is not my responsibility until it reaches my hands."

Marco stared into the distance, across the hard landscape of the valley, toward the mewling wail of coyotes that echoed through the night.

"You worry too much, Marco. I am El Rey Miguel."

But Marco appeared as if he hadn't heard. He cocked his head toward the howling pack. "They say that dead lovers come back as the coyote, and cry at night for the love they lost."

Miguel shook his head and turned away from his brother without another word. The rush of speed and adrenaline pumped through his veins as he made his way back to his truck, striding purposefully through the shadows of brittlebush and ghostflower.

Marco stood alone on the hillock, speaking only to himself.

"It will probably be the last sound heard on Earth."

PART THREE:

# Midnight Flyer

# Chapter 12

I was sitting at the folding table we kept inside the tent.

I had pinned back the flaps to trap what I could of the gauzy light and blunt the staleness of the air within. A low ceiling of lifeless clouds obscured the autumn sun and stilled the light breeze that had drifted through the pines all day; it left me slick with perspiration as I worked as quickly as I could to trim the buds off the plants Colt and Rick Montrose were humping down out of the forest. We'd been taking turns at the table since first light, one man cleaning weed while the other two piled five- and six-foot plants onto the Army surplus stretcher until the muscles of arms, legs and backs burned and ached and could take no more.

My fingers were nearly black with sticky resin, but it was the sweet, metallic odor of spent gunpowder that still hovered in my senses. My mind kept drifting, conjuring images of the firefight with the rippers the night before, and all the ways it could have well and truly turned to shit. I knew those fucking thieves would be back, but even the certainty in my gut couldn't stop me from second-guessing myself about pulling out early. And the thought of sending Rick Montrose down south instead of doing it myself was eating a hole in my stomach. It was like the odd thought that often crept into my head when I would dive from the deck of a boat as she lay at anchor, swimming out toward the horizon. What's the point at which it becomes dangerous to go any further? Of course, any soldier will tell you that it comes too late, when you know you've already gone too far.

❦

COLT AND RICK dropped the last of the day's load on the hard-packed floor beside me, the smell of sweat and damp earth mingling with the pot-infused stillness of the tent. The sweet fragrance of wet forest loam and the chatter of redwings in the pines hinted at a sense of peace which I couldn't share.

"What the hell happened to you?" I asked.

Rick Montrose was limping, one arm bleeding badly from a chain of scrapes and gashes that ran down one whole side of his body.

"Gravity storm," Colt smiled as he took off his cowboy hat. He wiped the perspiration off his forehead with the back of his hand.

Montrose ignored us both as he crossed over to the battered ammo box that served as our first aid kit. He fished out some bandages and antiseptic.

"Don't let Colt give you too much crap, kid," I told him. "I once saw him fall down a flight of steps outside a bar in Mexico, drunk as hell. If that place hadn't run out of stairs, he'd still be falling."

Montrose managed a smile as he daubed his bloody arm with a thick wad of cotton. He looked at Colt and shook his head.

"Don't get cocky," Colt said. "You could write the number of stupid-ass moves I've made on the back of a postage stamp. With a crayon." His eyes wandered across the table, landing on the bricks I had already wrapped and taped. "Making some headway, looks like."

I nodded, picked up a razor blade and started scraping the gummy resin off my fingers, gathering the shavings in a neat pile. By the time we were done cleaning the weed, we would collect a couple of dozen marble-sized balls of dark brown "Finger Hash" that would add another few hundred bucks to the till.

"Take a seat," I said. "We need to get the kid on the road in the next few hours."

I had awakened at about four o'clock that morning and taken the El Camino into town to top off the tank and fill the jerry cans at the Flying-A. I also used the time to reach out to my southern California contact on the station's payphone. Predictably, he was a little sketchy about connecting with Montrose—somebody he didn't know—so we agreed to modify the usual plan.

It was important that Montrose arrive in San Diego under cover of darkness, then check into a motel we both knew on a little side street off Rosecrans. My contact knew my El Camino from our previous business, so he said he'd be watching for it in the parking lot. Montrose was to keep himself holed-up for at least twenty-four hours so my guy could satisfy himself that Rick hadn't been surveilled, or worse. If everything proved cool, he'd reach out to Montrose sometime during the next day or so to set up the trade. If all went well, Colt and I could harvest the rest of the shit while all the cloak-and-dagger was going down in San Diego, and we'd be out of Humboldt County within the week. It added up to a hell of a lot of 'if's,' not the least of which was my ongoing concern that Montrose would somehow screw up. Or get busted on the way down. Or on the way back. Or that Colt and I could get all the dope hauled in without getting our shit blown away by the rippers in the middle of the night.

Then again, if it was easy, I suppose everybody would be in this business.

⊂══◆══⊃

TWO HOURS LATER I was going over the instructions with Montrose one last time.

"I got it, all right?" Rick said.

"Repeat it back to me. All of it."

"For *Chrissake*—"

"Just do it."

I listened as Montrose repeated everything I had told him, while Colt checked the knots on the rope that held the Jerry cans of extra gas in the bed of the El Camino.

"Where do you make your first piss-stop?" I asked him.

"Lathrop," he said, making me nervous all over again as he flaunted his youth with a sigh and a roll of his eyes. "I pull off into the boonies and refuel from one of the cans."

"Next?"

"Fort Tejon. Same thing."

"Then what?"

"San Diego. Siesta Cabrillo Motel. Check in, pay cash, and wait."

"What name?"

"C'mon, man."

"What fucking name do you check in under?"

"Rhodes. Rocky Rhodes. Okay?"

I had to smile.

"Okay," I said. "One last time. No pussy, you hearing me?"

"Listen, man—"

Colt shook his head. "Young, dumb and fulla cum."

"I'm telling you, Rick. There'll be more than enough bread for all the chicks you can handle once this thing is done. But until then, I don't care how blue your balls get."

"Fuck. Fine. Can I go?"

"Not yet," I said, and handed him a trucker's cap. "Tuck your hair up under this thing, and wear it until you get to San Diego."

His expression was incredulous. "I'm no redneck, man. I'm not wearing some Billy-Bob hat. Un-cool."

"This isn't the time to be letting your freak flag fly, Rick. Put it on."

Montrose shook his head sadly. ". . . so I tucked my hair up under my hat . . ." he sang. "Just like the song, huh?"

"Sure, man. Just like the song. We don't need you getting pulled over just because you look like a hippie. You got me?"

He did as I asked, then got into the car.

I leaned in the passenger side window. "Do *not* call anybody from the hotel. My guy will get in touch with me once you've made the deal."

"I know."

"Just making sure." It was the way I'd always done it. Payphone to payphone, prearranged, once the thing went down. Rick Montrose had no need to know the details, and I sure as hell didn't want him improvising.

"I got it," he said and headed out.

I watched him as he picked his way down the dirt road, still dogged by that empty feeling in my gut. There wasn't a chance in hell that I would have left Colt alone with Montrose after the aborted raid from the rippers—not if we were going to defend the crop we'd spent the past six months of our lives on. It would be like staking him out on an anthill. Still, it didn't make me feel any better, and I knew I'd be counting the hours until I saw Montrose driving back into camp. It was a bad feeling. And there wasn't enough weed in these mountains to make it go away.

"You look like you're sending your kid off to Boot Camp."

"I don't know that dude from Adam. He's *your* friend, Colt."

"He's my brother's friend. You're being paranoid."

"I am being 'hyper-vigilant,'" I said. "There's a difference."

Colt pushed back the brim of his hat and squinted in the afternoon glare. "Well," he smiled. "I do have to admit the kid is about half a bubble out of plumb."

Which was exactly what I didn't need to hear.

# CHAPTER 13

$S$teve Devlin drove hard, pushing his beloved '71 Barracuda from San Diego to Punta Enselma in just over four hours. Five years old, and the bright orange paint job could still blind you in direct sunlight. He had shelled out for every option from a Hemi dual-scoop shaker to braided wire tie-downs, and every part that didn't move had been dipped in chrome. It was all Devlin lived for outside of cash and ass.

Sonny Limon had been quiet for the first hour of the ride, which Devlin marked off to the ball Sonny had been in since the shooting in the arroyo. But once they passed through the border check and put the debauched shantytown they call Tijuana in the rearview, Sonny came back to life.

The plan called for the Zamora brothers to meet them at La Gaviota, a sun-faded beachfront cantina, at one-thirty that afternoon. With more than an hour to kill, Devlin pulled the car to a stop, flipped a quarter to a droopy-eyed boy who sat on the sidewalk outside, and told him to keep watch on the car.

The boy pocketed the quarter without a word and took up a place in the shade of a windblown jacaranda.

"Let's walk," Devlin said.

Sonny pushed his shades up the bridge of his nose, threw a glance across the rutted street, and locked onto an old man sitting in a tattered wicker chair. The old man was mumbling to himself, running his sandals across the hardpan that fronted a house that was little more than a corrugated metal lean-to. A goat was tied to a short rope, walking in lazy circles in a well-worn path marked by hoof prints and flyblown pebbles of dung. The old man stared back blindly, with eyes as clouded as milk glass.

Sonny pulled at his shirt where the sweat had molded it to his skin. "Hot," he said to no one. He felt as though he hadn't slept in days, like his joints were made of putty and his nerves like a junkie sweating a two-spoon load. An image of Maddie floated up behind his eyes, lying naked on their bed, curled softly beside some new and nameless lover. At Sonny's mandatory meet with the Department shrink, he was told that this was normal, that in times of extreme stress the brain was bound to leap unpredictably in any direction, or all directions at once. That's exactly how it felt now, like his mind was a monkey tethered to a chain. He turned back toward the old man with the goat, thinking that the man might be better off, blind and sitting alone in this cauterized landscape, expecting nothing. Sonny had to admit he had never been a proper caretaker of the things that were most important in his life.

Sonny caught Devlin looking at him, looking through him, more like. Like Sonny was some broken thing, or something that used to be there and had suddenly vanished. His agitated funk was replaced by a resignation so profound it seemed to envelop him like a cloud.

They spent the next half hour in silence, walking streets paved in little more than hardened mud and uneven stone. The sun bounced fiercely off the squat pastel buildings, plaster cracked and chipped and bristling with rusted rebar. Sonny Limon lost himself again in the brightly colored paper decorations that were strung across the square, and the tiny shops displaying woven baskets filled with fruit, vegetables and bread. The sere breeze smelled of cooking fires, sunbaked earth and the sea.

When they finally circled back to the cantina, they took two seats at the far end of a terrace that opened onto the beach. A gang of seagulls fought violently for food scraps among the foam and flotsam at the edge of the surf line. A galvanized bucket of Carta Blanca was delivered to their table, and Sonny watched rivulets of melted ice leak across the rusted metal and drip soundlessly to the floor. He pulled a chilled bottle from the bucket, popped the cap and put it to his lips while the jumping-monkey thoughts busted anew inside his head.

"Been thinking about this guy I knew once," Sonny said, tilting his face to the sun. "Nate Rudolph, this guy I knew back in high school. Had these big hands. These real big hands."

Devlin eyeballed his partner, trying like hell to get a fix on him. "Say what?"

Limon took another pull at his beer, wiped his mouth with the back of his hand. "I saw him right before he left for his second tour in 'Nam. I was thinking about what he told me. That the guys that survived over there were the ones who stopped giving a shit, just threw themselves into it like it was some kind of game they knew they were going to lose anyway. So, once they stopped giving a shit, it became this weird sort of trip for them. Like it was fun."

"You on something, Sonny?"

He snorted a laugh, sudden and dry. "What kinda question is that?"

Devlin rocked back in his chair, watching a small wooden boat cut a line of wake across the expanse of the bay. "What's your point, Sonny?"

"About what?"

"Your fucking friend, Nate or whatever."

"I don't know," Limon shrugged. "Seems like it should mean something. He's dead now, Nate is. Had big hands, though."

"Jesus," Devlin said. He reached into the bucket and cracked two more beers.

"How long we been partners, Steve?"

"Fuck, Sonny. Is this where you tell me I'm like the father you never had?"

"No," he said. The unexpected smile took years off his face. "More like the uncle who sneaks you beers at Thanksgiving."

"You thinking of going all Serpico on me? It's a little late in the day."

"I'm making my peace."

"And?"

"I just keep having this question buzzing around in my head: if you let somebody put the little bitty tippy-tip of his dick to your lips . . . does that make you a cocksucker?"

"What the hell is that supposed to mean?"

"Just don't want any more innocent people hurt by this thing," Sonny said quietly. "That's all."

Devlin shook his head. "There are no innocent people here."

MARCO ZAMORA stepped into the cantina, dressed in tight bell-bottom slacks and a white cotton shirt. He was wearing steel-framed sunglasses that were tinted a deep, electric blue. He was trailed by a nasty looking Mexican who was built like an icebox and dressed like a cross between a mariachi and a mercenary.

Devlin and Limon stood, eyed the men as they approached the table. Nobody smiled or made a move to shake hands. Devlin was the first to speak.

"Where's Miguel?"

"He does not leave the ranch so much these days." Marco's English was good, spoken quickly, but his accent was heavy. *He dunnut lev el rancho so mosh this daze.*

The big man wore a dust-encrusted cowboy hat, his eyes obscured by mirrored aviator shades. A bone-handled hunting knife protruded from a leather sheath clipped to one side of his belt. The cross-hatched grip of an automatic pistol peeked out of a holster affixed to the other. He hooked the thumbs of his broad-knuckled hands around a large silver buckle, planted his feet and stood silently behind Marco Zamora. The hands looked like they'd seen hard service.

"This is Esteban. He is the manager of Miguel's ranch. You are to come with us." Marco turned and started for the door.

"The hell are you talking about? You said Miguel was to meet us here."

"Change of plans. You are meeting *me*, so that you can come with me to the *rancho*. He is having a party and would like you to be there."

"Not a chance, *amigo*," Sonny Limon said.

Marco peeled the sunglasses from his face, tried to cool Sonny with a stare. He failed. "My brother will be extremely disappointed."

Limon took a step toward the younger Zamora, but Devlin stopped him with a nearly imperceptible shake of his head.

"I drive my own car," Devlin said. He took a hard look at Marco's eyes. He seemed spun out, speedy and jagged, the chemical odor of cocaine and whiskey sweat leaching from his pores.

Zamora turned to leave as he slid his blue-tinted glasses back in place, Esteban two paces behind. Sonny Limon stepped back to the table, felt the afternoon sun sting his flesh, but the heat of something else prickled beneath his scalp. He slipped a ten dollar bill from his wallet and wedged it beneath the bucket, then followed Devlin outside.

Outside, Marco was leaning against the door of a showroom-new '76 Trans Am. A silver T-Top with the outstretched wings of an eagle emblazoned on the hood. It was parked directly in front of Devlin's Barracuda. The smile on Marco's face was carnal to the point of lewdness. "You think you can follow me, Senor Devlin?"

"I can keep up just fine."

"But you will have to give me your guns."

The tidal surge of something primal snapped in Sonny's brain. "Fuck that," he said. "We're outta here."

Esteban turned his head toward Sonny, muscles flexing at his jawline, anxious to put a beat-down on the young *gringo* cop.

Devlin watched his partner's face, the empty look of give-a-shit insolence that had abruptly come to define Sonny Limon, and a dull, red ache began to throb behind Devlin's eyes. Things change over the course of a person's life, even if it is only a matter of perception. Regardless of the reasons, the changes that had lately been piling themselves onto Devlin's life were beginning to wear him down, and he was suddenly feeling every minute of his age.

"If you make a move on me," Limon smiled, "I will take a great deal of pleasure in kicking the shit outta you."

Across the narrow street, four boys chased a three-legged mongrel dog. They were laughing cruelly and pelting it with stones, its hindquarters already laid open and bleeding.

Marco made a ticking sound inside his throat, shook his head as they passed. "There is no need for that."

Devlin had to diffuse this thing, like *now*. The deal with Miguel Zamora was far too lucrative to allow it to go to hell just because Sonny was temporarily mind-fucked.

"Just give him your gun, Sonny," Devlin said finally. He slid his own from the holster strapped to his ankle, offered it butt-first to Esteban.

As the big man reached out, Sonny drew down. Esteban's reactions were instantaneous.

In the chaos of the moment, both Marco and Devlin pulled their guns. Four men stood in the heat of the Mexican sun, staring unblinkingly over the sights of their pistols.

Long seconds passed. Devlin felt an inexplicable desire to laugh out loud. An honest-to-God Mexican standoff. In Mexico, no less.

"I've got all day," Sonny said.

No one moved.

For a brief moment, Devlin's eyes cut sideways, taking in his partner with his peripheral vision before locking back on Marco Zamora. Something spooky there, Devlin thought. The serenity of a Buddhist monk about to douse himself with avgas and immolate them all.

"Put your guns away or—I shit you not—there will be hair on the walls," Limon said, his voice unnaturally calm.

Marco Zamora smiled unctuously, then slowly lowered his pistol. "It is only right, no? We have guns, they have guns," Marco said. "Esteban, put it away."

The big man remained still, only the reflection of Sonny Limon in his mirrored shades.

Devlin thumbed the hammer back to safety, and let his arm fall unhurriedly to his side. "My partner is getting a divorce," he smiled. "Women, huh? What I'm saying here is that this is not the kind of man you want to have pointing a gun at your face—a man who doesn't give a shit."

"Esteban," Marco said again.

This time he obeyed.

Limon let the moment linger before he returned his weapon to its holster. His eyes locked on Esteban's face.

Marco Zamora began to laugh. He tossed his head in Sonny's direction, but held his gaze on Devlin. "I like this one," he said. "He has big balls. Now let's go. This is no way to start a party."

Esteban remained on the sidewalk, watching the two Americans open the doors of Devlin's car and get in before he did the same.

Zamora's Trans Am pulled away from the crumbling curb and darted into the street, scattering the chickens that had been scratching aimlessly between the cobblestones. Devlin waited for the cloud of dust and exhaust fumes to pass over before lead-footing the accelerator and pulling up behind. Limon heard the tires spit gravel, pocking the undercarriage as they shot off down the road.

Devlin watched his partner from the corner of his eye. Sonny's face was a mask of stoicism.

"Just exactly how stupid are you? I swear, your brain's gotta be the size of a golf ball. I'm surprised I don't hear it rattling around when you walk."

Sonny was focused on something far off. "Just because they say 'action' doesn't mean you have to do something."

"You're gonna have to trust me, here, Sonny."

"I've always hated those words. I've said them before myself, so we both know what they're worth."

They slowed for a turn onto a dirt road that passed between the last cluster of hovels at the far end of Punta Enselma as Sonny's eyes cut sideways out the window. The four Mexican boys had caught up with the crippled dog. It was lying in a quivering heap at the side of the road, paws still twitching reflexively. Its skull had been crushed beneath a bloodstained cinderblock, encircled by a halo of flies.

# Chapter 14

The town of El Salto blistered up out of the brown hills and desert thorn like a sore.

After two hours of hard driving, the place appeared from nowhere out of the heat shimmers. Rows of boxlike buildings lined the first paved road they'd seen since leaving the cantina. Spectral striations of white cloud stretched across a sky bleached nearly colorless by the sun, their edges frayed and falling away in the chill currents of altitude.

Sonny Limon looked out the window at the nearly vacant streets. "What the hell is this?"

"It must be El Salto, the *padrino's* town. I've never been down this far."

Stray bits of trash slid from loose piles that had collected in the culvert and hopped across the street in the lifeless drafts that wheezed across the empty square. Stray dogs, chickens and goats roamed free, defecating in the alleys and narrow cobblestone side streets, while blank-faced children sought shade on the stoops of open doorways.

"Church looks new."

"These people belong to El Rey Miguel," Devlin said. "Keeping them happy buys a lot of loyalty. Plenty of eyeballs to watch his back."

The AC was cranked full, barely keeping pace with the bone-searing heat that seemed to pound them from every direction. Even with the windows rolled tight, the place smelled of dust and desiccation, of trash fires and night soil from the open pits and outhouses that lay behind the cracked plaster shacks and cactus wood fences tied with wire and twine.

"Asshole runs his world like a medieval lord," Limon said.

"Welcome to Mexico."

They followed Marco's Trans Am to the far end of town, where the macadam abruptly turned again to dirt and loose gravel, and made a sharp turn to the south. A shot-up Ford Bronco sat atop a monolithic block of concrete, like a monument. Bullet holes pocked the windshield and leaked rivulets of rust down the door frames, yielding to hard weather and the crusted stains of bird droppings. Sonny Limon watched his partner stare out at the makeshift shrine, his eyes tangled with thoughts Sonny couldn't guess at.

"I don't get it," Sonny said.

"A few years ago, another *padrino* tried to punch Miguel's ticket. He failed." Devlin turned away from the Bronco and followed the cloud of dust erupting from the car in front of them. "It's a reminder."

"Subtle."

"Yeah," Devlin said. "Like chewing foil."

◦━━✦━━◦

THE LATE AFTERNOON sun squatted over the low hills that trailed off to the west and cast long shadows across the grounds of Rancho Tronada. The compound was encircled by a high adobe wall topped with barbed wire and broken glass. Thick clutches of flowering oleander struggled to take hold in the dry soil along the fence line, but did little to dampen the undeniable impression of imprisonment within. Two guards flanked the only entrance, each holding an AK at port arms across his chest and a military grade walkie-talkie on his belt. Four more stood watch atop the roof of the main hacienda that occupied the far end of Miguel's estate.

The hacienda itself was fronted by a wide swath of gravel set out in an oval and surrounded by *lechuguilla*, yucca and knots of desert lavender. It had been constructed in the traditional style: two massive stories of pink-hued adobe and a red-tiled roof held aloft by vine-encrusted columns, which encircled a private garden within. A generous balcony jutted out over the main entrance overlooking the gathering below. A lone woman stood at the railing, hollow eyes tracing the line of the horizon and the sun that was falling away.

Once they had parked, Steve Devlin and Sonny Limon left Marco and Esteban standing beside their car. They passed slowly through the crowd, in the general direction of the grand vine-covered archway that marked the front entrance to Miguel's hacienda, feeling the eyes of the curious bore holes in their backs.

It looked as if the entire village had been invited to Miguel's fiesta. Men in straw cowboy hats and western dress were crowding about a fire-pit barbecue, pulling cans of Carta Blanca and Tecate from nearby coolers, talking easily and laughing among themselves. The aroma of *cabrito*—roasted baby goat—drifted in the arid evening air, mingling with the scent of gardenia and jasmine. Peasants in simple cotton shirts and sweat-soaked hats stood side-by-side with merchants in tan *guayaberas* and expensive Stetsons. Mechanics with grease beneath their fingernails spoke in animated tones with the manicured wives of local businessmen.

As Sonny scanned the crowd, he couldn't escape the feeling that there was something forced and abstrusely manic underneath the veneer of festivity.

"Where's Miguel?" Limon asked.

Devlin's gaze passed over the sea of faces. "I don't see him."

"Let's get this over with and get the fuck outta here."

A young girl acting as a waitress drifted past a cluster of men speaking in loud voices, a tray of chilled bottled beer balanced on one hand. She came to a stop in front of the two Americans. Without a word, Devlin took two, passed one to Sonny and popped the cap on his own. He downed half the contents in one long swallow as the girl turned away. "You need to get that look off your face, Sonny."

"What look?"

"Like you got scorpions under your skin."

Marco came up behind them, his platform shoes grating noisily on the loose gravel. "My brother is in the courtyard, beside the pool. He would like to see you. Come with me."

They followed Marco through a side entrance that opened on to a central courtyard encircled by the high walls of the hacienda. Wide Moorish archways belted the perimeter of both upper and lower floors, and protected the breezeways from the sun and wind.

A swimming pool the color of Caribbean jade rippled and sparked with the firelight of torches that threw shadows against date palms that reached beyond the tile of the roof.

Miguel was dressed in black, the only exceptions being the turquoise oval of his belt buckle and the deep red tint of the sunglasses he wore. Everything else—boots, shirt, vest, jeans—were black. His thick hair was swept straight back from his forehead, in need of a trim, and held in place by heavily scented oil. He was leaning against a bar that stood beside a cascading waterfall, a sheen of perspiration glazing his face.

"Senor Devlin," Miguel said, a broad smile splitting his face. He shook Devlin's hand warmly. "And this must be Senor Limon."

He stepped behind the bar and brought out a hand-blown bottle of amber liquor. "Let me offer you a drink. A fine tequila, from agave grown not far from Guadalajara. Very smooth."

"No, thanks," Limon said. "We can't stay long."

The skin near Miguel's eyes tightened momentarily, then broke into a grin. "I like that. A man with a sense of humor—a sign of intelligence, no?"

Miguel poured three glasses and handed them around. He gestured to a small table near the waterfall, and the three men sat. At the corner of Sonny's vision, he caught the motion of a guard as he rounded the corner of the breezeway, making his rounds.

Miguel shifted his gaze to Devlin as he sipped his tequila. "You received my gift?"

Limon shot a quick glance at his partner.

"A gift is what you get when nothing is expected in return," Devlin smiled.

Miguel smiled back. "Nevertheless, you received it."

Devlin made a show of looking at his wristwatch. "What's on your mind, Senor Zamora?"

"What's your hurry? You must learn to take your time, you will get more joy out of life." Miguel stood and paced a slow circle around the table, appraising Sonny Limon as if he were a racehorse. "A man cannot get to know another man in the space of only a few hours."

"Let me drop some knowledge on you, Miguel," Limon said, his tone sending a shot of heat lightning through Devlin's veins. "We don't have a few hours."

The *padrino*'s face went out of focus, like he was eyeing a thought inside his head. He took a lingering sip of his tequila before he spoke. "This is a celebration, my friends. Business talk is for tomorrow. For tonight, you will be my guests. I have rooms in the main house made up for you already."

Devlin eyed Miguel. Despite the man's outward demeanor, he could practically smell the speed in the man's sweat. This was not the Miguel he remembered. His hands were unsteady, like he hadn't slept in days, his face pale and seamed, the muscles in his cheeks about to vibrate his eyeballs right out of their sockets. He was reeling from the rocket ride, and coming down on a sea of tequila. In short, this was not a man to fuck with, not now.

"We'll talk tomorrow," Devlin offered reasonably.

"Tomorrow," Miguel agreed. "But tonight, we celebrate."

Sonny Limon didn't know what had just happened, but he knew it wasn't nothing. "What's the occasion?" Sonny asked.

"We are men," Miguel smiled, cupped his crotch in his hands. "We are celebrating that we have balls."

Sonny and Devlin went out the way they had come in, the sound of the waterfall receding as they made their way to the party outside.

"What was that about a gift?" Sonny asked as soon as they were out of earshot.

"It's nothing. A show of good faith. Got it tucked away in my sock drawer."

"Were you planning on telling me?"

"Sonny, shit man." Devlin said. "We've had a few things going on. Try to relax. When we get back to the world, I'll give you your piece, okay?"

"Piece of what?"

"You're starting to sound like my second ex-wife," Devlin said, pushing a path through the crowd in search of the bar. "The important thing here is that he's trying to show us off. That's what all this fiesta shit's about."

"We're fucked."

"He's not gonna burn us, Sonny," Devlin said. "But if you're gonna get fucked, you might as well lay back and try to enjoy the sex."

THE EVENING GREW perceptibly cooler as the sun sank behind the hills. At dusk, as night began to close in, the floodlights came on, throwing Miguel's hacienda into stark relief against a sky growing heavy with thunderheads over the coast just a few miles west.

Limon and Devlin stood apart from the main body of guests, watching as an elegant Mexican woman descended the stairs from the hacienda. She looked to be no older than thirty, a simple white cotton dress worn low on her shoulders and tied with a magenta sash around her slender waist. Her face held an expression of serenity, but as she drew closer, Sonny thought it was more like resignation.

She worked her way gracefully through the crowd, casting a nod or an unfinished smile to some, stopping only when she reached the spot where the two cops stood. Her eyes were deep amber, misted with alcohol. The glass she held smelled of mint and dark rum, and was ringed with half-moons of red lipstick.

"You are the Americans," she said. She studied them as if to memorize their faces.

"Pardon me?" Sonny said.

She tilted her chin and gazed out toward the lightning that popped silently inside the distant clouds. "Miguel found this place during a thunderstorm, did you know that?"

Sonny showed her an uncertain smile, said nothing.

"This is why he named it Rancho Tronada," she added.

"Thunderstorm Ranch."

"*Sí*," she said. "And now you are a part of it, too."

Miguel Zamora came from nowhere, his brother, Marco, at his side. "I see you have met my wife, Yolanda," Miguel said.

Marco placed a hand on her elbow. His knuckles showed white, and a brief grimace flashed across Yolanda's face.

"Take her back inside, Marco."

Yolanda Zamora cast one more look at Sonny Limon, burned a long glance into his face before Marco ushered her away. The look in her eyes was like a suicide note.

"My apologies," Miguel shrugged as he watched his brother escort her into the hacienda. "It appears she has rekindled her romance with liquor."

His eyes roved over his guests, then stalled abruptly when they fell on an officious-looking man with a vaguely fey manner, a razor-sharp part in his hair, who was overdressed for the occasion in a double-breasted business suit the color of desert sand. The man's complexion looked sallow and drawn inside the yellow globe of light under which he stood, his face creased with agitation.

"Excuse me," Miguel said. He strode directly toward the man at the far edge of the garden.

Limon and Devlin watched Miguel greet the man—who was clearly uninvited—then gesture with exaggerated courtesy toward the house.

Steve Devlin arched his brows, eyed Miguel and the well-dressed man as they entered the hacienda. He turned to Limon and smiled. "I gotta take a leak that's gonna peel the porcelain off the bowl," he said, and followed the *padrino* inside.

⚬━━✦━━⚬

SONNY LIMON wandered the grounds alone, nursing the beer that was growing warm in his hand. The night smelled of woodsmoke and roasting meat, and the sweat of the masses that laughed and danced to the music of the mariachis who wandered among them.

He found a place of relative quiet at the fringe of the garden, hooked a foot through the bottom rung of a split rail fence, and rested his arms on the post. Limon stared out into the desert, into the low shadows of mesquite and greasewood bushes outside the apron of floodlights. His eyes fell on a pack of feral dogs that wandered the top of a slow rise marked by the silhouettes of *pitaya* cactus, just inside the fence line, drawn by the aroma of *cabrito*.

"*Los perros de la lluvia.*"

The old man had come silently and taken up a place beside Sonny. He had casino eyes and a nose that looked as if it had been broken more than once, his voice flinty and hardened by cigarette smoke. He shook one from the pack in his thorny hand, lit it with a wooden match that he snapped to life with the nail of his thumb.

"Excuse me?" Sonny said, in English.

The old man gestured toward the rise, toward the lean and hungry dogs that roamed there. "*Los perros de la lluvia,*" he said again. "Rain dogs."

"Rain dogs?"

"*Sí,*" the man smiled behind his well-trimmed goatee, deep lines fanning from the corners of his eyes. "They have arrived here, one by one, each after having lost his way in a storm." He cast a glance toward the flickering purple sky. "They are caught out sometimes on a night like this, when the rain comes suddenly, and washes the scent of their trail away. They are lost, and cannot find their way back home."

"You live in El Salto?"

"No." He shook his head. "I have a ranch of my own not so far from here."

"Then you are a friend of El Rey Miguel?"

The old man mulled a thought inside his head, his lips drawn into a tight line. "Are you?"

Sonny laughed aloud, shook his head as he crushed his empty beer can. "No, Senor, I would not exactly say that I am his friend."

The man dropped the smoldering butt into the dust, crushed it under the heel of his boot and smiled like a thief. He extended a hand to Sonny Limon. "I am Eduardo," he said. "But most people here call me El Brujo."

# CHAPTER 15

The longer Rick Montrose drove, the more his mind drifted back to the firefight in the mountains the night before. And the more he replayed the scene, the more he began to feel like an honest-to-God gunslinger. Not just one of those phony Hollywood cowboys, but a real-life, dope-dealing, gun-toting badass. It was enough to make him feel like his nuts were as big as cantaloupes. Colt Freeland and the Boss might have started out treating him like a kid, but he had obviously proven himself, he thought.

He settled down into the seat and drove on, watching the billboards, traffic, and the city lights of L.A. fade into the rearview. Two hours later he pushed through the final long stretch of citrus groves and low rolling hills before finally pulling into San Diego.

He followed the directions he'd been given to the letter, and checked into the Siesta Cabrillo Motel in San Diego just after four in the morning. The moon had set several hours earlier and had left the night still and dark, a velvet sky pierced by a million pinpricks of light. To the west lay the bay, the Navy yards and barracks, the strip joints, massage parlors, and the expanse of the Pacific.

As he'd expected, the motel was a dump: a two-story battenboard walk-up with a breathtaking view of the parking lot that stretched all the way to the cinderblock wall that encircled it. As he'd been instructed, he parked the El Camino in the stall directly outside his ground floor room, where he could keep an eye on it through the unwashed, water-stained window beside the door.

A dim, bare bulb protruded from the exterior wall and cast just enough light for Montrose to find the keyhole. In the distance, police sirens cut through the ambient hum of freeway noise, and he felt the little hairs on the back of his neck stiffen. He felt like a kid coming out into the night after a Vincent Price double-feature at the Fremont.

He passed inside and shut the door behind him, sliding the flimsy chain lock in place. Like that would protect him from anything. Nearly three hundred pounds of fresh, green weed concealed inside the car right outside his window, and a chain lock across a hollow door was supposed to keep him safe.

A couple of hours ago he had himself convinced he was Butch Cassidy. Now, the reality of it all was beginning to hit home. This plan hadn't seemed so Mickey Mouse when he was hearing it from Colt and his asshole friend back at the camp, but it sure as hell seemed Mickey Mouse now.

Those guys had to know what they were doing, though, right? They'd been pulling this kind of shit for years. Sure, the guys could be weapons-grade assholes, but even Rick Montrose had to admit they were two tough motherfuckers, man. And smart. They wouldn't turn him out on some loosey-goosey operation. No way, right? Everything was gonna be cool. Right?

His wandering thoughts were making him squirrelly and paranoid. Nothing like a big fat toke to take the edge off. But that wasn't going to happen. Boss-man had been pretty damn clear about that. Montrose could see his point, he had to admit. Torching a J at this hour of the morning in a fleabag like the Siesta Cabrillo would send those sweet-smelling fumes floating all over the place. Might as well light the friggin' lawn on fire.

Rick Montrose tossed his duffel bag on the bed and rifled through it, looking for his toothbrush. The food he'd eaten while on the road had left his mouth tasting like ass, and he wanted a shower. A real fucking shower. When he was done, he'd take a little walk down to one of those Stop & Rob mini-marts and pick up a bottle of Annie Green Springs, maybe watch a little tube and try to get that wired-from-the-road feeling out of his system. Yeah. That would do it.

○━━┿━━○

MONTROSE WOKE UP the next day with a headache and a raging hard-on.

He looked for a clock, but the dump didn't provide one of those, so he patted down the nightstand, knocking the lamp and the empty bottle of apple wine to the floor in the process, until he found his watch. Shit. It was, like, two in the afternoon, and still no phone call, no knock on the door, no nothing. Colt Freeland had told him to hang tight for twenty-four hours—maybe longer—but, damn, he felt like bat crap.

He sat up in bed and felt his stomach turn over. The room smelled like mildew and cleaning solvent, and made him want to gag. He needed food, and like an idiot, hadn't even thought to pick up something for today when he was at the mini-mart. God, what a low-rent gig.

He went to the sink and washed his face, looked in the mirror and thought about shaving. Hell with it. His hands were shaking and he figured he'd be bent over the john, driving the porcelain bus, before he was halfway through the task. Besides, if he was a big-time drug-runner now, those cats should look kinda grizzled and tough, right? Take Colt Freeland, for example. Man, that guy had that kind of Texas cowboy thing down pat. Crumpled-up hat, three days' growth of beard, and pecs that looked like they'd bust the seams of his T-shirt. And the way he talked—on the rare occasions when he did—all slow and drawly. The other dude, the Boss, was pure southern Cal cool, but Colt Freeland could scare the hell out of you just by looking at you sideways. So, yeah, fuck shaving, man. Rick Montrose was a man on a mission. Rick Montrose was riding shotgun on a mondo load of killer bud.

Three hours later, he was bored.

Freeland always gave him shit about his short attention span. Maybe it was true. Still, all this waiting was like watching paint dry. He could only pace the room for so long. All they had in here for entertainment was a crappy Magnavox black-and-white TV sprouting a chrome rabbit-ear antenna jammed into the corner. The damned thing only pulled in three channels. How many episodes of *Beany and Cecil* and *The Andy Griffith Show* was he supposed to watch, anyway? Daytime television sucked.

He was hungry, too. Like he could eat one of those big-ass Budweiser horses, whatever they were called. Clydesdales, that was it. Anyway, he could eat one of those things, hooves and all. Great.

Now he was thinking about beer. A couple of those would go down pretty nice, too—a little hair of the dog.

Rick Montrose looked at his watch again. Five-fifteen. Which got him thinking. If he was supposed to sit tight for at least twenty-four hours—maybe more, the Boss had said so himself—that meant he shouldn't expect anybody to get in touch until sometime after four in the morning. He had plenty of time for a little feast before the meeting. Just stroll on down the street, grab a burger and a beer, then shag ass back to this rathole in time for *Columbo*. Stay up for *Don Kirshner's Rock Concert*, maybe catch somebody cool like Jethro Tull or Foghat. His luck, of course, it'd probably be the Starland Vocal Band.

But that wasn't the point. He crossed the room and parted the curtain. The El Camino was still there, exactly where it should be. The gas cans were still roped into the back. Everything was cool. So, why not? Everybody has to eat. Nobody said he was supposed to freaking starve to death. Right?

<hr>

SKYE DAYTON had been called a Stone Fox on more than a few occasions.

She was tall for a girl. Five-ten, firm, California tanned, ice-blue eyes in a heart-shaped face, and that long sun-bleached blonde hair—all natural—that always seemed to stop men dead. Which could be a pain in the ass sometimes. Especially in this place. The Draft Pick. Twenty-seven beers on tap, four pool tables, and sports memorabilia on every wall. And most days, a shithead on every stool.

Today was one of those days. Some baseball game or other had brought all the assholes out in droves, sucking down pitchers of beer like there was no tomorrow, and talking like *they* would be up there in the Major Leagues if only they hadn't taken that crappy job down at the loading dock. The testosterone in the room was so thick you could practically smell it over the chicken wings and burger grease.

Skye had to get out of there. She was too smart for this waitressing trip. She had always had the ability to think on her feet, knew in her heart there was something better waiting for her. Hell, she *deserved* better. That's why she had left home to begin with: four years ago, at seventeen, put Gopherhole, North Dakota in the rearview mirror and never looked back. Headed for California. Even if she had to hitchhike. Even if she had to pay off a trucker with a handjob or two. You did what you had to. But not anymore. She had her heart set on L.A. She had been able to set aside a little tip money, make a few acquaintances at the parties she was always being invited to. A few more dollars and Skye Dayton would make her play for Hollywood. Now *that* was the Major Leagues.

She was standing on the sidewalk outside the Draft Pick, smoking a cigarette, when Rick Montrose first saw her. She saw the familiar Oh-My-God look on his face. But he wasn't like most of the assholes in the place today. This guy was a lot younger, kinda cute in his loping, kind of hippy-dippy way. She liked his long hair, the way his eyes turned down at the outsides, a little sad maybe, like a puppy.

Rick Montrose stopped short of making eye contact, stepped up to the menu board that hung on the outside wall and made a show of looking it over. The girl just stood there, like she was wrapped in cool wind.

"You should try the burger," she said.

She dropped her cigarette to the sidewalk and he watched it roll over the edge of the curb.

"You eat here?"

"I work here."

He nodded lamely. "Nice place?" he asked, immediately feeling like an idiot. He had never seen a girl like her in his life. She was even foxier than Gina from the diner. Unreal, man.

"It's a hole," she said, showing him a half-hearted smile. "But they do a pretty mean burger."

"Okay, then."

She offered her hand. "My name's Skye."

"I'm Ricky," he said. Her skin was soft and warm. "Ricky Montrose."

"Nice to meet you, Ricky Montrose."

He followed her inside.

RICKY MONTROSE didn't give a shit about baseball. Not like all the other goons that packed the place. But he stayed, passed the next couple hours surrounded by burly daytime drunks who took turns hollering at the television screen and making suggestive verbal passes at Skye Dayton.

She brought a beer to the table Montrose had taken near the wall in the back where they racked the pool cues. Then she brought another when she delivered his double-cheese with fries, straying back from time to time for small talk during brief breaks as the afternoon wore on. He liked the way she moved, the way she looked him in the eye when they spoke. She seemed like a chick that knew what she was about. He liked pretty much everything about her.

The crowd thinned out when the ball game ended, until the only customers that remained were the pool hustlers and semi-pro barflies hunkering over their respective tables and trying to cool Montrose out with their flat-eyed stares.

The bartender reached up and switched off the TV sets behind the bar, then flipped another gizmo that activated the jukebox in the far corner. The room was instantly engulfed in the kind of twangy country shit that seemed to bring the inner redneck out of everybody but Montrose; and it wasn't long before he overheard familiar words that usually presaged trouble for guys who looked like him. Words like *hippie* and *fag* and phrases like *is that a boy or a girl?* and *get a haircut.* It didn't make things any better that Skye Dayton seemed to be paying Rick Montrose a great deal of extra attention.

He tossed a glance out through the door, saw the long shadows of late afternoon fading to black in the failing light of dusk as he polished off his most recent beer. The vibe inside was growing darker, too.

Montrose ordered one last draft and asked Skye for his check, hoping for a few extra minutes with her before he had to head back to the Siesta Cabrillo Motel. He wished these rheumy-eyed bastards didn't get to him the way they did, and he tried to console himself that it was only because he was outnumbered. But he couldn't help thinking about Colt Freeland and the Boss. If they were here right now, they'd stay for as long as they damn well pleased, talk to whomever they liked, and a big fuck-you if you didn't dig it. With those guys it was always damn the torpedoes and full speed ahead. He thought about Colt and his beat-up hat, the slow drawl and the dead stare.

Skye brought his beer, slid the check across the table and looked at him like she was trying to memorize his face. She waited in silence, just watching as he counted out his cash.

"There's five extra for you," he said. "It was cool meeting you."

She hooked a thumb past her shoulder, toward the bartender who was pretending not to eyeball her while he wiped down the counter. "Gotta put it in the tip jar, if you want to give me that."

"No problem."

She turned slowly and began to walk away. She pulled up short and returned to Montrose's table. "You're not from around here, are you?"

"Naw. I'm just down here for a couple days."

His eyes slipped past her shoulder and landed on the men at the next table. They made no attempt to disguise their leering expressions. Skye seemed to be trying hard to ignore the rude comments they made as they leaned in close to one another to share a laugh.

"Well, Ricky Montrose," she sighed. "That's too bad."

Skye threw him a smile that broke his heart, and threaded her way between the tables, past the assholes Montrose had been watching just a moment before. One of them waved her over, whispered something in her ear. She pulled back, appearing as though she was about to slap him, when one of the others slid his hand up under her skirt. He took a fistful of her panties and grabbed hold roughly.

Without thinking, Montrose ripped a cue stick from the rack beside his stool. He took two long strides toward them.

"You know, you got a bad look on your face, son," the big one said, laughing. "But I'll tell you what. I can see that this little girl likes you. So, how 'bout I let you sniff my finger before you haul your ass outta here. How'd that be?"

The first swing of the cue took the big guy across the bridge of the nose. Heavy clots of blood spattered into the air as he fell backwards off his stool, his head bouncing hard off the tile floor with a sickening, hollow thud. The smaller of the two leaped off his seat and drew back a left that was meant for Montrose's jaw, but the guy was a beat too slow. Montrose caught him in the ear with the heavy end of the stick and sent him sprawling into the booth behind him. Beer and broken glass rained down onto the floor. He was struggling to get back to his feet when Montrose laid him down for good. A vicious kick to the man's ribs left him gasping for breath and leaking heavily from his broken lips.

It all happened so fast, Skye Dayton didn't even have time to scream.

Montrose dropped the cue to the floor without another word, slipped five dollars in the tip jar and walked right out the door.

# CHAPTER 16

Skye Dayton caught up with Montrose before he'd walked half a block. She ran up behind him and reached for his hand.

His face glowed with a slick shine of sweat, muscles twitching with adrenaline burn-off. He was already wondering what the hell he'd done. He turned to her as they walked together in silence. The neon lights of Rosecrans Street flickered crudely against the darkening sky, etching clouds in purple fire behind her head.

"You have to take care of me for the rest of my life, now, you know," she said. "It's a Chinese proverb or something."

"Cut it out, man. I don't even know where that came from."

His gait was rigid, his eyes locked onto the middle distance, passing vacantly across the homes and cheap apartments that were carved into the hills beyond the freeway. Distant windows shone warm and yellow, peaceful and domestic. Regular people living regular lives. He was in over his head with this gunslinger stuff. It made him want to go home.

"I never had anybody stand up for me before."

He felt guilty hearing her words, unworthy. He wasn't sure if it was simple instinct to take those two guys down just for being assholes, having had to endure two hours of their ignorant redneck bullshit. Maybe he hadn't really been protecting her at all.

"That's sort of hard to believe," he said.

"My daddy worked on a ranch when I was a little girl back in North Dakota. I watched him work from can't-see to can't-see, then come home piss-drunk just so he'd have somebody to beat on. I spent my seventeenth birthday waiting for the Greyhound to Denver."

"Yeah, well . . ."

Maybe Colt Freeland was right about him. Maybe he was a spoiled rich kid, pretending to be a hippie, playing at dealing weed.

This whole thing was supposed to be a smile, man. But the past two days had been *way* more than he'd bargained for. The ups and downs were making him crazy, and he wasn't ready to deal with that kind of truth.

"That's a bummer," he said instead. "I'm sorry."

"Don't be," she said, a tiny smile hiding in her eyes. "I'm a city girl at heart. Now that you busted me out of that place, I can go to Hollywood."

"You should. Chick like you? You could be in the movies."

"You know what we should do? We should celebrate. We should party like rock stars."

<hr />

THEY WERE SITTING at the little table in the corner of Montrose's motel room sharing a brand new pack of cigarettes, a fresh one hanging from Skye's lips and a beer tucked between her legs. The room glowed blue from the TV in the corner, the sound turned down to nothing as they talked, pouring freely from a quart bottle of Bombay gin into paper cups. The warm flush of alcohol had fueled their conversation for a while, but Montrose soon found himself doing everything he could to neutralize Skye's growing restlessness.

"Where do you find a dog with no legs?" he asked.

She put her paper cup down on the table and chased it with her beer. "I don't know? Where?"

"Right where you left him," he smiled, shaking a cigarette from the pack.

"We *have* to get outta here," she said.

"I can't. I gotta stick around."

"C'*mon*. Just for a little while. I know a guy out in Lemon Grove. We can score a lid, roll a doobie."

"I can't." He peeled a match from the matchbook, scratched it across the strike-strip and torched a cigarette. "Hey, I got another one. What do you call a boomerang that doesn't work?"

"Ricky, seriously. We should go out to Lemon Grove."

He shook the match dead and dropped it into the ashtray. "I told you. I can't."

He was moving beyond frustration. One of the foxiest chicks he had ever seen was sitting five feet away from him. They were already half drunk, and he couldn't keep his eyes off her long, tan legs.

"It'll only take an hour, hour and a half," she said. "We can pick up a little pot and come right back. It'll be fun. I promise."

"I got all the pot we need right here." The words were out of his mouth before he even thought them.

"What?"

"Nothing. Never mind."

"C'mon, Ricky. Tell me what you said."

"Nothing."

She scrunched up her face, crossed her arms and put on a good mock pout. "You've got grass, and you won't even share it? Not even with me?"

"Look, I'm not . . . I'm supposed to meet some guys, that's all. I gotta stay here."

Skye's face brightened, showed him a smile of renewed interest. "What, you're like some kind of big dope dealer?"

He shook his head. "No, I'm just kind of, you know . . ."

"You are a mysterious man, Ricky Montrose," she purred. "Full of secrets." She moved closer to him, so close Montrose could smell the citrus from the shampoo in her blonde hair, the sweet tang of juniper on her breath. She ran a long, lacquered fingernail along the inside of his thigh. This was like the luckiest day of her life. If he was a dealer, he definitely had bread. L.A. was so close she could taste it.

"I don't have any secrets."

"Well, I do," she whispered. "Want to hear one?"

His throat went bone dry. "Yeah, sure. Okay."

She left her chair, knelt coyly at his feet and rested her chin on his knee. Her hand kept moving, gently stroking his leg. "When I smoke pot, I get very, very . . . mmm . . . *amorous.*"

◦═══◦

THE FIRST TIME they made love was in the shower.

The sweet smell of marijuana hung heavy inside the clouds of steam that roiled in the tiny room as he moved his hands along the tender curves of her body. He kissed her, gently at first, licking the soft, smooth skin of her throat as he caressed her firm breasts. Warm water sluiced down the length of her body when he turned her, felt her take him into her hand and guide him inside.

Her fingers splayed as they touched the wall, closing her eyes as she leaned into him, rocking her hips as she moved, the gentle motion of rolling waves. He listened to her breathing, her hoarse, rhythmic moans as he held her hips.

He heard her breath catch deep in her throat. She came up slowly, then shuddering, as she turned and kissed his lips.

⊶⊷

RICK MONTROSE awoke with a start, still entangled in the sheets of their lovemaking.

He tried not to wake Skye as he unfolded himself from the bed, reaching for the bath towel he had let fall to the floor when they had moved into the room from the shower. He heard her rustle softly, adjusting the blanket over the smooth curve of her hip while he wrapped the damp towel around his waist.

"What is it, Ricky?" she said. Her voice was a hoarse whisper of half-sleep.

"I thought I heard someone at the door."

She rolled onto her side, covered her bare breasts with a sweep of her arm, and watched Montrose put an eye to the peephole.

Shit, this was not the way it was supposed to go. They'd fallen asleep after the second time, and now the Boss' guys were here. Just be cool, he thought.

He unlocked the door and peered through the crack. Two thick-chested men dressed in ratty denims stood in the dark outside his room. One of them had unscrewed the light bulb that burned there and cast the entire scene in deep shadow.

The one closest to the door pushed past him. He wore a thick mustache across a broad, square face, and a dark blue Navy peacoat. He smelled of fruit gum and mothballs. "You Montrose?"

"Yeah."

The second one followed, closing the door with his boot. Montrose saw this one was taller, heavily bearded, and leaner than the first. He burned a glance at Montrose as he moved inside, eyes like muddy water, a faded fatigue jacket over a white T-shirt. Both had their hands thrust deep in the pockets of their coats.

Montrose crossed over to the bedside and reached for the switch on the lamp. What happened next happened fast.

The light the lamp cast was dim, but still enough to make Montrose blink furiously as his pupils adjusted from the dark. The two men didn't have that problem. They took one look at the bed, at Skye lying there naked, wide eyes half-covered with the back of her hand, fear-hardened nipples pressing against the cheap fabric of the sheet.

They both drew their pistols.

"Who the fuck is this?"

"Nobody, man," Montrose said quickly. "She's nobody."

Peacoat trained his gun on Skye's face. "Don't look at me. Roll over. Bury your face in the pillow."

Montrose's mouth went dry. This was not right. This was not right at all. "Calm down, man. It's okay."

Beard backed toward the door as he stared down the barrel of a steel-blue automatic, directly into Rick Montrose's eyes. "We're outta here. This is bullshit."

"Hang on, man. It's cool."

"I don't think so," Peacoat said. "You were supposed to be alone. *Alone*, dude. This is completely wrong. You fucked up."

"I've got—"

"Shut up. And tell your girlfriend to stop looking at me." He took another step toward the bed, brought the pistol within inches of Skye's face. "I told you to bury your goddamned face in the pillow."

They all watched her do it. She was shaking violently beneath the covers.

Beard looked to Montrose with those flat, swampy eyes, un-blinking as he thumbed the hammer of his gun. "You tell your guy that this thing ain't happening. You dig? You're lucky I don't just waste you both right here. You tell him I didn't fucking splatter your brains outta respect for him. But this is *not* going down. Not with fucking strangers all over the fucking place. I told him, man. I told him how I feel about fucking strangers."

"But it's cool," Montrose begged. "I've got the whole—"

"Shut up, shithead. This deal's dead."

"He's gonna kill me," Montrose said.

"Yeah? Well, he should. And *that* is a stone fucking fact."

PART FOUR:

# No Me Niegas

# CHAPTER 17

It was noon by the time Esteban led Limon and Devlin to the shabby, beaten-down motel in El Salto where Miguel was to meet them.

The party the night before had barely broken up when the thunderstorm had finally blown in just before dawn, dumping marble-sized drops of rain for three straight hours. Rivers of clotted water still flowed freely off the hard adobe, flooding the streets of that miserable town with thick brown mud that oozed down the alluvial plain. By late morning the rainstorm had passed, but a blanket of heavy clouds still lay across the sky, blurring the sun until it looked like little more than a dim glow inside a wet bed sheet. Anemic gray shadows fell across the windows and walls of the cracked plaster structures that fronted El Salto's only paved road.

They waited inside a dingy room on the second floor, Miguel's head bodyguard, Esteban, sitting silently in one of the room's two chairs with a shotgun propped against the water-stained wall beside him. Devlin and Limon took turns pacing. Neither wanted to sit on the soiled and crusty bedspread, or take up a place in the empty chair beside Esteban. The only window in the room was blacked out with heavy cardboard crudely taped to the sill and covered over with a layer of tinfoil—a testament, Devlin was sure, to Miguel's growing paranoia, even in the town he controlled like a medieval lord.

Steve Devlin hadn't yet had the chance to fill Limon in on what he had overheard outside Miguel's office door the night before, but it was clear that some of the heavy players upstream in La Plaza were making increasingly tougher demands on El Rey. It was also clear that El Rey Miguel was making some extreme moves of his own to remain where he was in the power structure. That Devlin and Limon were more important to him than before seemed likely, and as far as

Devlin was concerned, this was when the smart operators leveraged their positions. But that was as far as he got with his eavesdropping. Marco had found him standing alone outside Miguel's office door. For a guy wearing bell-bottom trousers and ugly Mexican platform shoes, Marco could move like a fucking panther. That, Devlin thought again, had been a little awkward.

Nobody spoke for a full half-hour, tension bordering on malevolence crowding the confines of the room that smelled of mold and dust and desperation. The big man rocked back and forth on two legs of the rickety chair, tapped the flat of his scarred and gnarled hand on the small table, in rhythm to something only he could hear.

From out of the silence, the door slammed inward, nearly dislodging from its hinges. Esteban instinctively grabbed for his shotgun as Limon and Devlin dropped to the grimy floor. The door cracked against the interior wall sending shards of broken plaster across the room like an explosion.

Miguel stood in silhouette in the doorway, sweeping the space with a .45-caliber six-shooter drawn from the hip, cowboy style. He laughed out loud as he holstered the gun and plopped down on the bed, his mud-laden boots tracing a wide brown arc across the bedspread as he crossed his feet and reclined against the headboard.

Miguel's brother, Marco, waited outside on the balcony and spoke briefly to the three armed men that had followed behind them. They stormed in quickly, checked the closets and bathroom and under the bed before nodding an all-clear as Marco pushed his way in. Only then did the men take up their positions outside, and shut the door behind them. Marco pushed his dark glasses to the top of his head as his eyes adjusted to the relative dark, and took the only other chair in the room.

"You must forgive Miguel," Marco smiled. "He has been quick-drawing on everybody all morning."

It was evident that neither of the brothers had slept. Both wore the same clothes as the night before, permeating the cramped space with the stale odor of cigarettes and sweat, vibrating with Bacchic energy that came off them like a plucked string. Devlin wondered when Miguel's drug use had slipped over the line from recreational to habitual, and when he had determined the need for this kind of protection in his own town.

"Forgive yourselves," Miguel said, made twin pistols from the thumb and forefinger of each hand, pretended to shoot down everyone in the room, then blew imaginary smoke from his imaginary guns. "Make us a *cigarillo*, Marco."

Sonny Limon shot an uncertain glance at Devlin as Marco shook a pair of smokes from a box of Marlboros he carried in his shirt pocket, drew a glassine bindle of white powder from another and laid them out on the table.

"Let's get on with it," Sonny said. This *pistolero* shit was getting out of hand.

Miguel slid the real pistol from his holster, stroked it with nearly sexual pleasure before bringing it to bear on Sonny Limon. "I like this one," he said to Steve Devlin. "He is impatient, but he says what is on his mind."

The younger cop didn't move. His eyes betrayed no emotion as the black hole of the barrel drew level with his chest. "You said we would talk business today. So, talk."

Miguel showed Sonny a hollow, flat-eyed gaze, kept him fixed in his sights as Marco did his trick at the tiny table, carefully removing the tobacco from the end of each cigarette, then using the hollow end like a shovel to scoop white powder into the empty paper cylinder. After twisting the end into a wick, Marco passed it to Miguel. Only then did he lower the pistol and reach into his vest for a butane lighter. They watched as he passed the flame underneath the cigarette to vaporize the cocaine, then take a long draw. In seconds the drug was circulating in his brain, bringing with it the feeling of super-humanity Miguel had come to crave.

Miguel turned to Devlin. Even behind the dark glasses, Devlin could see Miguel's attention focus on him like a blowtorch. "The nature of our relationship is about to change," he said.

"So I gathered," Devlin said. "The Miguel I knew never needed anybody to watch his back for him."

Black points of impenitence burned for a long moment in the center of his stare. "When one becomes a king, he often finds enemies growing in every corner of his kingdom."

"Be careful what you wish for, Miguel."

"I do not bother making wishes, Senor Devlin." The *padrino* chucked a short, dry laugh. "You know what they say: put a wish in one hand, and shit in the other. See which hand fills up first."

Across the room, Marco was chopping a small white rock into fine powder with the edge of a single-edged razor. He drew the pile into a series of fine lines and offered Devlin a short straw.

Devlin shook his head. "I don't put anything up my nose that doesn't have its thighs wrapped around my ears."

Marco shrugged and snorted a line into each nostril.

The room was silent for long seconds as Miguel gathered his thoughts. He looked toward the blacked-out window blankly before he spoke.

"For years it has been nothing but *pollos* and a few thousand kilos of marijuana," Miguel said. "And what is a few *pollos* to America, more or less? They will come out of this shithole and into your country for as long as there is money to pay them for the work your people are unwilling to do, am I not correct?"

Marco slipped on his dark glasses from their perch on his forehead, leaned dreamily against the wall as Miguel went on. Esteban remained as still as stone.

"I know you are smart, Senor Devlin. As is Senor Limon. If there is no stopping the traffic across your border, why not profit from the situation? In your own mind, you may even believe it might make things more orderly, more safe, no? And you may be right. But a man cannot become a king in that kind of business. He may become rich, but not a king. So, I have decided—how do you say it?—to branch out."

The smell of meat on open flames drifted up from the tiny restaurant below, mingling with the mordant odors of closeness in the room in a way that turned Limon's stomach. This man, Miguel, was not as Steve Devlin had described him. This man was a grandiose delusional and a dangerous paranoid, and his brother was a stone killer. Taking his bribes in the blind was one thing, but this was something else entirely. What felt most odd to Sonny, though, was the fact that he could no longer bring himself to give a shit. It felt as though it was all happening to someone else, someone outside of himself, someone whose boundaries had been blasted away, whose moral flesh had been corrupted beyond recognition. In that way, Devlin was right: if you're getting raped, you might as well try to enjoy the sex. And ever since Sonny had allowed himself to get on the pad, taken that very first dollar, he had been well and truly fucked.

"You know the limits of what we can do," Sonny Limon said.

"*Si, si*," said Miguel, his empathetic tone corded with ugly irony.

"What are we talking about here?" Devlin asked.

"We are talking about the future, Senor Devlin. We are talking about *la dama blanca*." The white lady.

"We know the balloon trick," Devlin said. "You want to send a bunch of *pollos* across the border with rubbers full of coke up their asses? Fine. We know the drill. All we have to do here is work out the price."

Miguel smiled and cast a sidelong glance at his brother who was also wearing an unpleasant grin. "I'm afraid that will not be sufficient for this."

"Why the fuck not?"

"Because that is much too limited and will take too long. We need to bring many kilos across at a time."

Miguel had no intention of spelling out the obstacles he faced on both sides of the border. The Pig, the Peacock and the *Maricon* could be dealt with. The fucking Peacock had made that clear enough at Miguel's party. But time was of the essence in moving it across if he was to do so without the Colombians discovering his deceit. As it was, it would take all the finesse in his power to convince them that their plane had simply never arrived. It wasn't a plan one could execute more than once.

"Jesus."

"So we need a new method," Miguel said. "We need you to help us find our way across your border. Quickly."

Sonny Limon began to speak, but Devlin briskly cut him off. "How much are we talking about?"

"One thousand dollars a kilo," Miguel said.

"What kind of weight are we talking about?"

Miguel pursed his lips, silent for several beats. "About thirteen hundred kilos."

"Fuck me," Sonny said.

Devlin shot him a sidelong glare, turned back to Miguel. "Make it two thousand a kilo."

Miguel had been ready for this. The ton of pure coke he had liberated from the Colombians would be stepped-on, diluted with powdered milk and baby laxative before being sent to the north. By the time it made its way across the border, his two thousand pounds of free cocaine would weigh nearly three thousand pounds—over 1,350 kilos, at a price of $20,000 each. And that was wholesale. Even after paying the vultures of La Plaza and these compromised American police, he was looking at a net profit of twenty million U.S. dollars.

"That would be more than two and a half million dollars to you and your friend, Senor Devlin."

Steve Devlin showed him a grim smile. "And that is a great deal of weight, Senor Zamora."

Miguel stood suddenly, brittle with impatience, and planted his mud-covered boots on the scarred surface of the floor. Bright flashes of light danced at the edges of his vision, sharp needles of pain prickled his scalp. He needed sleep. He wanted another taste of white powder.

"One other thing," Miguel said. "The details must be worked out tonight."

"Not a fuh—" Limon began.

"For two thousand dollars a kilo, my friend, it must be worked out right away." He turned slightly, facing Sonny Limon.

Sonny watched his own reflection in the mirrored lenses of Miguel's glasses, unsure of what he saw there.

"You, Senor Limon, will go with Marco to Tijuana. You will show him everything he needs to clear the path, then come back for Senor Devlin. You should be back in time for lunch tomorrow."

"I'm not leaving my partner here."

"Your partner and I have some details of our own to talk about while you are gone."

Devlin shook his head. "Don't sweat it, Sonny."

"Not a chance."

"You speak as though you have a choice." Miguel's lips turned down into an exaggerated frown. "If it makes you feel better, you can think of your partner as my insurance."

"What fucking insurance?"

"Insurance that you will do your part, and that you will return as quickly as possible. We have a saying here: *El perro mas pendejo sabe ladrar.*"

Even the most stupid dog knows how to bark.

# CHAPTER 18

Skye Dayton returned to the motel room to find Rick Montrose still pacing the floor.

He'd been at it for almost an hour, the time it had taken her to pick up a pair of deli sandwiches and a fresh pack of cigs. He'd already chain-smoked the ones from the night before, clouding the small space with a haze of acrid smoke that threatened to suffocate them both, his hands trembling like an old man every time he fired up.

"I am so screwed. I gotta fix this." He had been repeating the words, his personal anguished mantra, since dawn. "I am so dead."

Skye was grateful for the chance to have gotten outside, breathe some fresh air and think. She had come *that close* to leaving him there, just keep on walking; maybe even slink back into the Draft Pick, put on her apron and pretend that none of this ever happened. This guy who had started out as her hero and protector, who she had believed was her big-time ticket to L.A., was nothing but a gutless screw-up. She had even fucked him! Twice.

She changed her mind somewhere between Kamm's Deli and the Tic-Toc mini-mart. She popped the top off a bottle of Fanta orange soda, sat on the curb and thought the whole thing through.

On the plus side, there was the weed. She had a friend who could probably take a few pounds off Montrose, if he had that much. If she really racked her brain, she could likely think of a couple others, too. A few phone calls, and the grass was as good as cash. It might take a little doing, but she had never been this close before; so close she wasn't going to let all that bread just up and drive away.

On the downside, there was Ricky Montrose himself. He was coming apart at the seams. At first, she had thought he was cute. When he laid out the two assholes who manhandled her at the bar, she had thought she'd found somebody who could take care of her, someone she could hold onto, someone who could hold on to *her*. But, based on the last few hours of his near-incessant whining and hysterics, she concluded she had probably witnessed the single act of bravery in Ricky Montrose's entire life.

Eyes on the prize, though, she told herself. Get him to settle down and *think*.

"Ricky, c'mon, baby. It's gonna be all right."

"I am so dead."

"Ricky, sweetie," she whispered. Her L.A. dream was fading fast if she didn't get a handle on this thing, and quick. "Everything is going to work out fine. We just need to think it through, that's all."

"You don't know these guys. You don't know." Funnels of smoke blew from his nostrils, his long, uncombed hair obscuring a face that had the pallor of melted wax.

"We'll fix it, okay? We'll make it work."

Montrose shook his head. Colt Freeland was going to kick his ass. Probably worse. And if Colt didn't finish him off, the Boss sure as hell would. "You don't know these guys," he said again.

"Just stop freaking out, Ricky. Just be cool for a minute. Let's think about this."

"I gotta get outta here."

"Hold on a minute." Skye Dayton's mind was running a thousand miles an hour. "You still have the pot, right?"

He paced, didn't hear her, or acted like he hadn't.

"Ricky. Focus," she said, snapping her fingers. "You still have the pot, right?"

"Yeah, sure."

"How much?"

"About three hundred pounds. I am gonna get crucified. I'm serious."

Her heart pounded against her chest like she was coming on to a fistful of Black Beauties. Three *hundred* pounds? Jesus. This wasn't just going to be L.A. This was going to take her straight to Hollywood. Lower the drawbridge, citizens, the princess is coming home. "Remember I told you I know a guy? Out in Lemon Grove?"

"So?"

"So, I'll call him. Maybe he knows somebody who can take it off your hands, you know?"

"I don't think so."

"Ricky, think about it. What are your choices? At least, if you do it my way, you can take some cash back to where you came from, right?"

"Humboldt."

"Whatever. Did you hear what I said?"

"I heard you."

"You don't even have to go back if you don't want to. After all, *we'll* have the bread, right? And bread is freedom, baby."

Hope flickered across his face for one brief moment, then died stillborn.

"Not a chance, Skye. The guys I work for would hunt me down and kill me in my sleep."

"I'm with you, Ricky. We can go to Los Angeles, ditch the car. It's a big city, millions of people. How're they going to find you?"

"I don't know."

"Whatever you do, you're going to have to do it fast. You've got to make up your mind."

"I don't know. I can't fucking think right now."

"Ricky," she said. Her voice was hard-laced, like a reproving mother. "Look at me."

He did.

"You don't have any choices. You've got to do it my way. Let me make a call."

"I don't know."

"Ricky."

His body sagged.

"Okay," he sighed. "Okay. Call your friend."

She pulled Montrose close, cradled his head against her breasts and held him like a child. She stroked his tangled hair, kissed him softly on the forehead as she felt the fear leach out of him, felt the regularity of his hot breath through the fabric of her blouse. She kissed him one last time as she let him go.

"Where are you going?"

"Payphone," she said. "You want the motel to have a record?"

He shook his head, feeling stupid all over again.

"Take a shower, baby. Get some rest, okay? You just let Skye take care of everything."

RICKY MONTROSE had no idea where the hell he was.

He was behind the wheel of the El Camino, Skye Dayton beside him, both lost in silent tension interrupted only by the directions she gave him from time to time.

"Take a left at the next crossroad," she said.

"Here?"

"No. The *next* one, I said."

The painted striations of sunset had since faded to charcoal. The sky was a blank slate, void of moon or stars, blown clean by a brittle fall wind that charged the air with static electricity and sent dust and dry leaves raking across the twin beams of his headlights.

They were out in the middle of nowhere, turning left onto a narrow, unpaved service road, bounded on both sides by a heavy overgrowth of deadwood and tall weeds. Loose gravel ticked loudly at the undercarriage as Montrose steered the El Camino around the mounds and potholes that revealed themselves in the headlights, his palms damp with perspiration.

"You have any idea where we are?"

Skye Dayton didn't turn to look at him, only stared through the windshield, her expression washed with disquiet. "There's supposed to be a construction site up here somewhere."

A couple hours earlier, with the light of late afternoon washing over the city, this had seemed like a good idea. Like everything might just turn out all right. Skye and Montrose had gone over the plan a half-dozen times. He told her about the weed, how they would need time to unfasten the false bottom of the El Camino to get at the bulk of the pot. She would help unload that stuff while he disassembled the propane tank and got to the last twenty bricks. Sure, the guys back home were going to be pissed that he'd fucked things up a little, but what was the difference as long as he came back with the cash, right?

Now, pitching and rolling along a dirt road in total darkness, the reality was proving to be considerably more sketchy. It didn't help matters when he saw how Skye grew more skittish with every passing minute. This was *her* friend they were meeting out here.

"Listen, Skye . . ." he said. The sound of his voice startled them both, coming out of the heavy silence.

He saw her turn to him out of the corner of his eye. A sidelong glance revealed the yellow light that traced the contours of her face, the look in her eyes concealed in deep shadow.

"Listen," he began again. "If anything goes wrong out here . . . tell them I forced you into this, okay?"

"Cut it out, Ricky," she said.

"I mean it. I don't want you to—"

"There it is," she said. "Right up there. See it?"

A length of chain was stretched across the road a few yards beyond them, strung between a pair of steel posts. A hand-lettered sign rocked in the wind, saying something about authorized construction traffic.

Huge tractors had laid the land bare, scraped away the natural tangle of brush that covered the low, rolling hills, and left it looking naked and scarred. On the near side, the skeletal outlines of a tract of new houses sketched themselves against the sky, the ribs of some unholy litter of beasts bent on multiplying until there were no more hills at all.

"Pull over and stop," Skye said. "Flash your lights three times."

Rick Montrose did as he was told, looked off into the maze of lumber and brick and waited for the expected response. A moment later, he saw it. Three blinks of a flashlight coming from one of the unfinished houses.

"This is it," Montrose said. He leaned across the seat, kissed her gently on the corner of her mouth. "Remember what I told you. Anything goes wrong, I made you do this."

She looked away without a word, unable to meet his eyes. She watched him in the rearview as he walked around to the back of the car to wait. He crossed his arms and leaned uncertainly against the tailgate.

Montrose felt his muscles tense with the chill of cold wind on his clammy skin. The air smelled of machine oil and freshly cut wood; it was dead silent, but for the dry rattle of wind in the tall weeds.

Moments later, a man appeared out of the shadows, wearing a dark-colored windbreaker, a bandana tied across his face just below his eyes, and a Chicago Cubs baseball cap pulled low on his head. Two others, similarly dressed, pulled up short, waited a few yards behind. Each held some kind of rifle, hard to tell in the dark. But they were both trained squarely on Ricky's face.

"You got the stuff?"

"Got the money?" Montrose tried to be cool, but the tremor in his voice betrayed him.

The man closest to the car turned, gestured to one of the two behind him. When he turned back around he was holding a crowbar in one hand, smacking it firmly against the palm of the other. "Tell you what," he said. "Let's open 'er up and take a look first."

"Hey, man, hold on," Montrose said. "Gimme a couple minutes and I'll unscrew the bed-liner. No need to go prying it off and fucking up the car."

"Wish we could, but we don't have that kind of time, Chief."

Rick Montrose watched, a shotgun barrel pressed into the soft skin behind his ear, as the other two opened up the bed like they were peeling the lid off a can of tinned clams. From the corner of his eye, he saw Skye's reflection in the rearview mirror, mute and unmoving, as they stripped away the last bricks of dope.

"Bring the van around," the one with the crowbar said.

"What about the propane tank?" It was the one with the shotgun. The third one was already running back into the dark to retrieve their vehicle.

"Leave it."

"Skye said there was more in—"

"I already told you. Leave it." Crowbar and Shotgun locked eyes for a moment, then it was over. The van was pulling up beside them.

Rick Montrose seethed with impotence as, one by one, the heavy, duct-taped bags of pot were tossed into the back of the van.

Shotgun backed slowly away, holding Montrose in his sights, as Crowbar moved toward the passenger side of the El Camino.

"You coming, Skye?"

Skye Dayton got out, shut the car door behind her and deliberately made her way to the van.

"Skye?" Montrose said. "I did this for *us*. I did this for *you*." There was a simpering quality in his voice as it cut through the night. He hated himself for it even as it reached his own ears.

She shook her head slowly, the wind pulling loose strands of blonde hair across her face. She hugged herself tight against the chill and pulled her eyes away.

"Goodbye, Ricky."

◦━✦━◦

HIS HANDS WERE still shaking when he started the El Camino and headed back the way he had come. The dark of the moonless night felt as if it were closing in on him, leaving him sick with humiliation at the depth of Skye's betrayal, eclipsed only partly by his dread of returning to Humboldt in inexplicable failure.

He had made it all the way back to the paved county road, the lights of Lemon Grove in the distance, the glow of downtown San Diego rising up just beyond.

He was almost on top of them before he saw them. A dead-flat straightaway with nowhere to turn, nowhere to run.

Everything went into slow motion inside Rick Montrose's head.

He feels the heavy pulse in his neck, the pounding of his heart. His asshole is puckered so tight he feels like he might turn inside out. A hotshot of adrenaline speeds through his veins. Nothing but stray images as the gumball lights flash and throb. The white beam of a searchlight pins him to his seat. Cops, a half-dozen of them, stand with weapons drawn, shielded by the open doors of their cruisers. Gun barrels train on Ricky's bloodless face. He loses control of his bladder. An acidic odor fills the cab of the El Camino.

One of the cops approaches slowly, opens the driver's side door and drags Montrose out. He kneels on the pavement, fingers

- 149 -

interlaced behind his head, blinded by the spotlights, sweat rolling down his back, piss dripping down his legs. Two more cops approach. They cuff him. There is a squeal of leather as weapons are holstered.

"Mr. Montrose?"

Terror claws his skin like icy fingers. This is the realization of his worst nightmare. His mouth is dry as dust. He nods.

The cops toss him into the back of one of the cruisers. One begins to laugh.

Hot tears of panic fill Ricky's eyes as he descends back into reality.

"You want to tell me where it is, or shall we tear the rest of your car apart?"

Montrose moved his mouth, but no sound would come. This couldn't be happening. He nodded.

"You're looking at a twenty-five year jolt, son. Maybe more. A little cooperation from you might go a long way. You follow me?"

He nodded again.

"Let's start with where you've got it hidden," the cop said. "Where's the dope?"

It was over.

"The tank," he heard himself say. "It's in the propane tank."

Rick Montrose felt the steel bite into his wrists as he watched from the backseat of a cruiser, looking on as they unloaded a hundred pounds of prime weed, brick by brick, from a hole they'd kicked through the false front of the tank. Fifty bricks. Twenty-five years.

This whole thing was supposed to be a smile. A walk on the wild side. He wasn't the same as Colt Freeland. Or the Boss, either, for that matter. He was no professional dope dealer. This was just supposed to be a goof. A good story for later.

His head fell against the cold glass as he choked back his tears. He knew what they did to guys like him in prison. He'd never make it. Not twenty-five fucking years. He'd be pushing fifty years old when he got out. *If* he made it out, for Chrissake.

Situation like this, it's every man for himself, right? Those guys had to understand that.

Right?

# CHAPTER 19

An early morning rain shower left the trail slippery and cratered with treacherous pools of dead water. I pressed my way into town with greater care than usual, denying myself the pleasure of the periodic glimpses down through the cuts in the heavy foliage and into the silver gulch of the Mad River as I strained to keep the Yamaha upright. My eyes were fixed on the muddy trail, but my mind was locked on the call I was expecting from my contact down south informing me that everything had gone as planned.

I left Colt back at the camp to salvage what he could of our harvest and begin to break down the tents. With any luck, we'd be out of here for good—at least for this season—in less than three days. By that time, Rick Montrose would have returned with the El Camino so we could reload it and blow town with at least a little bit of cash and stash to show for our labors.

The cloud cover was beginning to break, but the wind that blew against my bare face and hands was brittle and cold. Small patches of bright blue sky behind the high mist gave me hope that we might have seen the last of the rain before we split.

The shops in town were just beginning to open their doors, storekeepers waving to one another across the park at the center of town as sidewalks were swept clean of fallen leaves. It was a scene from another time, and it never failed to bring a smile to my face. I always thought of it as Mayberry comes to California. With tie-dye.

As usual, the parking stalls in front of the diner were already filled, so I pulled the bike into a space in front of the hardware store about a block away and killed the engine. I liked to use the payphone adjacent to the statue near the center of the park. That way I could see if anyone tried to approach me from a full 360 degrees. In general, the people in town chose to remain blissfully detached from the realities of what made their local economy hum—though they certainly weren't stupid—and everyone seemed to get along in a live-and-let-live manner no matter what side of the proverbial hill one's income came from. Unfortunately, the influx of violence from rippers, not to mention elements of Organized Crime from certain countries south of the border, was beginning to manifest here, and the stress cracks were beginning to show. We were all a little more on edge than years past, more wary than we used to be. It was sad. It was unfortunate. But it was reality. So, like I said before, I like to use the phone in the middle of the park. I hadn't heard of anyone yet who did time for being cautious.

I looked at my watch and saw that I was a good half an hour early. I had expected the dirt trail would be a mess, but I still overestimated the time it would take me to get here. On the bright side, it would give me a chance to duck into the diner and grab myself a cup of coffee and a slice of Mrs. Kimball's homemade peach pie. Like I said, Mayberry with tie-dye.

⊶━┼━⊷

I LEFT A tip on the table for Gina, everyone's favorite piece of eye candy, and headed out the glass door. A small brass bell tinkled my departure as the door swung shut behind me.

The sun was shining brighter and dappled the drying pavement with yellow light and shadows cast by windswept storm clouds as I made my way back to the payphone. It rang two minutes later.

I answered without preamble before the second ring. "Everything good?" I said.

"No deal," the voice said.

"Excuse me?"

"Your boy brought a girlfriend to the party. You know how I feel about strangers. No deal."

I couldn't believe what I was hearing, and I felt the flush of heat beneath my skin. Goddamned fucking kid. "I gave him specific instructions."

"Well, he didn't follow 'em so good."

"Let me talk to him. We can try this thing again."

The din of street traffic spun down the line at me as he thought it over.

"Call me back in half an hour," I said. "Same number."

There was another long silence before he answered. "Half an hour."

I placed the handset back in the cradle with exaggerated care. My hands began to shake as a nearly debilitating wave of anger built inside my chest. I couldn't wrap my head around why the hell Rick Montrose would pull such an ignorant, dangerous stunt. All he had to do was sit in his goddamned room and wait. I couldn't wait to see him again so I could beat his ass into next week. In the meantime, I had a problem to solve.

I rifled through the contents of my wallet until I found the scrap of paper on which I had scribbled the number for the Siesta Cabrillo Motel, then dug into my pocket for more change. Three dimes, a nickel and two pennies. I was pretty sure that wasn't going to cover the cost of a long distance call to San Diego, so I wasted five minutes jogging across the park to the stationery store and back to get change for a couple bucks.

"Siesta Cabrillo Motel," a man answered. His voice was heavily accented with a sing-song Indian cadence.

"Can you connect me to a guest room, please," I said. "Mr. Rhodes."

I heard the sound of paper shuffling. "Rocky Rhodes?"

It didn't seem funny to me anymore. "Yeah."

"I will ring the room."

I let it ring ten times before I gave up. I fed another handful of coins into the slot and dialed again.

"Siesta Cabrillo—"

"Yes," I interrupted. "I just called a minute ago for Mr. Rhodes. He didn't answer."

"Perhaps he is away from his room."

He'd better fucking not be, I thought to myself. I was seething now, and barely able to contain it. "Could you do me a favor, please, sir?"

"How can I help you?"

"Would it be possible to check on Mr. Rhodes for me? Would you please knock on his door?"

"I don't know if I—"

"It is very important, sir, that I speak to him."

"This is an emergency of some kind?"

"Yes, absolutely. An emergency. Break down the door if you have to."

"I do not wish to have to break any doors . . ."

My hand was beginning to ache from my grip on the handset. "It was just a figure of speech, sir. Please take your key and open the door if he doesn't answer. It is very important. I will make sure he pays you an extra hundred if you'll just go and get him."

"A hundred dollars?"

"Yes."

"I will be right back."

Halfway through a wait that seemed like forever, an operator broke into the call and instructed me to insert more change. Several long minutes later the man from the motel came back on the line. He was out of breath.

"I am sorry but your friend is not in his room."

My temples throbbed with the sharp ache of impotent rage. "You checked everywhere? Even the bathroom?"

"Yes, everywhere. The rooms are actually quite small. Mr. Rhodes was not there, but his luggage is on the bed."

My mind raced through a thousand possible scenarios, none of them good. "Is his car still in the parking lot? A brown El Camino?"

"Will I still receive my one hundred dollars?"

"Yes. Would you please check for his car?"

"I will come right back."

Time was ticking away. I had a need to pace, but the cord on the phone was too short. "*Fuck!*" I said to no one.

"I am sorry, but there is no brown El Camino in the parking lot."

"You're sure?" I was trying to sound calm.

"I am certain."

"Thank you anyway."

"I will still get—?"

I hung up.

No car, no weed, no money, no Montrose. My heart pounded in my chest and I wanted to slug somebody. I was staring in frustration across the park's manicured lawn when I saw Colt Freeland come whipping around a corner behind the wheel of the Bushmonster. He barely slowed for the stop sign at the corner, gunned toward the curb near where I was standing, and skidded to a halt. He left his door open in his haste to jump out of the truck and jog over to me. This day looked like it was turning to shit at the speed of light.

"We got trouble, hoss."

"Yeah, we do," I said.

Colt looked at me blankly.

"You go first," I said.

"Rippers killed Junior Stavro last night. Colombians, it appears. Slit his throat and pulled his tongue through the hole. Colombian necktie. Jill got it even worse."

"Christ." I was starting to feel dizzy.

"I packed up everything I could and got us out of there. Gear's in the back of the 'monster. The Feds are gonna be all over this place."

"Montrose is missing," I added.

"Come again?"

The payphone rang and I picked up.

"I couldn't reach my guy," I said.

I could almost hear him shaking his head. "You got trouble, my man. Hang in there," he said and broke the connection.

∘═◆═∘

COLT FREELAND and I were seated in a booth at the back of the diner, hunched across the table and speaking in hushed voices, even though the morning crowd had thinned out and we were nearly alone.

"Let's deal with the Montrose situation first," Colt said. "Worst case."

"Worst case? The kid got pinched and he's squealing on us as we sit here."

"He doesn't know your name."

"He knows yours."

Colt chewed a toothpick and gave that a moment's thought. "That kid wouldn't know a donkey from a ring of keys," he said. "But he's surely not stupid enough to give anybody my name."

"I wouldn't wager the ranch on that."

"What about the car? The registration?"

"My mom bought it for cash from some dude three years ago. I never registered it."

"That cat's gonna have a helluva surprise when the DEA kicks in his door." He tapped a fingernail against his coffee cup and gazed out the window at the far end of the room. "I s'pose the smart move is to split up for a while. Just in case."

Colt had a place somewhere in the mountains across the border in Canada.

"You okay for cash?" I asked.

He nodded. "You remember when this used to be fun?"

I smiled sadly.

"I'm sorry things came down this way," I said finally. "Can't believe that about Junior and Jill, man."

Colt turned back from the window and looked at me. "Shit just happens, hoss. I don't tend to study on it."

"I thought we did everything we could've done. I thought we had things covered."

He unsnapped the pocket of his shirt. "This is for you," he said.

It was a small carving about the size of my thumb, a rabbit he had whittled from a chunk of fallen pine.

"For luck," he said. "I don't reckon a foot all by itself's gonna get it done."

"Thanks," I said. "And don't forget to watch your back."

"Don't worry on me," my friend laughed out loud. "It's you that's got the uphill run. I wouldn't strap on y'all's boots at the point of a gun."

"YOU TAKE THE truck," Colt said. "I'll take the bike. I'm just going up to McKinleyville and get my plane. You got a long road."

We were standing on the sidewalk beside the Bushmonster. The sky was a deep cobalt blue, dotted with white clouds.

Seemingly out of nowhere, the frighteningly familiar thrum of rotor blades cracked the silence overhead. Four black, military-style choppers sped inland at such low altitude and such incredible speed that we both instinctively ducked as if we were still soldiers in a hot LZ.

"Son of a bitch," Colt said.

"Here they come."

# Chapter 20

Sonny Limon and Marco Zamora drove past the guards at Rancho Tronada at about one o'clock in the afternoon.

The sun had burned away the gray sheet of inversion layer that clung to the coastal plain, and turned the sky a rich, clear blue. Now the midday heat seared hard, deep ruts into the mud that had washed the road all the way from Punta Enselma to El Salto, jarring Sonny's head as he rested it against the window, and making sleep impossible.

Fatigue wracked his body and his eyeballs danced with anxiety behind closed lids; he was unable to find any semblance of solace or justification for his complicity in a scheme that had suddenly run wildly out of control. Sonny Limon had come face to face with a hard reality as he sat inside one of the uneasy silences that marked the détente that existed between himself and Marco. He confronted the petty vanity of his own conscience. He recognized it for the contrivance that it was—little more than a failed attempt to pretend that he hadn't been neck deep in this shit well before this bastard Marco had ever slid the blade into that pitiful *pollo*. Hell, he was a dirty cop, a facilitator. Miguel Zamora's coke was going to move across with or without him. So, fuck it, right? In for a peso, in for a pound.

Marco and Sonny had spent the entire night watching the rhythm of traffic at the San Ysidro border crossing. And more long hours walking the fence at La Perla without uttering a word, taking note of the ebbs and flows of vigilance on the American side for any weakness in the system they could exploit.

"So what are you thinking?" Marco had asked him late last night. The moon was a waning crescent, low on the horizon.

"I think you're out of your mind moving the kind of weight you're talking about in such a short time."

Sonny turned his head only to see Marco's unblinking eyes staring back at him.

"And," he went on, "I think if it was me, I'd just keep doing what I was doing. Just keep stuffing balloons up my *pollos'* asses and sending them across. It's working. Don't fix it."

"It will take too long to move the weight."

"Then we're back to what I said before: you've got three choices."

Marco shook his head impatiently, reached into his pocket for his little silver vial of coke. He turned his back in the direction of the meager breeze and hit each nostril with a quick bump. "I already told you. We do not have access to a plane for this."

"Then you bring it ashore by boat—"

"*No tenemos ningún maldito barcos!*"

"Goddamnit. What kind of chickenshit operation are you guys running?"

Marco's eyes flashed with anger, then he turned his face toward the twinkling yellow lights far beyond the fence, across the arroyo. "Senor Limon, this has to be done quickly and quietly. My brother does not wish to involve any more people than necessary. No planes. No boats. No time."

"You need to listen to me, here," Sonny said. He held Marco's gaze, but pointed into the darkness. "You've seen what I've seen tonight. The crossing at San Ysidro is undermanned for peak traffic, always has been. The checkpoint at San Onofre is a joke. The BAG teams that operate along the fence here are spread out, but they're unpredictable and dangerous. You never know exactly where the patrol teams are going to be. Up until now, me and Devlin, we've been able to slide your *pollos* through the gaps. But that's because we know where the gaps are, and they've been relatively small groups. You with me so far?"

"*Entiendo. No yo soy un idiota.*"

"Relax, Marco. I'm trying to tell you that if you're not going in by boat or air, then you've got to overwhelm the system on the ground. Distract and overwhelm. You run about three or four times as many *pollos* through the fence as you usually do on the night you want to move. Some may get through, but many will likely be caught by the BAG teams. You want them to. If drugs are found, then a great deal of attention will be paid to those who are picked up. They'll have Jeeps and choppers like you've never seen. It'll create chaos that may even pull manpower from the checkpoints . . ."

Marco was silent for several seconds before pulling a pack of cigarettes from his pocket and lighting one. He picked a loose strand of tobacco from his tongue and stepped away into the darkness to think. Five minutes later, he was back at Sonny's side, grinding the butt beneath the heel of one of his pointy-toed boots. "Let's talk."

Two hours later, they had a plan. It would cost Miguel a few lost kilos, but the main body of his shipment would get through. There were no K-9 units at the San Ysidro border crossing, so it came down to a combination of audacity and bulldog courage on the part of El Rey Miguel.

Now, as they drove through the gates into Rancho Tronada, Limon was exhausted from lack of sleep and hungry as hell. But all he could think about was collecting Steve Devlin and getting the fuck out of Miguel's ranch, out of the shithole town called El Salto, and out of Mexico.

With their money.

The way Limon had it figured, if they left right away they could be back in San Diego by nightfall, and both Sonny and Devlin still had one day's leave left to sack-out before going back on shift. A cold beer and a good night's sleep in his own bed, far away from these cocksuckers, would go a long way toward setting Sonny's world back on its proper axis.

Marco pulled to a stop in front of the main house, and the two men got out of the car. A gust of hot wind hit them like a blast from a blow-dryer, kicking up eddies of brown dust and enveloping them in a leaden hush. A cluster of four-wheel-drive vehicles, their undercarriages crusted and dripping with sludge, baked in the hard sun outside the service building beyond Miguel's hacienda. From somewhere behind, muted canine ululations drifted on the broken drafts that vented across the Vizcaino. Otherwise, the place seemed deserted.

Marco cupped his hands to his lips and called out for his brother, but was answered by silence. Without trying again he made his way across the loose gravel toward the front door of the main house, Sonny Limon beside him, matching his stride.

It was cool and dark inside, soundless but for the echo of their footsteps on the hard tile floor. They came to a halt outside the door to Miguel's office. Marco pressed an ear to the heavy wooden door before knocking. Nothing. He twisted the knob, pushed inside and found the room empty.

"Miguel?" Marco called. "Yolanda!"

A door opened from somewhere upstairs. A moment later, a young Mexican woman appeared at the wrought iron railing. "Senor Marco," she said, her tone hovering between deference and obsequiousness.

"Susana, where is my brother?"

"I don't know, Senor Marco," she said. Her eyes slid away from his and focused on the floor. "I have been upstairs with *la Senora*."

"Call her down."

"I don't think—"

Marco didn't wait for her to finish as he took the stairs two at a time, his face flushed with anger. The girl made no move to intervene, only looked away in shame when Sonny Limon moved past her at the top of the landing.

Yolanda Zamora was seated in a chair beside an open window, her eyes fixed on the rolling brown landscape that stretched beyond the balustrade. Sheer white draperies luffed beside her on the uneven pulse of the wind.

She turned away from the window just as Sonny crossed the threshold and he saw her fix Marco with a flat, trenchant stare. Her face was the color of ash and marbled with bruises. She moved as if she was made of wax.

Marco's expression betrayed nothing. "Where is Miguel?"

She wore a long, multicolored skirt that fell to her ankles, and a powder blue blouse that had been badly torn. Tiny freckles of blood stained the collar and the sleeves where she had raised her arms to defend herself. But the sorrowful brown eyes Sonny had seen at the fiesta now burned with a steely strength.

"He is in the machine shop," she told him. She made the sign of the cross.

"My partner is with him?" Sonny asked.

Yolanda Zamora turned to Sonny, the rigor at the core of her expression falling away. "Yes."

Sonny watched her a moment longer, then turned as he heard Marco leave the room.

"Senor?" Yolanda called softly.

He stopped, faced her again.

"*Lo siento*," she whispered. "I am so very sorry."

⊙━━✦━━⊙

SONNY LIMON followed Marco through a side door into the machine shop that stood just inside the perimeter fence at the far edge of Miguel Zamora's compound. It was a two-story structure built of corrugated metal, opaque with a fine skin of *caliche* dust, streaked from the recent rain and pitted with fine points of rust. The strident sound of the dogs Sonny had heard earlier grew much louder as they neared the building, and he felt the sun's heat radiate from the exterior walls as he passed through the door and into the relative blackness inside.

The room was heavy with the smell of machine oil and sawdust, his eyes taking time to adjust to the blue-gray light that flickered unevenly from long fluorescent tubes suspended from an open-trussed ceiling. At the far end of the room, Sonny could hear, more than see, a small gathering of men. They spoke in rapid Spanish that sounded urgent and shot through with violence.

⊙━━✦━━⊙

STEVE DEVLIN heard Sonny arrive, or more accurately, the sudden hush that came over the men that surrounded him. His mind raced, bursting with fragmentary thoughts, flashes of white light screaming behind his eyes.

It had been the longest day of his life.

———

SONNY BLINKED, his vision finally having adjusted as they approached the circle of men.

"Jesus Christ," Sonny breathed.

The odor struck him then, like a solid mass, a nauseating heat-haze of human sweat, urine and the metallic electrical stench of charred hair and flesh. Steve Devlin was naked. His arms had been trussed behind his back, his wrists bound by duct tape and run-through with a thin chain that looped over a crossbeam high above his head. The sockets of Devlin's shoulders had dislocated, and he had been hoisted up in such a way that his toes barely brushed the concrete floor.

"What the fuck is this?" Sonny said, reaching to his hip for a pistol that wasn't there. "Cut him down!"

"This man can no longer be trusted," Miguel shrugged, resting a length of steel pipe on his shoulder, as if taking time out from batting practice. "What am I to think?"

"Bullshit," Devlin croaked. His words bubbled out in a viscous gout of blood.

Without hesitation, Miguel put the full force of his weight into an arcing blow to Devlin's kidney. His body swung like a broken puppet at the end of the chain. His head lolled to one side, both eyes swollen so thoroughly shut that Sonny could not see his eyeballs.

"Goddamn it," Sonny said, turning away. "Let him down."

———

STEVE DEVLIN was lost inside his agony.

Red curtains of pain washed him like a shower of incalescent cinder and he felt the edges of his consciousness closing in. But he knew the needle would come. Every time he thought he might mercifully slip away, they had hit him with a jolt of speed that re-awakened every nerve ending in his broken body and rushed him, quivering, back to reality.

"Let him down," he heard Sonny say.

His head filled with images. Maybe this was what it was to see your life flash before you. He saw Miguel's wife, Yolanda, at his door. She had awakened him during the very early hours of the morning, and been caught there trying to pass him a note.

"She is only a woman," Miguel had said to him. "If I cannot trust you with a woman, how am I to trust you with anything else?"

And they had brought him here.

Power was the only currency Miguel valued, Devlin knew. But Devlin had badly misjudged him, had lost touch with the depth of the changes in him. The *padrino*, he now knew, had become so lost to himself that he had completely put aside what most gamblers had at the heart of their commitment to their game: their desire to remain at the table. For Miguel it had turned upside down. The game, as he saw it now, was exclusively about the size and regularity of the gain. It was a dangerous line to have crossed.

The sting of the needle burst into the deep muscle tissue of Devlin's hip and brought the pain of every broken bone and dislo-cated joint, every ruptured organ, back to the white-hot center of his brain. He thought he heard Sonny speak again.

⊙══╪══⊙

"YOU'RE OUT OF your fucking mind," Sonny said, riveting Miguel Zamora. "You can't kill a cop."

Miguel was panting with exertion, half-moons of sweat darkened his shirt beneath his arms, and his face was slick and shining with perspiration. Esteban stood to one side, his purple lips curled into a bizarre leering grimace. The leather-handled hunting knife, clenched inside a gnarled fist, hung at his side. A man Sonny Limon had never seen before leaned against a workbench along the wall, his arms crossed casually, smoking a cigar now that he had finished pumping the hypodermic into Steve Devlin's skin.

Miguel cast a sidelong glance at Esteban, then trained his focus back on Sonny. "I think you will find, Senor, that I can do whatever I like."

Esteban took a step around Devlin's dangling body, pinned Sonny with a hard glare.

Sonny didn't take his eyes off Miguel. "If your man makes a move on me," Sonny said, "I swear to God, gun or not, I'll spatter his brain on the walls."

The room went flat with silence, punctuated only by the snarl and yelp of the dogs outside, and the thin, wet rattle of Devlin's breathing. Esteban's knuckles pressed white against the handle of his blade.

"Are you aware that your partner has been stealing from you?"

"I have nothing for him to steal."

"Oh, but you do," Miguel said smoothly. "Do you know about the diamonds?"

Sonny's stomach lurched, his gorge barely contained. He struggled to maintain a blank expression. He had no interest in feeding the man's fantasy.

"I have been paying you with uncut diamonds for the past month. Obviously, Senor Devlin cannot be trusted with women or any other items of value."

"That's bullshit. He's holding them for me."

Miguel read easily the lie behind Sonny's eyes.

"God, I like you," Miguel laughed. "I'll tell you what: I'll make you a deal because I like you."

Sonny didn't move, but watched Miguel prop the bloodstained pipe end against the wall and cross to the far end of the shed. He stopped in front of a large, metal roll-up door, bent to unlock the latch. He heaved his weight upward against the handle and threw it open, filling the foul-smelling room with blinding sunlight and the nearby sound of the dogs that had been penned up outside. Sonny recognized them immediately, though he had only seen them before from a distance. A dozen of them, maybe more. They were snarling and gnashing, throwing themselves against the chain link of the enclosure they had been herded into. Having gotten a stronger scent now of what was inside, they became frenzied, driven mad with the odor of fresh blood and charred muscle.

"I was planning to spend some more time with your partner, then let the dogs finish him. My men enjoy the sport. You would be surprised to see how long some people last when the dogs are upon them," Miguel said as he turned back toward the dark end of the room. "But seeing as I like the fire in your belly, Senor Limon, I will give you a choice."

Sonny was silent, unable to draw his gaze from the dogs that snapped viciously at the smiling rancheros that waited beyond the wire.

"Esteban," Miguel commanded. "Bring me Senor Limon's *pistola*."

Sonny watched as Esteban left the room, then brought his eyes back to bear on his partner. A viscid string of blood and mucous hung from Devlin's gaping mouth, and he could see the muscles twitch in his battered face as the amphetamine injection did its work in his system, bringing every pinpoint of agony into full focus inside his brain.

A moment later, Esteban returned with the gun Sonny had relinquished before leaving for his night along the border. When the big man gave it over to his boss, Miguel thumbed the release and checked the magazine with a nod of satisfaction, then jacked all the rounds. Satisfied he had left only one cartridge in the chamber, he rammed the clip back in place with the heel of his hand. The scrape of metal-on-metal echoed loudly in the room.

"Here is your choice, Senor Limon," Miguel told him. "You may put your partner out of his misery, or you may watch me continue as I was before you arrived. He can die quickly or very, very slowly. The choice is yours. Either way, it is in your hands."

Steve Devlin's body lurched at the end of the chain. "Shoot me, for fuck sake," he coughed.

Without hesitation, Miguel swung the butt of the automatic into Devlin's mouth, breaking three of his front teeth off at the gum line. "Shhh . . . You must let your partner choose for himself." He wiped the blood from the pistol grip on the leg of his pants.

Limon looked from Devlin to Miguel, then dropped his eyes to the weapon in Miguel's open palm. "I'm not going to kill my partner."

The *padrino* shrugged theatrically and turned to Esteban. "Then you had better fix Senor Devlin so he cannot get away from the dogs."

The big man nodded, moved behind the workbench and lifted a pair of heavy-duty bolt cutters from a pegboard on the wall. Sonny watched in sickened shock as Esteban came around behind Devlin, folded himself into a crouch and fit the tool's sharp blades to Devlin's Achilles tendon.

Steve Devlin arched and tried to writhe away, but could gain no traction on the floor that was slick with his blood and bodily fluids.

"Give me the gun," Sonny said.

Miguel remained still, taunting Sonny with his eyes as he hefted the automatic in his hand as though testing its weight.

"Give me—"

Esteban bore down on the long handles of the bolt cutter, forcing the blades through the gristle of Devlin's tendon, severing it with a savage grunt. Steve Devlin's shriek drowned even the continuous wail of the dogs. It sounded to Sonny as he had always imagined Hell.

"Give me the goddamned gun!" Sonny screamed.

"You are certain?" Miguel said, watching Devlin thrash in pain beyond imagining.

"Give me the goddamned pistol!"

Miguel reached toward Sonny Limon, the gun wrapped tight inside his fist. Sonny took hold of it, barrel first, but Miguel would not let go. Devlin's screams still echoed inside the shed.

"This is a lesson I want you to remember, Senor Limon," Miguel said. "*No me niegas.*" I will not be betrayed.

Sonny took the gun as the *padrino* released his grip. He slid the hammer as he took one long stride toward Steve Devlin's side. Sonny placed the barrel against his partner's temple. And squeezed the trigger.

The sound of Devlin's agony died instantly, and Sonny tasted vomit in the back of his throat as he watched his partner fall limp in death.

The room was silent, the hollow snap of gunfire momentarily stifling even the dogs. Miguel nodded slowly amid the thin haze of cordite and turned his eyes to Sonny.

"That was very good. It shows integrity. You are a better partner to him than he was to you, my friend." He leaned in close, his breath foul and hot on Sonny's neck. "But we are partners, now. You and I," Miguel whispered into his ear.

Sonny Limon doubled over and began to retch. He spat, but the metallic taste of Devlin's blood wouldn't leave his mouth.

"Cut this man down and give him to the dogs," Miguel told Esteban.

Sonny watched helplessly as they dragged Steve Devlin's broken body toward the caged, frothing pack. "You can't . . ." Sonny managed.

"I already told you, my friend," Miguel said, his voice laced with false resignation.

Sonny heard the dogs tear into Devlin's body with a ferocity he had witnessed only in films set on the African veldt. He fell to his knees and heaved himself dry.

"Esteban, give this man his diamonds," he heard Miguel say. Then he felt a hand rest on his shoulder.

"You are free to go now, Senor Limon."

# Chapter 21

Dull red clouds ranged across the darkening horizon as Sonny Limon passed through the town of Rosarito, the lights of Tijuana glittering in the distance.

He wanted a drink. He wanted several drinks, but he had promised himself on the long drive back from Rancho Tronada that he would think this through with a clear head. Carefully. One mistake, one misstep and he was fucked. But, goddamn if he didn't want that drink.

He'd had plenty of time to think during the long drive north, pushing Devlin's prized muscle car well beyond any reasonable speed. The synapses of his brain were firing like white hot flashes, and his heart pumped blood through his veins like a fire hose; a man without a single safe place to go, and no one he could trust. He had murdered his own partner. He was alone.

⚬━✦━⚬

HE TURNED LEFT off of Boulevard Fundadores and into a warren of narrow streets lined with shacks made from cast-off scraps of metal, tarpaper and plastic sheeting. Tiny shops, their windows plastered with handbills, sprang up among the squalor and cast a hazy light out into the street where shoeless children played.

Sonny approached Tijuana's commercial quarter with care, not wanting Devlin's car to attract undue attention among the throngs of tourists, hawkers, hustlers, and whores that would be wandering Avenida Revolucion. On the off chance that an investigation of Steve Devlin's disappearance led here, Sonny could not afford to be remembered as having been the driver.

It was here, on the edge of La Zona Tolerencia—the red light district—that he planned to ditch the Barracuda. If Sonny had any hope of getting through the next few days of his life, this car had to disappear. He knew it wouldn't last three hours in this neighborhood.

He pulled to a stop beneath a shattered streetlight, checked the rearview and scanned the darkened sidewalk to ensure he was alone. Satisfied, he killed the engine and stepped from the car. A riot of noise from the dozens of dance clubs, bars and strip joints a few blocks away carried on the dirty breeze that blew down from the canal and smelled of sewage, algae and brackish decay. Sonny cast another glance over his shoulder as he peeled a key from Devlin's key ring and inserted it into the ignition. He wiped his prints off the key, but didn't bother with the rest of the car. What was the point? There were any number of legitimate reasons why his prints would be inside this car. He had often been a passenger of Devlin's. Satisfying himself that both doors were unlocked, he pocketed the rest of Devlin's keys and walked briskly through the night and into the crowds and neon-lit confusion along Revolucion. With any luck the Barracuda would be stolen, perhaps even stripped, well before morning.

He had slid his pistol into the waistband at the small of his back and untucked his shirt to conceal it as a temporary measure, but once out on the avenue, he ducked into a *mercado* and bought a loose-fitting nylon windbreaker. When he reached into his pocket to pay the cashier, he was struck by an unexpected wave of vertigo as his fingers played over the small wad of folding cash Miguel had given him along with the small drawstring bag of opaque stones.

"Are you unwell, Senor?"

Sonny closed his eyes momentarily and shook his head. "I'm fine, thank you."

"You look unwell."

"I'm okay. Maybe too many margaritas," he lied.

The old woman nodded and smiled knowingly. Sonny handed her an American twenty and told her to keep the change.

Brassy strains of mariachi music drifted down from rooftop cantinas, fighting for attention amid the come-ons from titty-bar barkers, street beggars and the constant rumble of traffic that clogged the busy street. Sonny crossed at an intersection where a tourist was having his photo taken, standing beside a pitiful, hard-used donkey that had been sloppily painted with the black stripes of a zebra. Its eyes were milky blue and clouded by disease.

One by one, Sonny peeled the keys from Steve Devlin's key ring as he walked, dropping them into the sewers and storm drains he passed on his way to the Catwalk. He would follow that route to the bridge that spanned the Canal Rio Tijuana and merge into the flow of American pedestrians who passed through the border checkpoint on foot, having previously parked their cars in a lot on the U.S. side.

He was lost in thought again as his footsteps echoed in the street, and startled badly by a whispered appeal emanating from the alley beside him.

"Senor," the voice said. "Come! Here is cockfights. Very exciting. Many gamblings."

Sonny waved him off without a word and picked up his pace toward the border.

<hr />

FIVE LANES OF traffic spewed noxious fumes into the night sky as the vehicles idled, having no choice but to patiently wait their turn at one of the reentry booths manned by American border personnel. Mexican men, women and children by the dozen wormed their ways between the cars, hawking everything from candy and piñatas to pottery and stuffed iguanas to the passengers sealed within their air-conditioned vehicles.

Sonny took the footpath that paralleled the logjam of motorists, shouldered his way through the crush of last-chance peddlers, and fell into the pedestrian Immigration queue. Harsh blue neon spilled out of the wire-glass windows of the narrow building in which uniformed Immigration officers sat for endless hours scrutinizing the identification documents of returning U.S. citizens. He felt the first trickle of perspiration creep down his back and he wondered again whether there might be something different, something visible, he now carried in his eyes. Did he look any different? Did he look like a dirty cop? Like a killer? He briefly imagined simply turning around, walking away and losing himself in the crowds of this filthy city. Just for a couple of days. Just to get his shit together. But that was a fantasy and he knew it. The only choice Sonny had was to sack up and square things away back at home. First things first, he told himself, and tried to calm his breathing.

"Next," the INS officer said, waving in the general direction of Sonny Limon. "Identification, please."

Sonny slid out his driver's license from behind the plastic window in his wallet and handed it to the heavyset, bullet-eyed man seated behind the podium. The man examined it for a moment, looked at Sonny's face, and instead of returning the license to Sonny, slipped it beneath the metal claw of his clipboard.

"Tourist card?"

Legally, Sonny knew that if he admitted to having gone further south than Ensenada—which, of course, he had—he needed to have first obtained a tourist card. The fact that he hadn't done so could now pose a serious problem that would, at a minimum, get his name entered onto some list or other that could be used to confirm his presence in Mexico during the very time that Steve Devlin had gone missing. Sonny had never been a skillful liar. Nevertheless, he took a chance and removed his police ID and badge holder and handed them over. "A buddy and I just came down to blow off some steam on the Avenida."

The bullet-eyed man glared at the badge, then at Sonny. "So, where's your friend?"

"Lost him."

The Immigration man eyeballed him again. "You lost him?"

Sonny smiled and shrugged in mock resignation. "Yeah."

Bullet-eyes broke into a grin and handed Sonny his license, badge and police ID. "Wouldn't be the first time that happened down here. Have a good night."

<hr />

SONNY CAUGHT A cab outside a strip mall on the American side and gave the driver directions to an address about four blocks away from Steve Devlin's house. Twenty minutes later, he had the cabbie drop him near the neighborhood Quik Mart. He peeled off the fare, added a modest tip and waited until the taillights faded into the distance.

The moon had not yet risen, and a chill onshore wind had swept the sky into a clear and cloudless black. He took his time walking to Devlin's house, skirting the streetlights when he could, to retrieve the motorcycle he had left in Devlin's garage. Sonny had disposed of all but one of Devlin's keys during his long walk through Tijuana, including the keychain, which he had dropped into the slow-moving viscosity of the Canal Rio when he crossed over the bridge. He had retained the one he guessed would open the door to his partner's home.

From half a block away, he could see that the house was dark except for the pale yellow light that glowed from a fixture over the front door landing. Too much light. No concealment. Sonny cast a glance up and down the empty street and moved toward the narrow side yard. He opened the flimsy wooden gate that concealed a trash enclosure and led to the back of the house. He hid inside the shadows at the side entrance of the garage and fished in his pocket for the one remaining key, praying for just one tiny piece of luck. He slid it into the lock and twisted.

The handle wouldn't budge.

Story of his fucking life.

Sonny had guessed incorrectly.

He fought off a rising panic and furtively circled the house, checking every door, every slider and every window on the off chance that Devlin might have left one unlocked. No luck. Sonny was left with only one option.

He returned to the side yard and knelt quietly beside the door, waiting for cover, for the noise of a passing car, a plane flying overhead, anything to mask the sound of what he was about to do. He palmed a fist-sized stone he found in the weeds beside Devlin's trash cans and crouched impatiently in the shadows. The night seemed unnaturally silent and was doing a number on Sonny's already frayed nerves.

His knees had begun to ache by the time he got his opportunity. A large vehicle, a van by the sound of it, was coming up the street from the far end of the block. When it passed in front of Devlin's house, Sonny made his move and smashed the small panel of glass embedded in his partner's side door. Even with the cover of the van's passing, the racket seemed unbearably loud.

He gingerly reached through the opening, found the knob and let himself in. Open the garage, wheel the motorcycle outside, close the garage and get the hell out of here, he thought. But the other idea, the one he couldn't seem to shake, shot through his mind again. It would only take a couple of extra minutes. After all, he was inside now. Just take a quick look around. If Miguel Zamora had been telling Sonny the truth, Steve Devlin had stashed several thousand dollars' worth of raw diamonds somewhere in this house; several thousand dollars of *Sonny's* diamonds. There was nothing wrong with taking back what was rightfully his, was there? Five minutes, he told himself. Five minutes and I'm out of here.

◦───✦───◦

IT TURNED OUT to be closer to an hour.

Once he had started rifling through every drawer, every closet, every toilet tank, and every other conceivable hiding place in Devlin's house, Sonny recalled Devlin's offhand comment about his sock drawer. He had thought it a joke at the time, but having looked everywhere else, decided to take a shot. Sure as hell, in an enclosure beneath a false bottom of a dresser drawer, he found a small bag, not unlike the one he himself still carried in his pocket. That son of a bitch. Not real clever, but Devlin had never expected *his* place to be tossed, did he? Sonny hadn't wanted to believe that Miguel had told him the truth, but he had. Steve Devlin had been holding out. His partner had played him.

Sonny Limon pocketed the stones.

He rolled his bike out into the driveway and closed the garage door behind him. He slipped the clutch into neutral and pushed his motorcycle for two full blocks before he kicked it started and drove away.

It was time for that drink.

PART FIVE:

# Bitter Creek

# CHAPTER 22

Sometimes even the most fucked-up notion can make sense after your fifth or sixth Jim Beam. Any rational evaluation of cause-and-effect goes out the window and plans click into place that get executed with a precision that animate only the worst of our nihilistic fantasies.

Which is how Sonny Limon ended up at his ex-wife's house at two-thirty in the morning. Technically, the house was still partially his, since the divorce wasn't final for another couple of weeks, but Maddie wasn't big on technicalities that involved giving in to anything that might benefit Sonny. Which is why he lived in his shithole of a camper in the substation's parking lot.

He couldn't get her out of his head. This whole deal had him all turned around. His mind was a tangled mass of confusion, like rats were gnawing the soft tissue inside his skull, and his gut told him he had lost the last semblance of respect or manhood he might have ever possessed. Blood on his hands, dirty money in his pocket, and nowhere to put his dick even if he thought it might function properly. His life now consisted of nothing but chaos, upheaval and dread. The only thing he could seem to clearly lock onto was Maddie.

○══◄══○

"YOU'RE DRUNK," Maddie said through the tiny crack between the door and the door frame, speaking to him through the screen.

Sonny took a step forward. "I need to talk."

"It's two-thirty in the morning, Sonny. Go home."

Yellow light spilled from the porch light and cast half her face into shadow. That familiar look in her eyes and the set of her jaw told him she wasn't kidding about her wanting him to leave.

"There's somebody in there," he said.

"Go home. I mean it."

"This is my home."

Sonny could hear the sound of another set of footsteps inside the house, coming up from behind her. Masculine fingers curled around the edge of the door and yanked it open. A moment later, a man dressed in nothing but one of Sonny's bathrobes took Maddie's place in the doorway. He was shorter than Sonny, but broad across the chest and thick in the arms. He didn't have the eyes of a cop, but since she was such a sucker for a man in uniform, Sonny figured him for a smoke-eater. Asshole.

"Problem?" the guy said. Deep voice, but not much chest hair.

"Yvonne . . ." Maddie warned.

*Yvonne*, Sonny thought. My wife is fucking a guy named *Yvonne*? It just keeps getting better.

"Who the hell is this?" Sonny said, over the guy's shoulder.

"Take off," the guy said.

"Sonny—" she began, but the fireman—or whatever—interrupted.

"He was just leaving," he assured her.

Sonny felt the blood tingle beneath his scalp. This dickhead was talking about him like he was a piece of furniture.

"You want me to take care of this?" Yvonne said to Maddie.

"Go back to the living room, shithead, and mind your own business," Sonny told him.

He gave Sonny a hard glare. Or what Sonny figured must pass for a hard glare back at the firehouse. "Was I talking to you?"

"No," Sonny said. "That was *me* talking to *you*. You need to keep up with the conversation."

"Sugar," the fireman said. "Call the cops."

"I *am* a cop."

"You're a drunk."

Sonny's line of vision shrunk down to a point, and the whole scene was tinted in shades of red. "You are about to get the beating of a lifetime, *Yvonne*. You'll be talking about this for months, once you're back on solid food."

"Was that a threat?"

"Of course that was a threat. Fuck. You have a serious listening problem."

Maddie came from nowhere, stepping between them a moment before Sonny let loose a jab that would have punched through the flimsy screen and turned Yvonne the Fireman into a raccoon. She shoved her new boyfriend in the chest and told him to go back into the house, where he disappeared into the shadows.

"Good move, Maddie," Sonny said. "You just saved that guy a very serious session of percussive therapy."

She shook her head sadly, and cast her eyes down to her bare feet. "Nice, Sonny," she said. "Your solution for everything."

"I think I'm in trouble, Mad. I need your help."

From inside the house: "I'm dialing the cops."

"Jesus," Sonny said.

"Go home. This is over."

"Mad, please—"

"Goodbye, Sonny," she said.

And closed the door in his face.

HE WAKES UP in his camper.

He's still wearing yesterday's shirt, underwear and socks, but he has tossed his jeans into the sink. His teeth feel like they're wearing a sweater and his head is throbbing so hard it feels like his eyes might roll out of their sockets. He doesn't remember coming home. He doesn't remember much of anything. Only snapshots of disconnected moments. The last thing that rolls through his brain in anything like a continuous recollection is picking up his bike from Devlin's house. His heart skips a beat when he remembers something else. Sonny pulls his damp, balled-up jeans from the sink and rifles the pockets. He finds the little pouch of cloudy stones buried there and he feels his stomach turn over. He hangs on to the edge of the bowl's cold porcelain and feels like he's turning inside out.

A snapshot of Maddie slides behind his eyes as he empties his stomach.

A man named Yvonne threatening to call the cops.

Sonny wonders if there's a record of the call-out.

Ten-codes run pointlessly through his head. Ten-fifteen-F. Family Disturbance.

He has to think. He has to pull himself together. How long before Devlin's absence turns into a full-scale investigation?

Ten-sixty-five. Missing Person.

He heaves so hard that his eyes fill with hot tears. Sweat pops on his brow, his neck. His shirt is soaked with it. His hands are shaking and his bones feel like wax.

Steve Devlin's naked body dangling from a chain like a piece of meat.

His stomach surges again, but nothing comes this time.

A still photo of Devlin hanging lifeless. A bullet has sprayed half the contents of his brainpan against a greasy warehouse wall.

I am not a crook, Sonny thinks. Nixon. I am not a crook.

I am not a thief.

Get real.

Thou shalt not kill.

Has he left any of the Big Ten untouched? Maybe that one about graven images. He hasn't done that one, hasn't screwed that pooch quite yet.

Outside, the sound of cops coming out of morning briefing and heading for their squad cars. Laughter. Loud voices. Familiar voices. Muscular engines fill the air with throaty rumbling. Trunks loaded with field equipment slam shut.

He waits until the last of them leaves the lot to go Ten-eight and begin the day tour.

Sonny knows he wouldn't stand up under scrutiny. This thing with Miguel Zamora has spun so far, so fast, that it was probably forming its own solar system by now. His options weren't running low, they were down to zero.

There was no Blue Line where this was concerned. No lawyers. No nothing. He is way beyond all that. Beyond hope. Beyond the law. Beyond redemption.

The last of the black-and-whites has left the lot. It is quiet.

Sonny throws on a relatively clean pair of pants from the tiny closet, kicks on some shoes. He manhandles his bike onto the rack affixed to the back of his camper, straps it in place and locks it down.

Sonny slips into the cab of his truck and fires it up.

He stops at Denny's and orders breakfast. He writes with a cheap ballpoint on a yellow legal pad while he waits for his food. He writes while he eats. He writes while the waitress clears his plate. He writes until his hand cramps and his head hurts.

Half an hour later he stops off at his bank. He empties the contents of his accounts and starts heading for the border.

# CHAPTER 23

Miguel Zamora was not enjoying his lunch.

His appetite for food hadn't been much ever since he had ratcheted up his love affair with cocaine, so even the finest of meals wouldn't have held much interest for him. But more than that, it was the subject of discussion that was the primary cause of his distraction.

They were dining outdoors in the private courtyard tucked behind the high walls of the Mexico City hacienda owned by Comandante Rivera of the Federal Judicial Police. Servants dressed in white coats and black trousers came and went as they delivered elegantly prepared dishes of braised lamb, freshly baked rolls, vegetables and rice. All conversation ceased, of course, until the last of the plates had been placed on the table and the serving staff had disappeared back into the kitchen.

Miguel brought the glass of chilled wine to his lips, wishing for the hundredth time that he could slip off to a quiet corner of the villa and reward himself with a generous helping of the white lady. But this was probably the most critical component of his plan, if it was to succeed. It was vital that he sell La Plaza on the "disappearance" of the Colombians' plane, as well as his own diligent efforts to locate the wreckage and retrieve the contraband.

The Pig—General Diego Acosta—was the first to speak. As always, he was in full dress uniform in spite of the cloying midday heat. "The Comandante confirms that there has been no trace of our friends' lost delivery."

Miguel nodded as he replaced his wineglass on the white table linen. "That is correct. I notified the Comandante immediately when the plane failed to arrive. He had helicopters searching the area within hours of my call."

Comandante Rivera cast a glance at the General as he brushed nonexistent breadcrumbs from the lapel of his business suit. "We have had no fewer than three helicopters in the air from dawn to dusk for the past four days."

"And a dozen of my best men on the ground—" Miguel began.

"Plus another fifty of my soldiers," the Peacock interrupted. "We've looked under every stone, every weed, every clump of cactus and clot of cattle manure. Nothing."

"You are absolutely certain?" the General asked.

Miguel noticed the Comandante's reaction to the implied insult, and wondered idly why Dario Cruz—the *Maricon*—hadn't been included in this meeting. Two possibilities seemed likely. Either the Governor's man *had* been invited, but had elected to decline in order to distance both himself and the Governor from the possibility of a political embarrassment; or General Acosta and Comandante Rivera simply did not trust the man. *Interesting*, Miguel thought.

"I am—that is to say, *we* are, quite certain, General."

So it was "we" when the possibility of humiliation or failure existed. Typical of the Peacock, Miguel thought. The bastard. Still, to know a man's weaknesses is to hold power over him, no? The Pig, the Peacock, and the *Maricon*: three men with weaknesses, to be sure.

"And what of the Colombians?" the General asked.

Here was the heart of the matter that Miguel had been waiting for. The success of his deception depended on his performance in this moment. He dabbed at the corners of his mouth with his napkin and placed it beside his plate, careful to make meaningful eye contact with both of his tablemates before he spoke.

"I telephoned my man in Medellin the moment I finished speaking with Comandante Rivera. I informed them that I was doing everything in my power to locate the missing plane."

The General took a roll from the bread basket, tore it in half and sopped a dollop of fat-laden lamb juice from his plate. He stuffed it into his mouth and turned to face Miguel. "Are they satisfied with our efforts?" he asked.

"They are concerned, of course." A drop of juice dripped from the corner of the General's mouth, and Miguel had to look away before he could finish his reply. "But they also understand the risks associated with transporting their product over such distance and terrain."

Again, he was careful to look each man in the eye with complete sincerity. This was the moment. It was vital that they believe his lie, or at least the part that was a lie. He had, in fact, contacted the Colombians upon speaking with the Comandante and obtaining his pledge to begin a helicopter search. Their response, however, had not been quite as sanguine as Miguel had just stated. In truth, they were justifiably incensed, and were planning to dispatch a cartel lieutenant to Rancho Tronada if the cocaine was not successfully located. This was the part that Miguel had no intention of allowing La Plaza to discover. It was vital that Miguel remain firmly and exclusively in charge of the relationship with the Colombian cartel. To lose any component of control would be financial suicide. Quite possibly even literal suicide. Miguel had to be certain that there was not the slightest hint or implication, the smallest shred of doubt cast upon his integrity and his ability to continue to manage the relationship. What he had told his brother, Marco, had been the truth: this was not the kind of score one ever attempted more than once. On the other hand, once would be enough.

"I cannot imagine they will be happy to hear that we failed to find the plane," the Comandante put in. "Have you informed them?"

Miguel pushed his chair away from the table and casually crossed his legs. "I was waiting until I met with you gentlemen. If we are in agreement that we have done all we can do, then I will call them immediately upon my return to El Salto."

General Acosta arched a brow. "And if they decide to terminate our business arrangement?"

"I believe that is extremely unlikely. The American DEA has made it very difficult to move product through Florida, and the attention our associates have brought upon themselves in the California mountains is choking their distribution channels from the West Coast. The Colombians have little choice but to deal through us if they want access to the United States."

Acosta eyed the Comandante for a long moment, then shifted his gaze back to Miguel. "You sound sure of yourself."

I had better be sure of myself, Miguel thought. I have just bet my life on it. "I am certain that our friends can be made to understand that accidents sometimes happen, and that this unfortunate mishap need not affect the long-term success of our relationship." Miguel liked the way that had sounded. Cool. Calm. Confident.

"You will let us know if things do not go as you expect," Rivera said. It was not a question.

"Of course, Comandante," Miguel smiled, and rose to his feet. "Please give my compliments to your chef, and forgive my need to depart. I have a long flight back to Rancho Tronada, and this city traffic can be unpredictable."

Both men stood and offered their hands to El Rey Miguel.

He had only taken a few steps before he turned back toward the General and the Comandante. "I neglected to ask," Miguel said. "How did your little publicity stunt work out for you?"

Miguel was pleased to see something pass briefly across the Peacock's eyes before he responded. "Very well, thank you. It was unfortunate to have to destroy such a fine crop, but the public seems satisfied that we are doing all that can be done to rid our wonderful country of dangerous narcotics."

"I am delighted to hear that. It is important to keep the people happy." *You greedy, arrogant worm.*

"*Buenos tardes*, gentlemen."

THE SOUND OF Miguel's departing car had scarcely faded away when Dario Cruz strode across the courtyard and took a seat at the table.

"How much did you hear?" General Acosta asked the Governor's aide.

Cruz reached out a well-manicured hand to accept the wine Comandante Rivera had poured for him. "Most of it."

"Your thoughts?"

Cruz took a leisurely sip, tilted his face skyward and followed the slow passage of a cloud with his bullet-eyed gaze. "His claim to have contacted the Colombians is true."

The General cocked his head and seemed to reappraise the effeminate man that had always gotten under his skin. "And you know this how?"

"As you know, El Rey Miguel has no phone at Rancho Tronada."

"Paranoid," Rivera said.

"Indeed," Cruz said. "But you know what they say: 'just because you're paranoid doesn't mean they are not out to get you.'"

The General's smile was tight and disingenuous. "You were saying . . . about the phone?"

"Yes. Because Zamora has no telephone, he makes his calls from the exchange in El Salto."

"You have someone there?"

"Not exactly. But we do have the ability to check records from the phone company, to see what calls are placed—the general location and time."

"It's owned by the government."

"And nobody turns down the Governor when he has something he wants to know."

"Do we know what was said? Or better yet, the name of his contact?"

"It would be nice to be rid of our cocaine-worshipping *padrino*, but unfortunately, no. We do not have access to either of those pieces of information. Miguel Zamora runs a very tight ship, and the people of El Salto fear him more than Hell itself."

Dario Cruz enjoyed another sip of wine, then gently set the glass back on the table.

The General watched the man's effete mannerisms with distaste, stood and began pacing slow circles around the table. "And what of this missing plane?"

Comandante Rivera was insulted anew. He had already described the lengths to which he had gone to search for it, and did not appreciate the question being posed yet again. And by this preening *maricon*, no less. But Dario Cruz answered before Rivera could register his objection.

"Nothing yet," he said. "But I am working on it."

The General's expression betrayed genuine surprise. As the man at the head of the Directorate of Federal Security, he had always believed himself to be the country's preeminent spymaster. The Governor's aide had been correct when he said that the people of El Salto feared Miguel Zamora like the devil himself. And the *pistoleros* Miguel employed were nearly rabid in their loyalty to him.

Pleased at having disconcerted the General, Cruz crossed his legs and sighed. "Be careful not to underestimate the reach of the Governor's office."

Neither the General or Rivera could conceive of the implication.

"You're saying you have someone inside Miguel's organization?" The disbelief in Rivera's tone was unmistakable.

Dario Cruz showed them his most unctuous smile.

"Quite."

# Chapter 24

Three hours later, Miguel felt a tap on his shoulder.

"We are nearing the airstrip," his pilot informed him.

Miguel hadn't been sleeping, merely resting his head against the window with his eyes shut. It had been a miserable and bumpy flight, particularly as they passed over the crenellated mountains that marked the edge of the *bajada*. The sun had baked the barren soil all day, then mixed with the cooler air of late afternoon creating unpredictable updrafts that bounced the plane and made Miguel mildly sick to his stomach. Despite how little he had eaten while dining with the Pig and the Peacock, he could taste the sour residue of greasy meat at the back of his throat. He would be happy to have his feet on solid ground where he could properly celebrate his success. A few rounds of tequila with his brother, Marco, a bump or two of the powder, then a night spent reminding Yolanda how lucky she was to share his bed.

"*Gracias*, Xavier," Miguel acknowledged his pilot, and buckled his seat belt in anticipation of touching down.

YOLANDA ZAMORA woke from her nap with a start.

She had been dreaming and it took her a moment to regain her bearings. Blinking her eyes against the hard sunlight, she propped herself on an elbow and reached for the carefully folded towel that had been left for her on the table beside her poolside chaise. She adjusted the backrest and sat up, then used the towel to dab at the tiny dots of perspiration that now traced their way between her breasts, and dampened the cups of her swimsuit top. Yolanda moved one of the shoulder straps aside and checked for evidence of too much time in the sun.

From the corner of her eye, she saw that Esteban, Miguel's ugly bear of a bodyguard-ranch manager was still seated in the shade beside a banana tree, a rifle resting across his knees. He was smoking a cigarette and staring at her without shame. Yolanda felt dirty, defiled by the man's gaze.

For five days now she had been a virtual prisoner in her own home. A hostage. Ever since Miguel had discovered Rolando, the houseman, loading her luggage into the station wagon for her aborted getaway, she had not been allowed to roam more than a few yards beyond the hacienda's walls. With the exception of her time spent sleeping in her bedroom, Yolanda had been kept under the constant watch of either Marco or Esteban. To make matters worse, she knew her actions had cast suspicion on both Rolando and the young maid Susana, of whom she had grown most fond.

Since sharing that cigarette days before, Yolanda had made a great effort to bridge the inherent gap between their stations as Lady-of-the-House and maid. In fact, she had come to look forward to the moments she could arrange when Susana could speak openly, woman-to-woman, about her life. Yolanda had learned that Susana, not yet twenty years old, had been engaged to a young man from El Salto for over a year. A long time by Mexican standards. She was touched by the tenderness in the young girl's eyes when she spoke about her fiancé, the son of a store owner, working long hours in his father's *mercado* to save money to pay her dowry. More than that, Susana herself was sneaking a small percentage of her salary to him in order to speed the process. She was deeply in love, and hoped to consummate their marriage by year's end.

Yolanda could scarcely remember when she had last felt that sort of desire for her own husband. She cast her eyes to the wind-ruffled surface of the pool and was nearly consumed by her own sense of loneliness. She felt sick to her stomach.

She had started the morning with a small glimmer of optimism upon learning of Miguel's pending trip to Mexico City, harboring the hope that with Miguel gone for the day, she might find an opportunity to try again to make a getaway. But, obviously, Miguel had ordered the ugly monster, Esteban, to watch her every move more closely than usual.

Without a word, she rose from her lounge chair and wrapped herself in a towel. Her skin was hot and slick with the oil she had smoothed over her slender legs and body, and she moved toward the shade of the cabana at the far end of the courtyard.

Esteban stood and followed.

"I am going to the bathroom," Yolanda told him.

"Fine," he answered, but continued walking behind her.

"I'm thirsty," she said. "Please get me a cold drink and leave it on the small table."

Esteban smiled.

"Susana!" he shouted. "Bring the Senora an iced tea!"

Yolanda reached the door to the small powder room attached to the cabana and turned to face the ugly man. "If you don't mind . . ."

"Leave the door open." It was not a request.

The indignities were becoming almost too much to bear, but she refused to give him the satisfaction of showing her humiliation. She left the door halfway open, as he took up a post just outside, listening.

Minutes later she came out, summoned all her internal strength and walked past Esteban with her head held high, her back straight. She stepped past him without so much as a glance and returned to a seat beneath an umbrella, picked up a magazine and began thumbing through it.

The big man resumed his place beside the banana tree, seemingly unfazed and unmoved.

Yolanda's attention was caught by a pair of mourning doves cooing softly as they scratched the soil in the shade of a purple jacaranda and the words blurred on the page. She hadn't heard Susana approach.

"Senora," she said. "Your iced tea."

In the corner of her vision, Yolanda Zamora could see Esteban's eyes consume the girl, sliding over her like filthy hands. She didn't even want to imagine what was going through his mind.

"*Gracias*, Susana."

The girl stood beside her for a long moment, oblivious to Esteban's lecherous stare. Yolanda admired Susana's strength, grateful for this small act of grace, this act of feminine solidarity. At the same time, it saddened her to realize that this young girl had become the nearest thing she had to a friend.

"*De nada*, Senora," she said at last. "Is there anything else?"

Yolanda was about to respond when a commotion erupted on the other side of the high adobe walls. A brief bout of yelling was punctuated by the stutter of automatic weapons fire.

Esteban leapt to his feet and ran for the door, cocking his rifle as he disappeared into the hacienda.

Yolanda and Susana exchanged a look laced with both confusion and fear.

"You must go inside, Senora," the girl whispered. "Hurry."

"What's going on?"

Another burst of gunfire cracked in the distance and sent both women to the safety of the house. Once inside, Yolanda turned and sprang up the stairs to her bedroom. Susana moved in the opposite direction, the echo of her footsteps retreating down the long tiled hallway toward the kitchen, toward the sound of confusion and disorder outside.

∘——✦——∘

IT WAS THE first restful day Marco Zamora had had in weeks.

Reluctant as he was to admit it, the plan Miguel had concocted to rip off the Colombians—the plan that had once seemed so macho and bold—was now badly jangling his nerves. Miguel's behavior wasn't adding to his comfort level either. Nevertheless, Marco had taken the day as a welcome respite when Miguel announced that he had to fly to Mexico City to meet with La Plaza. Though it would never cross their minds to utter such a thing aloud, it seemed to Marco that the *pistoleros* seemed equally relieved. They all needed a break from El Rey's constant, manic presence.

He had spent the morning as he always did, making a circuit of Rancho Tronada in his Jeep, checking in with the men posted at their various points along the outside perimeter before returning to the hacienda for breakfast with Miguel. Yolanda no longer dined with them, taking her morning meal, instead, in her room upstairs.

Once they had finished, Marco drove his brother to the airstrip. The sky was a crisp and cloudless blue, with only the slightest of winds coming in from the coast. They waited together in silence as Xavier ran up the engines, warming them.

"Wish me luck," Miguel said. His eyes were bright, his smile expectant and genuine.

"I was hoping you would not need luck."

Miguel clapped Marco on the shoulder and laughed. "Everyone needs luck."

"Even El Rey?"

He took the jibe good-naturedly, as it had been intended. For the most part, anyway. "When has it ever hurt to have luck on your side?"

"In that case, *buena suerte*."

"*Gracias, mi hermano*."

Marco waved a cursory farewell, lingering in the morning sun as the twin-engine Cessna taxied to the end of the packed-dirt runway, turned and finally lifted off. He listened as the hum of the aircraft dopplered into the distance, waiting patiently for the dust of his brother's departure to settle back into the *caliche*.

He drove past the two guards at the hacienda's entrance gate a few minutes later, acknowledging them with little more than a brief nod of his head. Each returned his greeting in similar fashion.

Marco parked his Jeep beside the station wagon the house staff used to run errands, then entered the kitchen through the nearby servants' door.

Rolando stood beside the sink, humming to himself as he sliced away at some very nice-looking purple onions, lost in his work. He was a good-natured man with a propensity toward portliness, a man of few words and a fine cook. Marco guessed him to be in his early forties, though he could be five years off either way. With Rolando it was difficult to tell. He had worked for Miguel longer than any of the other domestic personnel, and had by virtue of tenure, if not his benign nature, become the *de facto* head of the household staff.

"Have you gone to the market yet this morning?" Marco asked.

Rolando turned suddenly, startled. "I am sorry Senor Zamora, I did not hear you come in."

Marco dipped his fingers into his shirt pocket and withdrew a small sheet of notepaper. "If you haven't yet gone into town, I would appreciate it if you would also pick up the items on this list and bring them to my quarters."

"No problem, Senor. I have not yet gone."

Marco handed him the list and retreated through the servants' entrance without another word.

Once back at his quarters, a relatively modest one-bedroom *casita* that stood well apart from the bunkhouse that the *pistoleros* shared, he opened a chilled bottle of Coca-Cola and took it outside to enjoy on the relative quiet of his patio. In the distance, he heard the baying of the rain dogs—a distinctly different cry than that of coyotes, who did most of their hunting at night—and wondered idly what they had cornered out on the open arroyo. A brief image of his last encounter with them, and the American cop, floated through his mind, but he closed his eyes and was soon enjoying the rare pleasure of a midday siesta.

He was awakened several hours later by the arrival of Rolando and the groceries Marco had requested. He looked at his watch, surprised to discover how long he had slept, and waited for the houseman to finish putting his provisions away before making his "rounds" again. This time, though, it would go much quicker: he would use one of the two radios that sat atop the desk in the corner of his small study to check in with the men.

Although Miguel had been unwavering in his opposition to the installation of a telephone, he wasn't so impractical as not to recognize the necessity for some means of communication both inside and outside the ranch. As a result, Marco's home also served as the communications center, which housed both short-range and long-range radio gear. With one, he could speak with the men stationed about Rancho Tronada via walkie-talkie-type radio telephones; with the other, he could reach the Cessna (when it was within a reasonable range) as well as the neighboring ranches, such as that owned by Eduardo "El Brujo" Chacon a few kilometers away.

Rolando was removing the last of the items from a cardboard box, placing them on the counter, and carefully organizing them inside Marco's pantry when the first of the rifle shots cracked in the distance.

Marco nearly knocked the man onto the floor as he raced from the room to retrieve the weapon he kept propped beside the sofa and bolted for the door.

○━━✦━━○

SONNY LIMON had not given much thought to the greeting he was going to receive when he arrived at Rancho Tronada unannounced, but he most certainly had not considered that it might be with a hailstorm of automatic weapons fire.

As he had pulled out of the substation parking lot, he was as wracked with fear and indecision as he had ever been in his life. Later, after stopping off at his bank, he had felt a little better. By the time he crossed the border at San Ysidro, he was nearly ecstatic. There was something liberating in the knowledge that he was all out of choices, and he felt a Zen-like calm overtake him as he pointed his beat-down pickup truck with the shitty little camper back to Mexico, into the only possible future that existed for him anymore.

Nobody gave him a second look as he passed through the narrow, rutted streets of El Salto. Sonny himself hadn't thought twice as he drove past the bullet-riddled Bronco that stood as a self-financed, self-aggrandizing monument to El Rey Miguel.

As he arrived at the gates outside the main hacienda, two guards armed with AK's shot out his tires and punched some brand new holes in his quarter panel. In fairness, they had been waving their arms and signaling for him to stop before they opened up on him, but Sonny had figured—incorrectly—that all he needed was to get close enough so that he could speak to them, tell them who he was.

He stuck both of his hands out the driver's side window, showing them he was unarmed. When he opened the door—unbidden by his captors—they had fired a line of warning shots that pocked the soil so dangerously close to his feet that it kicked up dust and stones on his shoes. It was then that the chaos ensued in earnest. Lots of hollering, running, and weapons being discharged into the air, culminating in Sonny Limon's being frog-marched in the direction of the machine shop at the point of a half-dozen gun muzzles.

Sonny yelled in vain, telling them who he was. He called for Miguel, promised that he was a friend of El Rey. He called for Marco. He even called for Esteban, but none of it did any good.

When they opened the door to the corrugated building that would live in Sonny's nightmares for whatever remained of his life, the familiar odor of machine oil, sawdust and death brought him, quite literally, to his knees.

◦►◄◦

SUSANA CREPT TO the kitchen window and peeked outside.

She watched as the first of the guards cautiously approached a shoddy-looking camper truck that had halted just yards outside the gate. Steam billowed from the front of the broken vehicle, tilting awkwardly on blown-out tires. The guards had their rifles held steady and aimed at the windshield, and a pair of hands appeared, as if in surrender, from the driver's side window.

Her mind raced as the sound of the remainder of the *pistoleros* bore down on the scene from all over the hacienda. She had never witnessed such a sudden eruption of violence, certainly not at Rancho Tronada.

To her left, on the kitchen counter, Susana spied a set of keys. She knew they had been left inadvertently by Rolando after returning from his morning trip into town. Almost without thinking, she picked them up and grasped them tightly in the palm of her hand.

In the confusion, Susana decided to take a risk. Perhaps the greatest of her young life. She felt sorry for the Senora, and knew that the mistress would be eternally grateful for an opportunity to leave this place. Grateful enough, Susana imagined, that she might even offer a generous reward. For Susana's part, she knew that if she succeeded in aiding Yolanda's escape, there would be no returning to Rancho Tronada. On the other hand, a reward from Senora could make it possible for Susana herself to leave El Salto once and for all in the arms of her fiancé. Susana felt vaguely guilty for harboring such thoughts of personal gain—she was not taking the risk for money, but out of respect and compassion. Still, she could not completely erase the hope that it might be just the thing that could help her begin a new life with the man she loved.

She ran from the kitchen, down the hall and up the winding staircase to the room of Senora Zamora. A quick glance in either direction confirmed what she already suspected: all the men had left to support the guards and their capture of the intruder. Susana knocked on the door, politely, but with greater force than usual.

There was no answer.

"*Senora!*" Her tone was urgent, but the volume was somewhere between a whisper and a shout. "It is me, Susana!"

Still no answer. Time was short. Susana did something she would never do, not in a lifetime: she gripped the doorknob and twisted.

Locked.

"Please! *Senora!*" This time, Susana hammered the door with the ball of her fist. Her heart raced, then jumped at the sound of another volley of rifle fire from the front gate.

The door flew open.

Yolanda Zamora stood at the threshold. She had obviously changed out of her swimsuit and dressed quickly, her face a mask of terror and confusion. Never before had there been an attack upon Rancho Tronada. It was unthinkable. What was happening? Where was Miguel? Part of her felt foolish and childishly desperate to think of Miguel at such a time, but the fact remained that he was a man of great strength, and a man who would know how to contain the threat that had suddenly arrived at her home.

"Senora, we must go!"

"What is happening?"

"A man in a truck . . . outside the gate . . . I don't know. The men are running in every direction."

To Susana, it appeared that the mistress was beginning to cry. "Please, Senora, you must go. This is your chance." Susana opened her fisted palm and displayed the set of car keys she held there.

Yolanda stood fixed, mesmerized.

Susana did the next thing she would never have thought possible; she reached out and grasped the hand of the lady of the house. She gripped her firmly and pulled her into the hall. "We have to go *now!*"

This time Yolanda acquiesced. Better, Susana thought. The lady seemed to be coming out of her stupor and was beginning to understand the opportunity the stranger's arrival had delivered to her. They ran hand-in-hand to the staircase, paused to confirm that they were unobserved, and made their way down to the kitchen.

There was much yelling now, coming from the direction of the machine shop. None of the *pistoleros* occupied their proper posts. Susana glanced out of the window again. The area was empty. The men had apparently secured the intruder and taken him away.

Susana and Yolanda moved quickly to the back service door, threw it open and made a frantic dash for the car.

# CHAPTER 25

I pulled into town at a little past noon.

I had been on the road for almost twenty-four hours straight, careful to watch for speed traps all the way from Humboldt to this little village on the Mexican coast, stopping only for gas and the occasional drive-thru burger. I was wired to the gills on coffee and NoDoz, which only fueled my growing paranoia and my seething anger for that worthless ass-clown, Rick Montrose. Since I couldn't be certain whether he had been pinched by the cops or simply run off with Colt's and my weed, I was forced to assume the worst. So, not wanting to spend one more minute on the U.S. side of the border than I had to, and having no clue as to what Montrose might have spilled to the authorities, I pushed it as far as I could before I knew I had to stop and get some rest. I skipped the customary visit to my mother's house, instead holing-up where I finally felt relatively safe.

I parked the Bushmonster in the dirt lot behind Rosa's house and climbed down. My legs were shaky from fatigue and over-the-counter speed, so I took a few seconds to stretch before I grabbed the canvas rucksack off the seat and went around to the front door.

Rosa was waiting for me in the shade of her tiny veranda, her meaty arms spread wide in greeting. "I thought that was you!" she said to me in Spanish. Her smile was as warm as the day, her face framed by a pair of long black braids that were just beginning to show their first fine strands of gray. "You and your ugly truck!"

I dropped my duffel and was immediately enveloped in a hug that nearly squeezed the air from my lungs. "One of these days you're going to kill me," I told her.

She took me by my shoulders and held me at arm's length, shaking her head and displaying her silver-capped grin. "How long has it been?"

"Two, three months?" I offered.

"It is good to see you. You need a room? How many nights?"

"I'm not sure."

Her expression changed to one of concern. "Trouble?"

"No," I tried to assure her. "No trouble."

"You take the room at the back. I'll get your key," she said as she turned and waddled inside.

I never understood why she bothered with keys, though I suspected it had more to do with it making her feel like the innkeeper she imagined herself to be than with security. She returned a few moments later and pressed a worn brass key into my hand. I reached into the pocket of my jeans and peeled a couple twenties off the roll.

Rosa shook her head. "This is too much."

"Let me know when it runs out."

She showed me a matronly smile and kissed me softly on the cheek. "Go and get something to eat. Your hands are shaking."

⊙══✦══⊙

"YOU SEE THAT man over there?" Ramon asked me, jutting his chin in the direction of a thickset man sitting by himself at a table beyond the corner of the bar. He had spilled himself into a metal folding chair in the shade of a palm-frond *palapa*, his scarred, working-man's hands wrapped around a sweating can of Carta Blanca. The clothes he wore looked slept in, his eyes turned inward, lost inside his own thoughts.

"Yeah," I said.

"Who do you think he is?"

I looked at the guy again. Deep lines etched his sunburned brow and channeled rivulets of perspiration down the sides of his tired face.

I shook my head, took the last pull from my Modelo, aimed the empty can past Ramon's shoulder and tossed it toward the rusted metal barrel that served as a trash can. It bounced off noisily, and landed in the sand between his feet.

"Who gives a shit," I said.

It had become a game when things were slow, and they almost always were. A new face was something to talk about, and Ramon always liked the stories I'd make up for him. Especially if I was drunk.

It's one of the reasons I drank here instead of any of the other makeshift stalls that dotted the beach. He jammed a wedge of lime into the mouth of a fresh beer and slid it across the plywood counter, as I rocked the legs of my unsteady stool into the sand. I knew that he was waiting me out.

"What?" I said finally. "You think just because he's a *gringo* I should know him."

Ramon shrugged and took a seat on the chipped and rusted metal cooler that contained the beer he sold. He smiled knowingly and leaned back against the corrugated metal wall in a way that made the palm frond ceiling rattle and shake. A few months earlier, a *chubasco* had rolled in and blown the old roof into the bay, along with a few dozen chairs from up and down the beach. After the storm passed, I helped the locals dredge the chairs up out of the shallows, but Ramon's roof was a goner. We rebuilt it using old two-by-fours, metal pipe and palm fronds. At least the next time it blew away, nobody would give a damn.

I shoved the lime wedge through the mouth of the can and took a long pull, then leaned in on my elbows so I wouldn't have to talk too loud.

"I'm not up for this today, Ramon."

"I think I recognize the guy," a voice said from a couple stools down. The speaker was one of the two skeevy-looking white dudes that I'd been trying to ignore since I'd arrived at the bar. They looked like the kind of guys that'd be more comfortable selling cigarettes in a subway.

Ramon nodded. "Yes," he said, and tapped a finger against his temple. "This is what I am thinking."

I twisted around on my stool for a better look at the breaking waves. The last thing I wanted to hear were these two greasy idiots spewing bullshit, and I definitely didn't want to engage in conversation.

"You know what a treetop flyer is?" the taller of the two offered up.

Ramon's English was pretty good, but still a little weak on slang. When things were slow, we sometimes taught each other words that would come in handy if you ever wound up in jail. But I could tell he didn't know that one.

"*No se*," Ramon said.

"A pilot," the guy stage-whispered. "A kind of bush pilot. Flies low so nobody sees him. *Comprende?*"

Excellent, I thought. This is just what I need.

"Ah, *si*." The guy really had Ramon's attention.

"Last time I saw that man, he was flying a load of *mota* from San Rafaelito up to California."

"Cool it," I said, and turned to face the two loudmouths. "That's enough, man."

"Was I talking to you?" the tall guy said to me.

"And you know this man?" Ramon egged him on.

He nodded sagely. "Yes, but I thought he was dead. Heard he was shot by the *Federales* outside of Matamoros. That was three years ago. They took his plane, his pot, shot him and buried him in the weeds beside the dirt airstrip."

"And yet, here he is," Ramon said, totally digging the story.

I had always liked this little village because it was quiet, off the beaten tourist path, and above all, safe. The last thing I needed was for two wandering jack-offs to blow into my space and start telling drug dealer stories. This was not a good thing for me.

"Shut the fuck up," I said.

"Excuse me?" The other guy—the heavyset cat—responded this time.

"I said, 'shut the fuck up.'"

He looked at his buddy and snorted a laugh, then turned back to me. "And you are?"

Sometimes you've got to be ready to leave hair on the walls. "I am the guy who's gonna put a beat-down on your ass that's going to make you *wish* you had a wolverine down your pants instead," I said. "Now how about you knock off the bullshit, and leave that fucking dude alone."

The tall one cocked his head and looked at me over the top of his shades. "You should buy this guy a beer, Ramon. He's wound up a little tight."

"I think maybe *you* should buy the *cerveza*," Ramon replied.

A hot breeze blew the smoke from a cooking fire across the beach and made my belly growl. I'd had enough of this bullshit anyway, and I had no interest in trouble.

I stood, reached into the pocket of my jeans and peeled a couple of wrinkled bills off my shrinking bankroll, and handed them to Ramon. "Thanks for the beers," I said. "And buy one for the stranger there. He'll need it if he's going to have to put up with these two dickheads."

I couldn't really afford to be tossing cash around, since I was carrying all that I had; that is to say, all I had left of the bread I'd collected from selling the Mexican Red I brought back from my mercy run to Eddie's place. It was going to have to last me until I could reach out and make arrangements for some sort of Western Union deal. I flashed on that fucker, Rick Montrose, again and felt myself go hot behind the ears. Still, I felt sorry for the sad-looking cat who had become the unwitting punch line to these assholes' unfunny joke, so buying him a beer seemed like good karma.

"I'm hungry," I told Ramon as I turned away. "I'm going down to Luisa's."

"I will hold your calls," he said. Another of our old jokes. I could see he was feeling badly, and trying to make amends.

I stepped out from under the makeshift roof and into the searing sun. Even with my sunglasses on, I had to squint against the glare that flashed off the rippling green water of the bay. *Bahia de los Mestengos.* Mustang Bay. There was a legend that a Spanish galleon had once run aground here with a load of horses meant for the conquistadors. The horses that survived had run wild and bred, then migrated north into the cooler elevations. The closest thing I'd ever seen to a horse since I'd been here was the pair of tired burros they used to haul bricks to build the new bakery.

Luisa had a lean-to shed at the other end of the beach where she cooked thin strips of meat and whole fish over an open fire. A torn canvas tarp had been stretched between a pair of palm trees and some lengths of galvanized pipe, and shaded the rusted metal tables where her husband usually sat. Today, he was sprawled across one of those tables, sleeping. A skinny mutt dozed at his feet, absently pawing the flies that landed on its nose.

"*Hola*, my friend," Luisa smiled. "*Tiene hambre?*"

"*Si*, Luisa. *Necesito sus pescados frescos.*"

"*Con cerveza?*"

I slugged the last of the Modelo I'd brought with me from Ramon's, and shook the empty can. "*Si, por favor.*"

Luisa showed me the space in her smile that her two front teeth had once occupied, then reached down into a cooler for my beer. The dog startled when the can snicked open, then lost interest and started licking his balls.

While I waited for my food, I pulled a postcard and pen from the pocket of my shirt and settled in to write a cryptic note to my mother back in southern California. I wanted her to know I was okay, but didn't want to give the Man too much info on my whereabouts. I knew she would understand, she knew the drill. Just spending a little time south of the border.

I had finished writing as Luisa came back with my plate. Two small snappers stared up from a pile of rice on a paper plate, their flesh perfectly singed from the fire. I jabbed them with my flimsy metal fork, and the meat fell free of the bones. That first bite tasted as good to me as anything I had ever eaten.

"Ees hokay?" Luisa asked me after a few minutes. "*Mas cerveza*, maybe?"

"*Esta bien*," I said, and I took the other beer she offered. I looked at my watch for no reason, and began to feel my jagged and speedy edges morph into the beginnings of a smooth early afternoon buzz.

A flock of frigate birds circled low over the bay, making that mournful sound they make, and I watched a pod of dolphins break the surface beneath them. A breeze began to waft in from the south, pushing a thin ribbon of clouds across the far horizon, and stirring the smoke of Luisa's open fire. She watched me unbutton my shirt, lean back in my chair, satiated, and finally begin to relax.

I must have dozed off, because the next thing I knew, I damn near jumped out of my chair when somebody came up behind me and grabbed me by the shoulders.

I turned around fast, my heart hammering in my throat.

"Goddamnit, Enrique," I said. "You scared the shit outta me."

It was Luisa's husband, up from his siesta, a bottle in his hand, and a big grin on his unshaven face.

"Come have a drink with me," he said. "Luisa! *Musica!*"

Luisa found a station on the little AM radio that hung from a wire at the back of the lean-to, and turned it so the speaker pointed out toward the tables. Enrique grabbed two mismatched plastic cups from behind the counter and a pair of fresh beers.

I was groggy from my brief nap, and my shirt stuck to my back, but I managed to stand up long enough to move to where Enrique was pouring his homemade tequila and sit myself back down.

Enrique bobbed his head happily to the rhythm of that Mexican polka crap with all the accordions, and handed me a cup. I chased that first taste with a cold Modelo that went down easier than I'd like to admit. The first time I'd tasted Enrique's cactus juice, he'd almost busted a gut laughing at me while I tried to catch my breath after tossing back a three-finger shot as though it was shelf tequila. By now, I knew better.

One by one, Enrique's friends showed up, some with bottles of their own, until the late afternoon found eleven of us filling up that small space under the torn canvas, passing bottles from hand to hand, and watching the sun fade slowly from the sky.

Like I said, booze is not generally my drug of choice, but I justified my behavior by telling myself that tequila wasn't exactly booze. And before too long, the world was tilting sideways and I knew I'd better hold on like hell or slide right off.

# CHAPTER 26

Susana and Yolanda were nearly delirious with their good fortune.

They had timed their escape perfectly, passing through the temporarily unmanned gate scant seconds before two of the guards returned to their posts. The arrival of the stranger had Miguel's men so distracted that they failed to notice the dust cloud trail of the women's departure floating away on the wind.

For her part, Yolanda Zamora was so giddy from the rush of adrenaline and sudden sense of freedom that she began to laugh out loud, gripping the steering wheel with a manic strength that threatened to squeeze blood from her palms. She couldn't remember the last time she had driven herself anywhere, and was struggling to keep the station wagon from fishtailing on the loose gravel road. Still, she was exhilarated, laughing when she glanced to her right and saw Susana wedged into the corner of the passenger seat, eyes wide, clutching her armrest with both hands.

Yolanda's mind was racing, too. Where to go now that she had made it outside the gates? Two choices: to head north at the crossroad marked by the monument of her husband's shot-up Bronco, bypass El Salto and travel as far as they could before stopping for fuel; or she could attempt to seek sanctuary with their neighbor, Eduardo "El Brujo" Chacon. Yolanda's eyes flitted down to the instrument panel. Gasoline. She hadn't thought to look until this moment. She was relieved to see that it held just over a half-tank. Thank God. That would be sufficient to get them well on their way. She made her decision and made for the crossroad a kilometer or so beyond the rise.

<br>

"YOU SHOT MY fucking truck."

Sonny Limon had been dragged into the chain-link enclosure at the back of the machine shop, and locked inside. The last time he had seen it, it had been occupied by a pack of wild dogs. The dogs were gone, but their malevolent odor remained.

Marco Zamora smiled at Sonny through the wire. "It is not often I hear a man on the wrong side of a cage make accusations toward me."

"It's not an accusation. You shot the living crap out of my camper."

Marco shrugged. "That appears to be the smallest of your worries."

Sonny was unfazed. The past forty-eight hours of his life had changed him in ways he himself was only beginning to understand. What he knew for certain was that he was not afraid of Marco Zamora. Or El Rey Miguel, either. That part of Sonny was as dead as Steve Devlin.

"Where's Miguel? I want to talk to him."

"Talk to me."

"Thanks. I'll wait for your brother."

Esteban planted a vicious kick against the cage. "Show some respect, *pendejo*. You're lucky we didn't kill you."

Sonny eyed the big man. "You assholes are lucky you didn't kill *each other*."

"Enough of this bullshit," Marco said. He pointed at two of the men. "You two stay with Senor Limon. Everybody else get back where you belong."

Esteban was the last of the men to file out into the afternoon sun. He tossed a parting glance over his shoulder at the American in the cage and smiled as he slammed the door behind him.

Marco stood in the empty driveway, the barrel of his rifle resting on his shoulder. He swiveled his head from side to side, then called out, "Rolando!"

The houseman shambled out from the narrow walkway that lead to Marco's *casita*. He could see that Marco was obviously unhappy about something, though confused as to what it might be.

"Where is the car, Rolando?"

"What?"

"The car. Where is it?"

A cold chill of panic coursed through him, and he ran to Marco's side. He saw that the space where he had left the station wagon sat empty. "I parked it here, Senor Zamora. Where I always do."

Without warning, Rolando was dropped to the ground by a savage blow from the stock of Marco's gun. He sat on the hardpan, dazed, as a thick ribbon of blood and saliva flowed from his nose and mouth.

"Esteban, check on Yolanda."

The big man gazed dumbly at the bleeding houseman.

"Do it!" Marco shouted. "Now!"

<hr />

YOLANDA SLOWED AS she approached the rise in the road.

It was not much of a rise, but enough that she could not see beyond it, and she knew well that there was barely enough space for the safe passage of oncoming traffic. She steered cautiously toward the edge, careful not to let the front end slip onto the soft soil at the shoulder, or worse, into the ditch just beyond.

She gripped the wheel tightly still, though the near lunatic laughter of before had faded into a terse and steely silence. Yolanda glanced sideways and saw that Susana's eyes were tightly shut, her hands knotted into white-knuckled fists.

"Try not to worry—"

They reached the crest as she spoke to comfort the girl.

It happened quickly. The screech of brakes and a cloud of dirt and tiny stones. Yolanda's car swerved sideways as she cranked the wheel to avoid being sideswiped. There hadn't even been time to notice the color of the vehicle that had nearly killed them. She felt the rear end slide and fishtail into the shallow ravine. She couldn't see beyond the front end of the car, engulfed as they were in the fog of fine dust that had been cast into the air by their near miss.

Susana rubbed her shoulder where it had struck the dashboard, and winced. An expression of concern displaced her fear when she looked back at Yolanda. "You're bleeding."

Yolanda wasn't certain she had heard correctly.

"You're bleeding," Susana said again. "Your head. I think you bumped it on the wheel."

Yolanda brushed at her forehead with the back of her hand. It came away smeared with her blood. "Are you all right?"

"Fine, Senora. Just my arm. I am fine. We have to go."

"Yes, yes," Yolanda said. She nodded and immediately regretted it. "*Un momento*."

"We must go, Senora. *Inmediatamente*. I can drive."

Her mind was moving so slowly. She needed only to sit for a few more minutes.

"Senora, we can trade places," Susana urged. "Come, slide over here. I will come around."

The car was canted at an odd angle, so it took all the strength Susana could muster to force open the door. Her shoulder throbbed in time with her racing heart as she stepped around to the other side. She pulled up short and felt as though her breath would not come.

"Is everyone all right?"

He was standing in the middle of the road, smiling as though he had expected something like this. It was not the kind of smile Susana ever wanted to see again.

"Xavier will wait here with the car. I will send someone to fetch them," Miguel said. "The two of you can ride back to the ranch with me."

"*Si*, Senor Zamora," Susana whispered. "We were only—"

"Shhh," he said. He placed a finger to her lips, as if he were speaking to a slow child.

⁓⟊⁓

MIGUEL AND THE women arrived at Rancho Tronada ten minutes later.

As he drove past the gates, he saw that Marco and Esteban were preparing to depart in Marco's Jeep, each man armed with an AK-47 slung across his shoulder and a sidearm holstered at his hip. When they saw that it was Miguel behind the wheel of Xavier's pickup, their expressions grew sheepish and grim. There would be hell to pay for their lapse.

"Senor Miguel—" Esteban began, but El Rey cut him off before he could say any more.

"Take the women inside. And watch them this time."

Marco approached his brother without a word and stood beside him as they watched Esteban march Yolanda and Susana inside the hacienda. There was no doubt that Miguel was furious—it was coming off him in nearly tangible waves—and Marco did not relish having to tell him that there was yet another part of the story to be told.

He steeled himself and finally spoke. "You saw the broken truck outside the gates?"

Miguel reached into his shirt pocket and withdrew a cigarette. He flipped open his silver Zippo lighter and exhaled a stream of smoke, his eyes locked on Marco's. He raised an eyebrow questioningly, but did not speak.

"It is the American policeman. He arrived unexpectedly. There was a great deal of confusion, and—"

"Where is he now? Senor Limon?"

Marco gestured toward the mechanic's shed. "In the cage."

El Rey Miguel raised his head and squinted into the sun. His face emptied of emotion, like a receding tide. He took one last drag from his cigarette, dropped it to the ground and crushed it under his boot. "Send someone for Xavier," he said. "He's waiting with the station wagon beside the road about three kilometers from here, just beyond the rise. Tell them to bring a chain to help tow it from the ravine."

Miguel turned and strode toward the machine shop, leaving his brother to do as he had been told. It was all he could do to contain his anger. His day had been, for the most part, a success. To come home after such a day only to discover ineptitude and unwelcome surprises of this magnitude was delivering him to the edge of an eruption of violence. He could feel it prickling beneath his skin.

Sonny Limon had propped himself in the corner of the enclosure, sitting on the floor and humming softly to himself. He shaded his eyes with his hand as a wedge of bright light preceded Miguel into the room. The imprinted image of El Rey's silhouette floated in his brain as his eyes readjusted to the dimness inside.

Miguel pulled up a chair beside the chain-link pen, straddled it and stared at Sonny. He took his time lighting another Marlboro, then shook the pack and offered one to him. Sonny rose to accept it, placed it between his lips and leaned toward the wire. Their faces flickered in yellow light as Miguel touched the flame to Sonny's cigarette.

"So, how do you feel, Senor Limon?" Miguel asked.

"Like I've gone bear hunting in a meat suit."

Despite his mood, Miguel had to laugh. At least this one had *cojones*.

"What brings you back here so soon. I thought we had finalized our arrangements."

Sonny paced to the rear of his cell and leaned against the wall. "Well, my situation has encountered an unexpected change."

"Change?"

"Especially the unexpected kind."

Men like Miguel Zamora either wanted you dead, or living inside the lies they create. That's all. That's their game and those are the choices they give you. It was time to change the menu. "Yeah, well," Sonny shrugged. "Life. You know."

Miguel's eyes narrowed as he studied Sonny Limon. It was not difficult to see that something inside the man had transformed.

"Here's the thing," Sonny said. "I have a choice to make, but I need your help to make it."

"Go on."

"I can't be a cop anymore, Senor Zamora—"

"You think you can come to my ranch . . . my *home* and shake me down?" He laughed dryly. "I must admit you are not very smart, but you must have *huevos* like coconuts."

It was Sonny's turn to smile. "Oh, this isn't a shakedown. This is a straight-up business proposition."

"By all means, then, let me hear it before I feed you to the dogs."

"Then listen up, because it gets a little complicated. See, before I left the States I stopped off to meet with my banker. I left two envelopes in a safe deposit box that only he has access to. One envelope is addressed to the captain of my squad, and contains a simple letter of resignation. The other is addressed to the DEA, Border Patrol, and the FBI. That second one is a real motherfucker, too, Miguel. There are names, dates, detailed descriptions of the routes we set up for you to move your product. It's really something. Real newsworthy shit.

"Thing is, I need your help deciding which one of those letters I should tell my banker to put in the mail."

Miguel could feel the muscles twitch at the corners of his eyes. "I should shoot you right now."

"You could do that. Of course, if my guy doesn't hear from me by tomorrow morning, the second letter goes out. I'm guessing it would take less than seventy-two hours for this place to be swarming with black helicopters raining a shitstorm down on your world. You could probably run, but your life as El Rey Miguel would be over forever. Hell, I bet some of your own people would spend their last peso to put your head on a pike."

"Nobody blackmails me. Nobody."

"I'm sure they don't," Sonny said. "Besides, that's such an ugly word."

"You saw what happened to your partner. That could be you."

"I suppose, but you'd best not let me die. Starting tomorrow, my banker is expecting a call from me every morning, bright and early. When he picks up the phone, he will ask me—at random—one question. It will be one of about a hundred personal questions to which I've supplied him the answers in advance. One wrong reply, and that second letter goes out. Immediately. Game over."

"So, I will torture you until you provide the correct ones to me."

"I figured you'd think of that. Problem is, you'll never know if the responses I give to you will be true until it's too late. Frankly, I don't think I could even remember all the questions."

"Then I will kidnap someone you love. Your wife, perhaps."

"*Ex*-wife. Go ahead."

"Your mother."

"Dead."

"Your father. Your brother. Your sister."

"Also dead; and I'm an only child."

This bastard seemed to have thought this through. "Then I will keep you imprisoned. You may make your call each morning, and return to the comforts of your cage. It will be a less-than-desirable life."

"C'mon, Miguel. I'd give a false answer the very first day, and you'd never know I lied."

"What do you want?"

"I can no longer return to the United States. I wish to remain in your employ, and continue to collect the, ah, 'commission' you promised to my partner and me. I figure five, six months. Then I'll be gone. You'll never see me again."

"And if I refuse? If I don't believe you?"

"You've got your choices and I've got mine, Senor Zamora. I know you're a businessman, but I never figured you for a gambler."

"You've given me a great deal to think about."

"I'll need a vehicle, too," Sonny pressed. "Free roam of the ranch, and a nice room in the main house."

"You're a sonofabitch."

"But I can be *your* sonofabitch. Just don't think too long."

It had been a long time since Miguel had found himself pressed into a corner. He had sorely misjudged Sonny Limon, had thought he could control him by making him a murderer. It had never crossed his mind that this man could summon the backbone to do what he had just done; it had never crossed his mind that Sonny Limon could simply walk away from his country, his family and his police career. Miguel still had to place that call to the Colombians and inform them that he had failed to locate the "lost" cocaine. That was no small hurdle, either, but one he had believed himself prepared for. Now that La Plaza appeared to be prepared to back his story, the pieces were finally in place. This was not the time to take a chance that this compromised cop was telling the truth, and would blow the whistle on the entire pipeline. If that came crashing down, Miguel was a dead man.

There was one thing, however, that Miguel could do—needed to do immediately—to reassert his dominion. Certain scales needed to be set back into balance. For the time being, he would put up with the smug American.

"My trust in you comes with a price," Miguel said. "There is something I need you to see."

# CHAPTER 27

Esteban was not a man who was easily cowed.

But he had to admit he had been humiliated by having been treated as a common *campesino* by Miguel Zamora. The only silver lining, if you could call it that, was that he had not been berated in front of the men. That would have been an untenable loss of face, very difficult to recover from. Still, he had been responsible for allowing an opportunity for the Senora's escape—even if it had been in the service of protecting Rancho Tronada from an unexpected intruder.

As he had been instructed, Esteban took the two women into the courtyard where he held them at gunpoint as they sat together in a pair of straight-backed chairs near the waterfall at the far end of the pool. The Senora wore an expression of defiance as she watched him pace inside the shade of the open *pasillo*, but the little maid, Susana, was nearly catatonic with fear. Esteban liked that she could not bear to look at him, and savored his feeling of power. Her eyes were locked onto the space between her feet, rocking gently as her lips moved with the recitation of some silent prayer. He felt something stir inside his trousers and he forced himself to look away.

The late afternoon sun had begun to fall behind the high walls and cast long shadows across the ornate brickwork and ceramic tile pathways that wound themselves about the poolside gardens. Before long, the floodlights would come on and the night would arrive in full. And not a moment too soon. Esteban wanted little more than to put this day behind him.

The approaching echo of heavy footfalls brought him to attention.

Marco was the first to emerge from beneath the high archway of the hacienda. He had Rolando's arm gripped firmly with one hand, and a roll of something that looked like silver tape in the other. Miguel followed not far behind; his expression was blank and immobile, which Esteban knew from experience masked a dangerous and unpredictable rage. The fourth man to emerge, however, took Esteban by surprise. It was the American he had last seen in the dog cage, and he was walking along with the Zamoras as though he was an invited guest.

Esteban had no intention of questioning a single thing. He hadn't survived this long by being a fool. No, he would get through the rest of this worthless day by doing what he was told, and staying out of sight until tomorrow when, perhaps, El Rey might have cooled off. He didn't have to wait long for the first of his orders.

"Gather the rest of the household staff and bring them here," Miguel said.

Esteban responded immediately by running—not walking—inside the hacienda to bring the remaining cooks, chambermaids and gardeners back to the courtyard. In less than three minutes he had them all assembled and standing at ragged attention in a line facing El Rey.

Miguel spoke softly at first, directing his comments to those who had just arrived. Their eyes were cast submissively downward, making no contact whatsoever with Senor Zamora.

"Please look at me," Miguel said.

There was an uncomfortable shuffling of feet before, one by one, each managed to look in the general direction of the *padron's* face.

"It is a sad day at Rancho Tronada," he continued. "Because today I discovered that two people—two trusted household servants who have for years been in my generous employ—conspired to kidnap my wife."

To Miguel's satisfaction, he saw the instantaneous display of dread on the faces before him, heard their collective intake of disbelieving breath. From her seat a few feet away, young Susana began to sob aloud, the intonation of her prayers taking voice.

Rolando began to struggle, momentarily pulling away from Marco before his captor dropped him to the ground with a vicious elbow strike to the houseman's stomach.

"It is impossible for me to believe that I cannot even trust those who have been in my employ—in my own hacienda—to remain loyal to El Rey Miguel when he is away for only a few hours! If someone had told me this, I would have said it was unthinkable, for I love you like a father loves his children."

Rolando was trembling visibly, shivering, terrified. His fear was made all the more potent upon hearing Susana's keening cries. He had done nothing wrong, not really. He hadn't tried to kidnap anyone. If he was guilty of anything, it was stupidity; he should never have let the car keys out of his sight. He had a wife. He had a family. Surely, Senor Miguel would have pity on him.

"But sometimes," Miguel said. "Sometimes a father must punish his children in order to teach them the important lessons of life. And the most important of all of life's lessons is loyalty.

"I give each of you my trust by allowing you into my home, by paying your salaries and helping you take care of your own families. Without trust, what do we have? We have nothing. We have less than nothing.

"So I want you to understand clearly: When I give you my trust, it comes with a price. That price is your loyalty. It is important that none of you ever forget this."

Miguel turned to his brother and nodded.

The small group watched in horror as Marco forced Rolando into a heavy iron lawn chair. He held him in place as he fought in vain against the younger, stronger man. Esteban wound loops of silver tape around the houseman's wrists, pinning them to the chair, then did the same to his ankles.

Tears streamed from Rolando's eyes, chin quivering as his lips opened and closed in a silent scream, like a fish left to die on the dry slats of a pier.

In the seconds it took to confine Rolando, Yolanda had transitioned from stony defiance to incredulity to paralyzing fear. She knew her husband could be cruel, but this display was so far beyond any of her most nightmarish imaginings that she was unable to catch her breath. Lightheaded, she was certain that this poor man was about to receive a bullet to the back of his head. It was a bullet that was rightly meant for her; this man was innocent. She inhaled a ragged breath and screamed for Miguel to stop.

At El Rey's bidding, Marco and Esteban went immediately to Yolanda's side and silenced her. For good measure, they did the same to young Susana, and the two women were brought closer to where Rolando now struggled in his chair. Both women had been bound at the wrists, their lips sealed shut with silver tape. It had taken only seconds.

With order restored, Miguel nodded once again to Marco and the big man.

"Loyalty, my children," he intoned, shaking his head slowly in a display of mock despair.

The sun had sunk behind the far mountains and dimmed the sky to a bruised purple. One by one, the lights inside the courtyard snapped on as their sensors detected the approaching night. The pool, too, was suddenly illuminated, glowing in hues of turquoise and blue, and cast marbling shadows on the faces gathered there.

"I think that's enough, Miguel," Sonny hissed. He had held his tongue long enough. "They get it."

El Rey scanned the faces arrayed before him before he answered.

"I do not think you understand," he said. "This is as much for you as it is for them, Senor Limon."

In one swift move, Marco and Esteban cast Rolando, still struggling against his restraints, into the deep end of the pool. Yolanda felt her knees go weak as she watched him sink, resting momentarily on the tiles at the bottom before the chair tipped slowly backward. Seconds ticked by like hours as they watched the old man drown, his eyes as wide as saucers, his head thrashing from side to side in agony and terror. The muscles of Rolando's arms and legs flexed wildly as he fought against his bindings, seeking a breath of air that would not come.

And then he lay still, eyes and mouth thrown open in a final silent scream.

The silence was a palpable thing, broken only by the brittle sound of palm fronds rattling inside the ascetic breeze.

"Sweet Jesus," Sonny whispered.

Susana felt herself on the edge of fainting. She had known Rolando, had loved him as one might love a kindly uncle. He had been guilty of nothing, and now he was dead. Her own desires had led to this, and she knew without question that the stain of sin was hers to bear. If Rolando's was the fate of the innocent, then she had no doubt that her own should be far worse. She prayed for God and the Blessed Virgin to forgive her, for a miracle to intercede and save her from the death she had surely brought upon herself.

"Esteban," Miguel said. His voice echoed inside the walls of the garden. "Take the girl. She is yours to do with as you wish. When you tire of her, you may share her with the men, if you choose."

Susana had no way of knowing that in the coming hours, she would find herself no longer wishing for intercession but for death itself.

⚬━◆━⚬

IT WAS DEAD dark when Sonny Limon climbed out of bed.

He had spent the past several hours tossing beneath the sheets, unable to sleep, unable to think, unable to *stop* thinking. He stepped out onto the balcony of the enormous guest room that Miguel had provided him, and stared into the black sky. He stood naked in the desert air, letting it cool his skin as it dried the perspiration that had dampened the sheets of his sleeplessness. The moon had long since set, but a semaphore of starlight blinked behind the slow passage of clouds across the horizon. He guessed it was well into the small hours of morning, but he had left his watch on the nightstand. He didn't really want to know.

Sonny had tried hard to drink himself to sleep, but had succeeded only in awakening the demons that now resided inside his head. Across the compound, he could see the dim glow of light that still shone inside the bunkhouse. When the wind blew just right, he could hear the riotous shouting of the men inside those walls. They had been at it for hours without end. Savages. Every fucking one of them.

He turned from the balcony and went inside, closing the heavy doors behind him. Sonny crawled back into bed and buried his face in the pillows. He willed his mind to calm itself, but the visions remained behind his eyes like echoes rising from a deep stone well until he finally drifted into a fitful sleep.

An hour later, he was awakened by the unmistakable report of a handgun.

⊙━━✦━━⊙

MIGUEL'S LEGS HAD begun to cramp from all the pacing.

He'd been circling the edges of the room for a long, long time, pausing only to draw another fine line of powder across the smooth glass surface of the table beside the window. It was the only thing he felt he could count on anymore. He took a tightly rolled bill of currency between his fingers, tilted his head to the tabletop and felt the familiar burn in his nostrils, the back of his throat.

He cast his gaze toward the bed where Yolanda lay, eyelids fluttering with dreams, a dark nipple showing itself from beneath the rumpled sheets. He sat down, naked, in the wooden chair near the window, and picked up the revolver that rested on the table beside the flickering candle. Miguel watched his shadow dance on the white plaster wall as he thumbed the chamber release and absently spun the cylinder. The noise brought Yolanda awake, and she rolled to her side and watched him.

Miguel wore the bored and angry expression she had come to fear more than anything. He motioned to her with his fingers; she knows what he wants. She is a prisoner in every way.

Yolanda rolled out from under the sheets and stepped across to him, stealing a glance at his face as she tilted her head and looked at him. She placed a hand on one of his knees and knelt between his legs. From the corner of her eye, she watched him appraise her as she took him in her hand and slowly stroked him. He saw her red lips form an O around him, and a thin line of bright blood trickle from her nose.

"*Puta*," he said, and slapped her again on the side of the head. "I should have given you over to Esteban."

Yolanda recoiled and curled into herself, bringing her knees up under her chin and trying to daub the blood away with the back

- 218 -

of her hand. Miguel gazed openly at the thatch of black hair at the nexus of her thighs.

"Let's play," he said.

Miguel tilted the barrel of the revolver toward the ceiling, opened the cylinder and allowed the heavy cartridges to fall to the table. He took his time as he stood each one on end in a neat little row, like a child arranging toy soldiers.

A tiny twitch of a smile pulled at the corner of his eyes as he replaced one brass shell into the chamber and spun the cylinder. He snapped it shut with a brisk snap of his wrist, and without a word, placed the barrel to his temple and squeezed the trigger. Click. His teeth shone white as he grinned in the half-light cast by the candle at his elbow.

She feels the fear steal across her face now, real fear. Yolanda has seen him act crazy before, especially when he's snorted too much *yeyo*. There is a watery fire in his eyes, and his lips are pulled back tight against his teeth.

"Your turn," he smiled.

Miguel grabbed a fistful of her hair and dragged her to the bed. She shook uncontrollably as he stabbed the cold, hard barrel of the revolver into her womb. His eyes locked on hers as he thumbed back the hammer and fired a second time. Click.

She shuddered and nearly lost control of herself, panting shallow breaths as he brought the barrel to his lips and licked it. His eyes locked on hers as he studied her fear. He felt himself stiffen again and swung the gun in the direction of a potted plant that rested on a pedestal at the far corner of the room. He squeezed the trigger. For a moment, the room flashed white and the vase exploded with the impact of the bullet as it rammed a jagged hole through the plaster wall just beyond.

Miguel was on her a moment later, clawing her like a panther, the smell of sulphur mingling with the damp, musky odor of their tangled bodies as he forced himself inside.

# CHAPTER 28

Heat shimmers radiated off the sunbaked sand and transformed the desert into a sea of quicksilver that stretched all the way to the horizon.

The interior of the truck was stifling, but Sonny was lost in thought. In fact, his mind had been running at full gallop all morning. He stared out the windshield, past smears of juice from the bugs that had spattered there, squinting against the glare and trying unsuccessfully to ignore the heat and Miguel Zamora's erratic driving. A single bodyguard accompanied them, some nameless *pistolero* who had obviously drawn the short straw after a long night of unspeakable debauchery with Esteban and the rest of their crew. He was riding in the open truck bed with an automatic rifle gripped tightly against his chest, a bandana tied about his face and a slouch hat pulled low against the roiling rooster-tail of dust that the truck kicked up.

As they had previously agreed, Miguel was taking Sonny to the telephone exchange in El Salto to make the first of his expected daily calls to Sonny's banker. Of course, Miguel had his own phone call to make, and he was not looking forward to playing the part of loyal Mexican lackey with the Colombians. But it was a necessary final installment in his plan to liberate their coke.

There had been little conversation between the men during breakfast, and Sonny's inquiry as to the pistol shot he had heard in the early hours of the morning drew a silence that had been unbroken up to this very moment. It was obvious that Miguel was beyond simple distraction and had moved to something more closely resembling the restless agitation of a caged animal. His eyes practically vibrated behind his dark glasses, and his skin smelled of stale sex.

Miguel drifted from thoughts of Colombians and stolen blow to the present matter. He still wasn't certain that he believed Sonny Limon, but he harbored no illusion that this was the time to take on additional risk. If the American was telling the truth about his protection arrangement, then the few more months' worth of payoffs to Limon would be a small price to pay. If Sonny was lying, well, Miguel would never know if he had been lying, would he? He needed something to clear his head, something to push these thoughts away for a few minutes of peace. For now, he would settle for the distraction of music.

From the corner of his eye, Sonny saw Miguel snatch an eight-track tape from a box on the seat, shove it into the player, and crank the volume to a level that rattled the filthy glass. It was an old-style *corrido* whose lyrics spoke of glamorous outlaws and revenge and the gratitude of amber-eyed senoritas. Sonny listened absently until the words were lost inside the blare of accordion and *bajo sextos*.

The music seemed to put El Rey in a better frame of mind as he tapped out a rhythm on the steering wheel and sang along with the tape. When the song came to an end, he snapped off the volume and spoke to Sonny for the first time in over an hour.

"You like Ramon Ayala? Los Bravos del Norte?" He waved absently at the muted tape deck.

Sonny eyed him for a long second, amazed anew at the man's mercurial mood swings. "He's fine."

" 'Fine?' " Miguel scoffed. "He is one of the very best in Mexico. One day they will write songs about Miguel Zamora!"

"Sure they will."

"You really think so?"

*Sure, you sick fuck. They'll be heroic, beautiful songs about gang rape and the murder of defenseless old men.*

"You are El Rey Miguel, no?" Sonny said instead.

His answer seemed to please Miguel greatly, and he turned the tape player back on and sang the rest of the way into town.

◦━✦━◦

THE NARROW SIDEWALKS were crowded with the business of Market Day.

Long tables were piled high with fresh fruit and vegetables, loaves of fresh bread and sweet cakes. The limp carcasses of ducks and plucked chickens and great red sheets of flayed meat hung on hooks in storefront windows, flyblown and growing dark in the heat of the advancing day.

Miguel's bodyguard took the lead as they exited the truck and crossed the cobblestone street toward the telephone office. A gang of young boys, the oldest of whom could not have been more than seven years old, ran into the street and gathered around Miguel, hands outstretched, noisily begging him for loose change. He shooed them aside as he would a brood of chickens, playfully kicking the slowest of them in the backside before he could scramble away.

Miguel directed the guard inside the building to clear whatever customers might be using the facilities there. It was a task with which he seemed quite familiar.

Sonny stopped short of the door and motioned Miguel to one side.

"Don't even think about tracing my call," Sonny said.

"We have discussed this already."

"Any harm comes to my banker, any attempt to coerce him in any way, my attorney will release that letter to the Feds. Do not make the mistake of thinking I am bullshitting you."

Miguel shrugged innocently. "Senor Limon, why do you wish to insult me?"

One by one, a half-dozen men and a pair of old women shambled out the door and quickly melted into the bustle of El Salto. Far from appearing annoyed by the interruption, they all seemed relieved to be excused from any interaction with Miguel Zamora.

Once the last of the civilians had finally been cleared out, the guard took up a conspicuous position at the main entry and waited as Miguel led Sonny to the cashier's counter at the back of the dingy office. Sonny peeled off a handful of badly worn pesos and was directed to a booth at the far end of the room. Miguel leaned against the counter, drew a thin black cigarillo from his shirt pocket and lit up as he watched Sonny make his call.

Less than five minutes later, Sonny emerged from the cramped booth, returned to the counter and waited for his change.

"Looks like you're good for another day," Sonny said, turned and left Miguel to his business.

⌁

SONNY'S CALL HAD gone according to plan, and had purchased him another day among the living.

"Wait here," Miguel's nameless bodyguard had ordered him when he had exited the telephone exchange office. "Senor Zamora will not be long."

"I don't think so, bro," Sonny replied. "I believe I'll take a walk instead."

Sonny wandered aimlessly through the narrow streets. In the distance a church bell tolled the hour, and he knew he should be hungry, but felt nothing more than a craving for something that might settle his nerves. Perhaps if he found a small restaurant, the smell of food would ignite his appetite.

He turned left down a narrow alley where the smooth paving gave way onto hard-packed soil and gypsum dust. The white light of midday glared brightly at the opposite end, from which Sonny could hear the hustle and stir of commerce echo down between the walls mingling with the smells of woodsmoke and roasting meat. Overhead, a line of pigeons cooed from their perch on an electrical wire that sagged between the pastel buildings, and a man slept in the shade of a doorway, oblivious to Sonny's passing.

Sonny shaded his eyes as he emerged from the relative dark of the alley and into the town's central plaza. As on the main street, the central square was lined with colorful handcarts piled high with handmade goods: *ristras* of dried peppers and hard Indian corn hung on the wire beside clusters of cook pots and tinware in the shop windows that bordered the *zocalo*.

A church dominated the far side, its doors shut tight against the heat. Just beyond lay a thin ribbon of water running inside a shallow ravine where women knelt doing their wash along the flat rocks. Naked toddlers and young children played alongside, throwing stones and making shapes in the sand and mud with dry staves of wolf willow.

Sonny dismissed a fleeting impulse to enter the cool darkness of the cathedral nave, turned instead and took up a seat at a small table in the open air outside a cantina across from the bandstand. A few moments later, a hawk-faced waiter appeared beside him and asked for his order.

"How cold is your beer?" Sonny asked.

"Is good. Very cold."

"Tecate, then. And a bottle of Cuervo."

Deep lines formed on the waiter's brow as one eyebrow shot skyward. "A whole bottle, Senor?"

Sonny peeled off several more crumpled bills and set them on the table. "*Por favor.*"

Sonny drank in silence as he watched the people of El Salto go about the business of their day, savoring the burn of the liquor he tossed back, waiting for the familiar glow to clear his mind. He studied the faces of the vendors, the barefooted children that played among their stalls, and was washed with shame by the feudal subservience that Miguel Zamora had imposed upon their lives, onto this village of dust and disrepair. Now Sonny himself had become complicit in their subjugation. He cast a baleful glance across the plaza, threw back another Cuervo and forced himself to look away.

He closed his eyes and drew a deep breath, trying to relax and allow the tequila to work its magic. He felt his stomach lurch anew when his mind drifted to thoughts of the night before. God only knew what had become of the poor maid. Good Christ. As carefully and securely as he had devised his plan to keep himself alive, there was no question in Sonny's mind that he'd better sleep with one eye open and grow another set in the back of his head. There was also no question that he needed Miguel's bribery bread now more than ever. That money was going to have to last a while; lately the thought of heading down to Costa Rica, buying a little place on the beach and disappearing had grown from fantasy into a full-fledged necessity . . .

Somewhere along the way he had allowed himself to slip into a half-sleep occupied by images he knew he would spend the rest of his life denying. He came awake suddenly, glancing at his watch to see how long he had been out. He was relieved to know it had been only a few minutes, though the sun had shifted and pushed the shade of a *guamuchil* tree across the walkway and cast his table in irregular light. It must have been the cause of his sudden awakening.

Sonny removed the dark glasses he had been wearing and tucked them into the pocket of his shirt. His head was still buzzing with dark thoughts, so he poured himself another shot of Cuervo and knocked it back. He dried his lips with the back of his hand and focused aimlessly on the stand of tall carrizo cane that grew beside the stream where the women did their wash.

"You are enjoying your afternoon in the square?"

Sonny nearly knocked his tepid bottle of Tecate to the ground.

"I am sorry," the man said. "I did not mean to sneak up on you. May I join you?"

The man looked familiar. He was in his sixties if he was a day, his skin dark and deeply lined, with a neatly trimmed goatee. But his eyes danced with something at once youthful and powerful and laced with amusement. It was something Sonny hadn't seen in anyone's eyes in a long, long time.

"We met a week or so ago," the man said. "The fiesta at Rancho Tronada."

It came back to Sonny then, a conversation about the dogs. "El Brujo."

"The same," he smiled and gestured to the empty chair at Sonny's table. "Do you mind if I sit?"

The hawk-faced waiter appeared at El Brujo's side before Sonny had a chance to answer. The tray in his hand held two fresh Tecates and a second shot glass. The old man nodded politely as the waiter set the unordered drinks on the table, then nervously backed away into the recesses of the cantina.

"Please," Sonny said at last.

Silence stretched between them as Sonny poured the tequila.

Sonny raised his glass to the old man. "Here's to you, as good as you are. Here's to me, as bad as I am. As good as you are, and as bad as I am, I'm as good as you are, as bad as I am."

El Brujo sipped slowly as he watched the American throw back his head and empty his glass with a practiced flip of the wrist.

"You are Irish?" the older man asked. "You do not look it."

Sonny's eyes registered surprise that El Brujo would recognize the hoary ethnic toast. "Not me," he said. "Just something an old friend of mine used to say."

"I see."

"Another?" Sonny offered.

"I try to limit myself in the hours before sunset." El Brujo was pleased to see that the American accepted the little fib innocently enough. It was always best to gather the pieces with a sober mind. "But please, enjoy yourself."

Sonny raised the Tecate to his lips and savored the cool chaser. "Name's Sonny, by the way."

"A pleasure," El Brujo said. "So, what brings you to El Salto, Senor Sonny?"

"I had to make a phone call."

The answer seemed to puzzle El Brujo.

"You mean why am I here with Miguel Zamora?"

El Brujo showed him the palms of his hands and a little frown, as if it were none of his business, though this was exactly what he had meant by his question. "A man may keep any friendships he chooses. It is none of my affair, and I apologize."

"Miguel Zamora is nobody's friend." He realized too late what he had said.

Long seconds passed as El Brujo watched the American appear to shrink inside himself.

"You are quiet," the old man said finally.

"I'm drunk."

"Perhaps so. But mostly you are quiet."

"It is not very restful at Rancho Tronada," Sonny said, and turned his face toward the distant sound of children playing at the creek's edge.

"There is trouble?"

Sonny continued staring into the distance, adding nothing, wishing he could grab that last statement about Miguel and cram it right back into his mouth.

"Senor," El Brujo broke the silence. "It is not the sharing of bread that binds men together, it is the sharing of enemies."

A narrow shaft of sunlight spilled through the leaves overhead and caught the half-empty bottle of tequila in its glare. Sonny shook his head. "Some people are damned from the day they're born."

"With respect, I disagree. The damned are complicit in their own damnation."

"And what about salvation?"

"Do you have something for which you need to atone?"

He was about to reply when he noticed El Brujo shift his gaze beyond Sonny's shoulder, to something behind him. Sonny turned and saw Miguel Zamora striding purposefully toward their table, the nameless bodyguard at his side. Even at a distance it was easy to read his agitation. Miguel looked as though he had enough electrical current running up his spine to light him up.

"Don Eduardo," Miguel said as he reached the table. "A surprise to see you in El Salto."

Sonny noticed the old man made no attempt to rise. Instead, El Brujo lifted his arms and gestured broadly toward the town square. "It is Market Day."

"So it is." Miguel smiled, but it was clear that his nervous system was on tilt. "And I see you have met my houseguest."

Miguel regarded the man with a deference Sonny had never seen him display in the presence of anyone, but there was something feral lurking there, too.

"We were just about to order lunch," El Brujo said.

"That is unfortunate," Miguel answered. "I need to take him home. Perhaps another time."

Sonny watched the exchange with interest. It was obvious that these two men were accustomed to circling each other like dogs.

"But I insist," the old man smiled. "Let your friend enjoy his meal. I will bring him back to your *rancho*. It is on my way."

Before Miguel had a chance to reply, the old man snapped his fingers and the restaurant owner appeared instantly tableside. Had the gesture been made by a man of lesser standing, it would have been considered rude to the point of insolence. Somehow though, Sonny saw, El Brujo possessed an elegance and force of will that engendered both respect and fear in everyone he encountered. Even Miguel Zamora chose not to argue any further the point of who would drive Sonny back to Rancho Tronada.

⚬⚊⚊╫⚊⚊⚬

"YOU DID NOT enjoy your meal?" El Brujo asked as pushed his empty plate toward the center of the table.

"It was fine," Sonny answered. "I haven't had much of an appetite. I apologize. That was kind of you."

Over the course of the past hour, the two men had fallen into a companionable pattern of conversation.

"You will forgive me if I tell you that you look very bad. Tired."

"Thanks."

"When was the last time you slept?"

"I don't remember."

"There is a *farmacia* across the plaza. They will have something that could help you with that."

"I don't know."

"You don't know what?"

"I don't know if I want to sleep too soundly inside El Rey Miguel's hacienda. I think I'll stick with my friend Mr. Cuervo," Sonny said.

"Tequila is not always our friend. Especially when it is rest we seek."

"You are a wise man." Sonny smiled, but there was a deep sadness inside his eyes.

"Why do you think they call me 'El Brujo'?"

Why, indeed, Sonny thought. But there's no question you scare the shit out of everybody in town, and it seemed like more than simple superstition. On the other hand, what did Sonny know about the social dynamics of a bumfuck town that was jammed into the ass end of Mexico like a suppository?

El Brujo studied Sonny's face. "We spoke earlier of atonement," he said softly.

"I'm too far gone for that."

"A man can do so in many ways." The old man lifted his *cerveza* from the table and drank. "So how is Senora Yolanda? She is a fine young woman."

The abrupt change of subject caught Sonny off guard. He felt the rush of heat run up his neck, and he knew that El Brujo had read him.

"You know her well?" It was all Sonny could come up with. He felt he was drifting far into the deep water, but could do nothing about it.

"Her father and I were once friends."

"And now?"

He shrugged. "Things changed when she married Miguel Zamora."

"Miguel seems to have that effect."

A wistful shadow passed across the old man's features, then was gone. "Please tell me she is well."

"That atonement you were talking about? I don't imagine it starts with a lie."

This time it wasn't sorrow that flashed in El Brujo's eyes, but he contained it almost immediately. When he spoke, his voice was as soft as the wind. "You are right, Senor Sonny. A sincere penance should not begin with a lie. But I suspect that God would smile on the man who could make it true. Yolanda is a lovely girl, and deserves the Lord's protection."

Sonny leaned back in his chair and watched the old man stand and signal the waiter for the check.

"As it turns out," El Brujo said. "I have an errand of my own before I take you back to Senor Zamora's. Wait here and I will return for you shortly."

EL BRUJO brought his car to a halt about a hundred yards from the main gate of Rancho Tronada. The guards eyed them from a distance, then grew bored and turned away.

"I enjoyed our lunch together, Senor Sonny," the old man said, and offered his hand.

Sonny shook it firmly. "*Gracias*. So did I." He pushed open the car door and stepped out into the light of late afternoon.

"Take these," the old man said. He was holding a prescription bottle in his outstretched palm.

"What is it?"

"Valium. It will help you sleep."

"Thank you, but—"

"You may find you have some use for them," El Brujo interrupted. "It is always better to have and not need, than the other way around, no?"

There being no point in arguing, Sonny thanked him again and slipped the bottle into his pocket.

"*Vaya con Dios*, Senor Sonny."

# CHAPTER 29

I don't remember walking home, but that's where I was when I woke up.

I was stark naked, but for the watch that was still on my wrist, my clothes in a pile at the foot of my bed. My mouth felt like cotton and tasted like something you'd hose out of a dog pen. I reached up to rub my eyes and was rewarded with an unexpected bolt of pain that shot from my eye socket to the base of my jaw.

I was coming out of that twilight place between sleeping and waking, trying like hell to recall the night before, and not having much success. The last memory I could come up with was passing around a bottle of *sotol* with Enrique and his pals, listening to them tell stories and sing along with the radio. After that, nothing. That recollection was immediately followed by one of those moments of sheer panic, when the adrenaline shoots through you so fast that you feel dizzy and your arms go numb. My money.

I dug through the pile of clothes on the floor and checked the pockets of the pants I'd been wearing the night before. I was momentarily grateful to find my wallet and driver's license where they belonged. That is, until I discovered that all my cash was gone. All but about two hundred wrinkled pesos I kept tucked behind a flap in my billfold. Two hundred fucking pesos. That's like twenty bucks in real money.

My heart skipped a beat and my legs went weak. I sat down hard on the corner of the bed. I told myself to think, try to remember, but nothing would come. There wasn't a chance in hell that Enrique or his friends would have rolled me. Nor was there any possibility that I could have burned through my bankroll in one night at Bahia de los Mestengos; I'm not sure it's even possible to blow that kind of bread in this town.

I told myself to try to relax. I'd get dressed and go find Enrique, ask him what had happened. I even allowed myself to hope that Enrique might have taken custody of my money so I wouldn't lose it, as drunk as I had been. Yeah, that was good enough for the moment. I would hold onto that thought while I pulled myself together.

I drew back the curtain that separated the main room from the toilet, and ran some lukewarm water in the sink. It came out cloudy and brown like always, but eventually ran clear enough. While I waited, I examined the shiner that now decorated my left eye and the crusty scabs that had formed on my swollen knuckles. The only words my aching brain could put together were, What the fuck? I filled the basin and gingerly washed my face, dunked my head in deep and soaked my hair. The water felt cool as it ran down my back, and I soaped up a washcloth and gave myself a good scrubbing. I tossed on a clean pair of pants, a light cotton shirt, my sandals, and headed out into the daylight.

The sun pierced my eyes like hot needles the second I opened the door, and I had to duck back inside for the shades I'd forgotten. I pushed the wet hair off my forehead and gave it another go. Better. It was unusually quiet, only the bleating of goats and the rattle of wind in the dry palm fronds overhead.

I walked slowly through town, such as it was, and back toward the beach. Scrawny dogs chased scrawny chickens, and the dirty brown faces of half-naked children stared out at me from open doorways. I stopped off at the *panaderia*, bought a couple of rolls and ate them as I walked down past the pharmacy, past the laundry, past the tiny plaza where an old man sat in the shade strumming a cheap guitar.

The smell of the sea drifted on the wind that blew a dust devil up from the road, the only sign of traffic being the battered silver bus that idled out in front of the cinderblock shack that passed as a bus station. A cloud of blue smoke choked the air behind it, and I looked up the hill toward the old church. A couple of days from now, though, the plaza would be alive with little boys chasing each other, little girls dressed all in white, teenagers strutting and posing—a scene from a different time altogether.

The *pasteles* I had bought at the bakery had started to settle my stomach, and I allowed myself a small glimmer of optimism. I tossed the old guitar player a heavy silver coin I had received in change, turned down the small dirt track that led past the post office and off toward the beach.

Most of the food stalls were only beginning to show signs of life, so I wasn't all that surprised to find Luisa and Enrique's place uninhabited. They lived in an old trailer that was parked on the flats behind their open-air cantina, and I knocked gently on their door.

"Enrique!" I called. "Hey, Enrique, get up!"

I heard some rattling around from inside, stepped back and waited.

A few seconds later Enrique appeared wearing a tattered pair of striped boxer shorts and an undershirt. His sleep-heavy eyes were as red-rimmed as mine, but were, thankfully, otherwise unmarked. He rubbed the stubble of his beard as he blinked back the onslaught of daylight and stared at me.

"Sorry, man," I said. "But I need to know if you've got my money."

He yawned. "What money?"

I felt my stomach turn all over again. "The money I had on me last night. I thought you might have held onto it for me. I was pretty damned wasted."

"This is true," he smiled weakly. "What happened to your face? You ran into a wall, maybe?"

"I was hoping you could tell me."

"*No se*, my friend. You were fine when you left with your friends."

"What friends?"

"Your two *gringo* friends."

Fuck. A new surge of heat coursed through my veins. "You ever seen them around here before, Enrique?"

"No. Never. Tell you the truth, *amigo*, I do not much like the way they look."

"Yeah," I said. "Well, you're a good judge of character."

I needed to find those ganky cocksuckers, and now there was only one place I could start looking. I thanked Enrique and turned back the way I had just come, and went to find Ramon. He was the only one who might know who those shitheads were, or where they were staying.

"Thank you, Enrique," I said as I turned away. "I'm sorry to wake you."

"*No problema.* Just be careful. There are very many walls in Mestengos," he chuckled. "But they are more easy to avoid in the daytime."

Mesquite and bougainvillea grew thick beneath the palms on either side of the trail, and choked it down to a narrow path. My eyes were fixed on the outer edge of the bay as I approached the bend that opened onto the beach. I was lost in my fantasy of beating the shit out of the thieves who had ripped me off, so I didn't see the guy hiding there inside the heavy tangle of weeds. An arm shot out of the bushes and grabbed my elbow.

"You don't want to go down there," he whispered.

I looked hard into the shadow and saw it was the Aussie photographer who I'd seen around town from time to time, but whose name I could never remember. He was clearly distressed, his face pale with concern.

"What's going on?"

"*Federales,*" he said.

"How many?"

"Five or six, I think."

I could hear them in the distance then, but only barely. I caught a few words when the breeze blew just right. Raised voices, rapid fire.

"Were they carrying guns?" I whispered.

The photographer nodded.

"Shit," I said.

There was some more shouting, closer than before, then the sound of heavy boots coming in our direction. I shot a glance at the photographer and put a finger to my lips. He gave a quick nod and we both backed deeper into the thorny bushes, trying like hell to keep from making too much noise.

I knew what we were both thinking as we hid in there, a couple of long-haired *gringos*, waiting for the fucking Mexican law to press the barrels of those big, black automatic rifles into the back of our heads and frog-march us off to some jail nobody ever heard of, placing bets on how long two hippies could keep their asses pressed to the wall.

For a moment I flashed on making a run for it. In that moment, I felt a tiny pinch of nerves at the base of my skull, that place where my head balanced tentatively on my spine; the precognitive pressure of an eyeball behind a gunsight boring into the exact spot where the slug would take me, penetrate the skin, sever my spinal cord, and knock me into the dust. Bad idea.

I don't know how long we waited, but neither of us breathed until we heard the sound of those boots marching out to the main road and away toward the plaza. I crawled out first, my shirt completely soaked through with nervous perspiration, and gave the photographer a come-ahead. He took one quick look over his shoulder and we both moved fast for Ramon's.

RAMON WAS SETTING up his tables and chairs when we got to his place, wiping them down with a wet rag. He looked startled by our sudden appearance.

"What happened to you?" he asked.

"I thought you might be able to tell me."

"You are *locote* my friend," Ramon said. "The *Federales* were just here."

"I know," I said. "What did they want?"

"They were up and down *la playa*, talking to everybody." There was something in his voice that wasn't right.

The photographer was breathing hard and looked as though he might pass out. He folded himself into one of Ramon's chairs and put his head between his knees.

"What's going on, Ray?" I asked. Ramon was definitely off his game, and his nervousness was becoming contagious.

"You know the man we saw yesterday? The tree pilot?"

I thought back to the grizzled-looking dude with the thousand yard stare. "That was just a story those fuckheads made up, man," I said. "They were just putting you on."

Ramon's eyes cut from side to side, finally landed at me. "He is *muerto*, my friend. There was a struggle and then somebody shot his head."

I felt the photographer's eyes on my back, but didn't turn around. "Who the hell did it?"

"Nobody knows. Maybe it is about the drugs."

"That was a bullshit story, Ramon! Those guys were lying to you!" My pulse was pounding behind my bruised cheekbone, and it felt like everything went into slow motion. I tried to get my voice back under control. "What did you tell the *Federales*, Ramon?"

Ramon answered me with only a blank expression that didn't give me any comfort.

"What did you tell them, Ramon?" I asked again.

There was a long silence, then his eyes slid off my face.

I felt a hint of breeze against the cool wetness of my shirt, heard the small waves break against the beach of Bahia de los Mestengos as my head throbbed in time with my racing heart. I heard the frigate birds cry out over the bay, and I knew I didn't have much time. My shot at retrieving my stolen cash had just been blown away. All I could do now was to take my chances in the Bushmonster, make the run down to Eddie "El Brujo" Chacon's, and hope to God I had enough gas to get there.

# CHAPTER 30

"Motherfucker!"

"Try to calm down," Marco said.

Miguel Zamora had returned from El Salto in a particularly venomous mood, and was taking it out on the billiard balls that skittered violently across the table.

"That wrinkled old man made me look like a fool!" Miguel persisted.

"Here," Marco offered. "Have another line and let's try to think clearly."

"Calm down? Try to think clearly? This is your answer?" he said as he tipped his face to the mirror.

"We need to think clearly."

"Good. Yes. Let's think clearly." He wiped his nose on his shirt-sleeve, crossed to the bar at the corner of the billiard room and poured a generous ration of Scotch into each of two crystal tumblers. He handed one to Marco and helped himself to a deep swallow of his own.

"First," Marco began tentatively. He was anxious to get his brother to focus on more important matters than his perceived slight. "When did our Colombian friends tell you we should expect our visitor?"

"They were not specific. Only that he should arrive within a few days. Which means we will need to get our supply lines moving faster than I had originally planned."

"Is that wise? A sudden movement of cocaine that is supposed to be missing?"

"Only a small amount. We need the cash flow. La Plaza—the bastards—burned our marijuana, remember?"

"Still—"

"Still there are mouths to feed."

Marco could not argue that fact. "A small amount. We will try out the route Senor Limon and I determined. We will use the *pollos*."

"Fine."

"It is important that we maintain outward appearances."

"What is that supposed to mean?" His tone made it clear that he was becoming agitated again.

"You know what that means, Miguel," Marco said. "We need stability. Order."

"Fuck order."

"Miguel—"

"You were not there."

They were talking about El Brujo again.

SONNY LIMON watched El Brujo's car disappear down the long dirt road, turned and walked with exaggerated care toward the guards that stood at the entrance of Rancho Tronada.

"*Alto*," one of the guards ordered when Sonny approached the gate.

Sonny complied, stopped in his tracks and flashed a toothy grin.

"*Necesitamos para buscarle*," the guard told him.

Again, Sonny did as he was told, and waited for the pat-down.

"*Que es esto?*"

"Pills," Sonny said. "For sleeping. You probably haven't noticed, but it's been a little tense around here."

The guard turned to his counterpart, raised the bottle into the air and shook it so that it rattled like a maraca. They shouted back and forth for what seemed like several minutes, until Sonny lost interest in the process.

"Listen," he said in their language. "Take the fucking things, or give them back—I don't give a shit. Just let me pass so I can go to my room."

His lack of interest in the pills seemed to satisfy them. The guard handed them back.

Sonny returned the bottle to his pocket and proceeded through the gate. "You assholes could complicate a staring contest," he muttered to himself, this time in English.

He heard the unmistakable sounds of a heated discussion coming from the billiard room as he crossed the foyer into the main hacienda. He considered going directly to his room, but on second thought, decided it might be interesting to see what had sparked such a lively conversation between the brothers Zamora.

⚬══✦══⚬

SONNY STOOD OUTSIDE the billiard room and listened to Miguel and Marco's muffled voices through the unopened door. Ordinarily, he imagined, he would not have heard much of their conversation, but with their voices raised as they were he was able to catch almost everything.

"Senor Limon would not discuss our business with El Brujo," Marco argued. "Limon has as much at stake as we do."

"That's not what concerns me. And stop calling him 'El Brujo'!"

"That is what he is called."

"That is what he is called by superstitious fools."

Marco would not relent. "That is what many people believe. Some even believe he is *nagual*."

"Of course, my mistake," Miguel spat. "Eduardo Chacon is magical and can turn into an animal. He can prowl the night at will. How stupid of me. The man made me look like a fool!"

"He did no such thing."

"You were not there! He commandeered my houseguest right in front of my face."

"It was only lunch."

"It was not only lunch. It was disrespectful."

"And what should you have done instead? Shoot him in the middle of the *zocalo* on Market Day? The people would turn on you like dogs."

Miguel didn't answer.

"You have made your point, Miguel. We delivered Rolando's body to his family. And Susana has been returned home, as well. The town will be talking of nothing else but the importance of loyalty to 'El Rey.' Let their gossip do the rest."

This seemed to mollify Miguel, for he was silent for several seconds.

"You offered to compensate the girl and her family?" he asked finally.

"Of course. And also for Rolando's funeral. You will need to attend."

Miguel became quiet again. "I still do not like being treated like a woman."

"No one thinks you are a woman, Miguel."

The argument between the men seemed to have reached an end, so Sonny knocked on the door and entered without waiting for acknowledgment.

Miguel looked at Sonny as though he had dropped in from space. "You enjoyed your luncheon with Eduardo Chacon?"

"Who?"

"El Brujo," Miguel snapped. His tone was laced with sarcasm.

"It was fine," Sonny answered as he made his way to the bar.

"The old man asked about me, I suspect?"

"In fact, your name did not come up. He did inquire as to the Senora, though." Sonny couldn't resist the opportunity to prod Miguel's obviously prickly state of mind.

Sonny was rewarded handsomely. That bit of information seemed to make Miguel's face twitch as though he had cockroaches under his skin.

"And you said?"

"I said I hadn't seen the lady of the house since yesterday."

"Nosy old man."

Sonny decided to press the point. "He seemed rather fond of Senora Zamora. He mentioned that he had once been a friend of her father's. He asked that I pass along his good wishes to her."

Sonny watched Miguel's eyes ignite. To say that Miguel was skittish would be an understatement; he could see that this particular tantrum was about to escalate to epic proportions.

"Thank you for passing that along, Senor Limon." Miguel's lips split into a menacing smile. "I believe I will pass along his greetings to the Senora personally."

⊶⊷

SONNY HAD TO shut the door when the screaming began.

He was shooting billiards by himself, trying to block the sounds from his mind, when Marco reentered the room.

"You have to learn to take things easy, Senor Limon."

"Like you do?"

"*Si*. Like me."

"Go fuck yourself. You and your brother, too."

"Have a drink," he said as he stepped to the bar and refilled their glasses. "This is not an easy business. Things are complicated, and the natural order must be enforced."

"The natural order. Good one, Marco. And Yolanda? She enjoys being raped by her husband?"

"It is not rape when it is your wife."

"So she is free to leave anytime she wishes?"

Marco removed a pool cue from a rack affixed to the wall, turned slowly, and lined up a shot. "There are no guards on her door."

"That's not an answer."

Marco watched with satisfaction as he sank the nine ball in the side pocket. "A very fine shot, no?"

"What about the girl?"

"What girl?"

Sonny felt the pulse begin to pound in his temples. "The maid, goddamnit."

"You mean Susana."

"Yes. Susana."

"She has been returned to her home. She will be fine in a few days."

"I'm sure her family was appreciative."

"Money makes miracles, Senor Limon. You should know this as much as anyone."

"Again, fuck you."

Marco stood, restored the cue to its place in the rack and fixed Sonny with a glare. "You should remember who you are talking to. I am trying to be patient with you."

"Thanks." Sonny was unmoved. "You and your brother are exceptional hosts."

"This town belongs to El Rey Miguel. Everything and everybody in it. If it were not for him, there would be nothing."

"There's already nothing."

"You are wrong, Senor Limon. There is power. Without power, *then* there is nothing. Sometimes people need to be reminded of this. To maintain the balance."

"I've already told you, I'll help you move your shit. I've helped you move your *pollos*. The minute I get my money, I'm gone. You'll never see me again. But don't try to feed me that bullshit again. It's beneath even you."

"As I have already said," Marco smiled over the rim of his glass. "People do not always remember to be grateful. Reminders are sometimes necessary. Read your Stalin."

"Yeah, you guys are givers."

"I do not care for your sarcasm."

Sonny placed his glass on the bar with exaggerated care. "You had better remember who *you're* talking to, as well, Marco. What we have here is a standoff. That's the only 'balance' you need to concern yourself with. But you'd better keep a close eye on your brother, *amigo*, because it looks to me like that motherfucker is getting dangerously close to running off the rails."

# CHAPTER 31

The Club de Oficiales de la Ciudad de Mexico boasted one of the finest views in all of Mexico City.

Not only did it occupy the top three floors of the historic Edificio Real, but the roof garden as well. Its dining room and bar were widely rumored to be among the best in the entire Distrito Federal, though few would ever have the privilege of seeing them firsthand.

Its members were primarily high-ranking military officers, both active and retired, and membership was strictly regulated. Once a year, a list of names would be placed into nomination, the candidates interviewed rigorously, and finally voted upon by a special committee. One blackball, and membership was denied. No exceptions. To say that one was a member of the Club de Oficiales, was to say that one was both a man of means, and a man capable of great discretion.

It was for both of these reasons that General Diego Acosta—the man Miguel Zamora had privately dubbed 'The Pig'—had chosen the Club as the location for this unplanned meeting of La Plaza. Nothing spoken within these walls would ever leak to the world outside.

The General and Comandante Rivera of the Federal Police had seated themselves at a comfortable table at the far corner of the roof garden bar, well away from any of the other members. General Acosta had almost run out of polite inquiries after Rivera's wife and family, when the third in their group finally arrived. Late, as usual, the General noted, and made a show of examining his watch.

The Governor's First Assistant, Dario Cruz, made no attempt to apologize for his tardiness, much to the annoyance of the older men. He was well aware of the fact that they viewed him as something of a dandy, but it mattered little to Dario Cruz. His sexual predilections aside, he was equally aware that—for the moment at least—the

Governor's office held the most important key to the success of La Plaza. Which meant that, like it or not, Dario Cruz held the high hand, and he enjoyed wielding it.

"Good evening, Senor Cruz," the Comandante offered politely.

"Good evening, Comandante. General Acosta."

The words were barely out of his mouth when a waiter appeared beside their table. Like his comrades, Cruz ordered a twenty-one-year-old Scotch.

"You have been here before, Senor Cruz?" the General asked. "I have been a member since I was a Colonel, and never tire of this view."

Cruz ignored Acosta's implicit slight, and leaned back in his chair. "I am sorry we have to meet at such a late hour, but I thought it best that we waste no time in discussing our present circumstances."

Neither General Acosta or the Comandante liked the sound of those words. "Go on," Comandante Rivera said.

"I have received word from my sources that there is growing unrest in El Salto."

"What kind of unrest?"

Cruz was about to respond, but was interrupted by the waiter returning with his drink. "First," he said once the waiter was out of earshot, "it has been confirmed that Miguel Zamora did, in fact, make contact with the Colombians."

"That is what we asked him to do."

"That much is true. However, it seems that the Colombians are unhappy and are sending an emissary to meet with him within the next few days."

"When exactly?" the General asked.

"We don't know yet." Cruz savored the bouquet of his fine whiskey before he continued. "But that is not the real problem."

The General was growing impatient with the preening *maricon*. First, he calls for an emergency meeting of La Plaza, then he dallies here sipping my Scotch and doling out information like bread crusts to ducks.

"The real problem is that it seems Miguel Zamora is losing control. In the past two days alone, he apparently—and I say 'apparently' because they still fear him enough in El Salto not to bear witness directly—murdered a long-time member of his household staff by drowning him in the swimming pool. That same day, he turned a young maid over to his *pistoleros* to be repeatedly abused. The girl survived, though I don't know how."

The General and the Comandante traded looks of disgust.

"There was some reason for all of this?" Rivera asked.

"It appears that Miguel Zamora is coming increasingly under the influence of cocaine, and growing quite paranoid as a result." Dario Cruz gave the men a minute to digest this before he went on. "Ordinarily, these things would only trouble me slightly. After all, the way a *padron* runs his operation is his own business. If he feels the need to make an example of certain people around him, then there must be a good reason. Unfortunately for us, his timing is extremely poor, and his recklessness could jeopardize the Colombian relationship."

There was silence around the table as the men of La Plaza contemplated the lights of the city that spread out beneath them. After what seemed like several minutes, it was the General who spoke first.

"It is unacceptable to lose the Colombians after we have come so far," he said.

"Agreed," Comandante Rivera added. "But equally unfortunate to lose the diamonds. Such a clever operation."

Cruz looked from man to man, and leaned in close. "It is conceivable that the money laundering aspect—the diamonds, that is—would not need to be put at risk, that the current system could remain intact."

The General studied Dario's face. *What is he not telling us? There always seems to be something held back.* The General would speak to the Governor himself at the first opportunity about that. There had to be trust within La Plaza. In the meantime, though, it seemed best to take Cruz at his word.

"This is a large step we are considering," General Acosta said quietly. "One that could potentially—in the worst case—cast light on La Plaza. Something none of us would relish, I'm sure." He turned his eyes on the Governor's man. "I suggest that you meet with Zamora in person, Senor Cruz, and look into his eyes, before we make our decision. We cannot afford to be mistaken."

Comandante Rivera nodded his assent.

"I am in complete agreement," Dario Cruz smiled and quaffed the last bit of whiskey from his glass. "I will make arrangements first thing tomorrow."

"Kindly keep us informed."

"As always."

# CHAPTER 32

The night came down like a hammer, more collision than transition from gray twilight to full dark.

I had spent my last hundred pesos at a Pemex station somewhere south of San Ignacio, and been praying ever since that I had enough fuel to get to my trailer at Eddie's place. I don't think I took my eyes off the rearview for more than five seconds at a time for the first three hours after leaving Bahia de los Mestengos, which was about how long it took my heart to stop pounding against my tonsils.

I looked at my watch and was surprised to see that it was a little after ten o'clock. I would have guessed it was much later, burned out as I was by the constant electrical charge that had been arcing between the twin poles of my psyche: debilitating anxiety and unmitigated rage.

I started to feel a little better when, about fifteen minutes later, I passed through the town of El Salto and knew I was getting close, though my fuel gauge was nearing the flat-line. My headlights slashed the darkness of the narrow street and cast long shadows against the low buildings of concrete block and cracked plaster. Weathered rebar and TV antennae poked through flat rooflines, clawed the air like fingers, like bent and rusted slashes against a moonless blanket of sky.

I reached the crossroads a short time later, the one marked with the shot-up Ford Bronco. I made a right turn onto the *caliche* road and pushed my way through the last few miles of a long, long drive.

⊙━✦━⊙

I SAT OUTDOORS on my ratty lawn chair beneath a sky lit only by pinpoint stars and the blue-white wash of the Milky Way, and twisted up a bone from the little bag of shake I keep inside my trailer. I was too exhausted to sleep, so I just sat there in the desert night, listening to the bay of a distant pack of dogs.

It seemed like a lifetime ago, Humboldt. A week ago, my biggest problem was making sure the rip-off artists didn't put too big a dent in my crop before the Halloween harvest. Now it was gone. All of it. Junior Stavro and his girlfriend murdered by South American gangsters; Colt Freeland on the run to God-knows-where; that useless douche bag Rick Montrose either ripping me off or selling me out; and it was anybody's guess what my "friend" Ramon had told the *Federales*. Jesus. None of this had to go down this way. But I was coming to believe that human beings are, at their core, little more than frightened, greedy, evil bastards who will gladly turn any kind of paradise into a shithole if it serves their self-interest.

I torched the J, closed my eyes and took a long, deep drag.

I exhaled slowly into the warm breeze.

When I opened my eyes again, Eddie Chacon was standing in front of me, wreathed in a cloud of silver smoke.

"Shit, Eddie!"

"I heard your truck."

"You scared the crap out of me," I said and offered him a hit of the doob.

"You always say that," he said.

I reached into the space between us and offered it to him again.

"No," he said and waved away my invitation. "But, thank you."

"Excuse me? Did I hear you correctly?" I kidded.

He seemed distracted, and did not reply.

"And I always say that because you always seem to sneak up and scare the shit out of me," I told him.

"You are not a difficult man to sneak up on when you are smoking," he smiled. "It is good to see you, my friend, but this may not be a good time to be here."

I could barely see his face in the dim light that escaped from the interior of my Airstream, but it was enough that I could tell he was in an unusually serious frame of mind.

"What's going on, Eddie?"

"I am not completely certain, but there is something in the air. Something bad."

"No shit," I agreed, and helped myself to another toke. "That's why I'm here, man."

He looked newly concerned.

"I had a little trouble of my own," I added. "I had to split from Humboldt. Maybe for good."

"I am sorry to hear that. Tell me what happened."

So I gave him the CliffsNotes version. Told him how I had heard the news on the car radio my second day on the road. That the black choppers the Feds had flown into the Humboldt forest had captured twenty tons—repeat, *tons*—of weed the first day alone. But not without a fight. It seems that they also encountered all kinds of very serious defenses: anti-personnel mines, trip wires, grenades, and a bunch of other nasty shit that had killed two DEA officers. The Colombians had fought back and turned a simple dope raid into a day-long firefight, and as far as I was concerned, turned that peaceful little corner of California into a fuckapalooza that would make it unwise for any of us to go back there for years to come. Something else niggled in my brain that told me that Rick Montrose had supplied them with a little intel, too. There were miles and miles of fields hidden inside those redwoods, and inasmuch as I had stopped believing in coincidence, the whole situation had a funny odor to it. Colt and I hadn't bugged-out a moment too soon.

"So you were left with nothing," Eddie said, when I had finished.

"Pretty much."

"What of your man, Montrose?"

"I'm guessing he's dodging dicks in state prison right about now."

"And you came directly here? To this place?"

"No," I said. I took another hit, and stared out into the darkness. "I stopped off in Bahia de los Mestengos. I stay there sometimes."

"And?"

"There was a little trouble with the *Federales*. A *gringo* was murdered, and I think somebody pointed at me."

"This was someone you knew? This man who was murdered?"

I shook my head. "Never seen him before in my life."

"And you did not kill him?"

"I'm not a killer, Eddie."

He looked into my face, studying me as though for the first time. "That is not entirely true. A man does not live without having the map of his life written somewhere on his face."

"I was a soldier. That's all."

"As was I." Eddie shook his head and sighed deeply. "I apologize."

He turned his back to me and contemplated the night, as I had done a few moments before.

"How many people know about this?" he asked, sweeping his arm in the general direction of my trailer.

"Nobody," I said. "Just you and Colt."

He was silent as he processed all I had told him, and took several steps into the shadows. "I think you had better stay with me."

"What?" I said dumbly. I pinched the cherry end of my joint and snuffed it. When I was certain it was cold, I pocketed the roach.

"Come," he said. "Now."

<hr/>

IN THE EARLY days of our relationship, Eddie and I had conducted our business at his home. It had been a long time since I had last been inside it.

It was a large, simple, single story ranch-style place with white plaster walls and a red tile roof. The landscape consisted of native cacti and aloe, *sacahuista* and monkey flower. Vines of pink bougainvillea crawled freely along the exterior walls, amid clusters of palms that had been planted in urns of hand-hewn stone.

He guided me inside, through a pair of heavy doors and into a low-ceilinged foyer. "My room is there, at the end of the hall," he pointed. "You may take any of the others."

"Eddie—"

"Wash up, if you like," he interrupted. "I will pour us a drink and meet you in the sitting room when you are ready."

I took a room near the kitchen, tossed my ditty-bag on the floor beside the bed and did as he suggested. It had been a while since I had experienced the simple pleasure of cool, clean running water on my face.

When I came back, Eddie was seated in one of the two well-worn leather chairs beside an unlit fireplace that graced the far wall of the sitting room that adjoined the kitchen. A bottle of tequila and two glasses sat on an end table beside him. My stomach lurched slightly at the sight of the bottle, but I took my place in the empty seat and joined him. His face was void of expression and his eyes looked as tired as mine. I had never seen him in such a state, and I found myself at a loss for words and feeling vaguely guilty for having brought my problems into his life. Without a word, he poured two fingers of gold agave into the glasses and handed one to me.

"*Salud*," he said, and lifted his glass in my direction.

I did the same.

"I am sorry, Don Eduardo," I said. "I didn't mean to—"

"Please," he said. "Life is complicated, but friends are friends."

I didn't know what to say.

We drank without words until we had emptied our glasses. He refilled them both and looked as though he was about to say something, when the sound of a ringing telephone came from somewhere at the other end of the house. He lifted his glass and took a sip as he rose from his chair, then walked slowly in the direction of the phone.

A large picture window faced out toward the entrance of the house, and I stared into the stillness of the late hour. I heard Eddie's voice, muffled though it was through the thick adobe walls, speaking in rapid-fire Spanish. He seemed to listen far more than he spoke, and returned to the sitting room within minutes. His face betrayed no emotion, but I knew he was troubled by the way he folded himself into his chair. More troubled, even, than before.

"Don Eduardo, if—"

"I have always enjoyed your company," he said as he emerged from the depth of his thoughts. "Please do not start calling me that."

"Okay, Eddie."

He smiled then, and met my eye. "Better," he said, and lifted his glass again. "You are familiar with Miguel Zamora?"

I was unprepared for the change of subject, but my old friend was clearly operating in a world of his own. I rolled with it. "'El Rey' Miguel."

Eddie chuffed. "'El Rey' indeed."

I waited him out.

"Miguel Zamora was not always the way he is now," he said. "He was once very promising. A very bright and handsome young man. Educated and charming."

I nodded.

"He has fallen under the spell of the *yeyo* and things have begun to lose their balance. This is a dangerous time for you to be here."

"You already told me that. I want to help you, Eddie."

He seemed to look right through me as he considered what I said. "Trouble is likely to come sooner rather than later. This is not trouble you want to be a part of, I assure you."

"Eddie, I'm here. I have nowhere else to go. You've always been a friend to me, and I have no problem doing what needs to be done."

He held his glass to the light and examined the contents like a wine connoisseur, rotating it slowly as he studied the amber candescence.

"You fought in Vietnam," he said.

"A lot of people fought in Vietnam. It's nothing I tend to brag about."

"But you know what it is to fight."

"I did two tours. You put your boots on the ground, you do your shit, and come back home. That's it. That's all I know."

"Then you know all you need to know for this fight."

"The phone call just now," I asked. "It was a warning? A threat?"

"I did not need a phone call to warn me of anything."

I watched him as he smiled sadly, placed his tequila on the table and studied the tile floor between his feet.

"When the finger points to the moon," he told me. "The idiot sees only the finger."

PART SIX:

# A Good Day in Hell

# CHAPTER 33

We were up the next morning before the sun. Eddie had made coffee and laid out an assortment of *polvoron, molletes* and *galleta de canela* that looked fresh from the bakery. While I could see that he still carried a burden, his mood had improved decidedly with a decent night's sleep, as had my own.

"You've got enough here for an army," I said as I drank my black coffee.

He looked at me from beneath a heavy brow. "Let us hope not."

I took my coffee and some pastries to the sitting room, and made myself comfortable in the chair I had occupied the night before. Through the picture window, I watched the first pink brushstrokes of the sunrise as I ate, watched them intensify from fine traces of saffron and hyacinth to great washes of sulphur and scarlet across the sky. I recalled the old sailor's adage about red skies at morning. Without thinking, I touched the shirt pocket where I kept the small carved rabbit Colt had given me for luck.

I stood and returned to the kitchen where Eddie was standing at the sink, watching the sunrise just as I had been.

"When you are finished, we should get started," Eddie said without turning around.

"Let's rock," I said, taking a last gulp of coffee and placing my empty plate on the counter.

He led me down the corridor, past a small alcove packed tight with radio gear and a small desk, past his bedroom to the end of the hall where it dead-ended at a doorway at the back of the house. It was a room I never had a reason to see, let alone enter, before. Eddie withdrew a ring of keys from his pocket and worked the first of a pair of dead-bolt locks.

My expression betrayed me when he pushed the door open and snapped on the overhead light.

"Holy shit," I said.

He laughed.

There was enough crap in that room to arm a small militia. There had to be a dozen .30-caliber M1 rifles lined up neatly along one wall. Beside them lay a crate of M16 automatics, several metal boxes loaded with Claymore mines, spools of heavy wire, and a mounted pegboard that displayed an assortment of handguns ranging from Smith & Wesson .45s to small caliber revolvers.

"You want to tell me what we're getting into?"

"I wish I could."

"El Rey Miguel?"

"Maybe," Eddie shrugged. "Or it could be the Colombians. Or the Federal Police. Perhaps even the Army. On the other hand, it could be no one."

"I don't get it," I said.

"There aren't too many victims in this life, but there are many volunteers." Eddie clapped me on the shoulder. "I made a promise to myself a long time ago that I would never volunteer for victimhood."

I tossed my head toward the far corner of the room. "What's in the safe?" It was a big fucker, too.

"Not now," he said firmly. "First things first. It is getting light outside."

<hr/>

BY MIDDAY WE had strung a perimeter with Claymores, and booby-trapped the living shit out of my trailer.

I placed the charges while Eddie unspooled the det-wire. It had been sometime since I had worked with anti-personnel mines, but I remembered well how unsafe the electrical firing devices could be. Premature detonation could ruin your whole day, so I was careful to connect both firing wires to one terminal on the trigger until the time came to actually set them off. I didn't like the idea of setting the things in Uncontrolled Mode, nor did I completely trust their stability—not knowing how long they had been in storage—so I rigged them all for Command Detonation. Which meant we could trigger each weapon individually, by hand, when we needed to. It also meant we had to string the wire all the way back to the house.

Claymores are nasty little bastards that fire steel balls of shrapnel across a sixty-degree arc and a distance of a hundred meters. One man sets the device into the ground while the other attaches the wire. We decided to run them in a daisy chain, which made it long, tedious work, but we labored together seamlessly, laying down a pattern of interlocking fields of fire that would take out anything that came inside our defenses.

Eduardo Chacon proved to be quite nimble for a man of his age.

"You're pretty good at this," I said. "Speaking for myself, it's been awhile, you know?"

"I was not always an old man."

"I have never thought of you as an old man, Eddie."

"I am happy to hear you say that," he said, and became serious again. "Age is not magic, you know. Wisdom does not come with the passage of time alone. Any fool can get old. I know many people who lived into their very late years and gained no wisdom at all. It is very regrettable."

"I understand."

"I hope you do. Because most people grow old inside their skin, but gain nothing here," he said, touching a calloused finger to his chest, then to his temple. "Or here. Just because a person has a head of silver hair is no reason to impart respect to him. You understand this, too?"

I told him I did.

"There are few second chances in this life, my friend. Do not fail to take the ones that belong to you."

"I didn't survive two tours in 'Nam to have my nuts blown off for a few kilos of somebody else's blow."

WE WERE SEATED across from one another at a rough wooden table on Eddie's back patio, field stripping and lubricating the weapons we had selected for ourselves from Eddie's arsenal. I was taking particular care with a beauty of a Colt 1911 .45 pistol that was just like the one I had carried as a sidearm back in Indian Country, and it felt more comfortable in my hand than I would have liked to admit.

Eddie was lost in himself again, concentrating on running a cleaning brush through the barrel of a matte black Beretta.

"Nine mil?" I asked, making small talk. "Isn't that a little light?"

"It is chambered for forty caliber shells," he said without looking up from his work.

"Cool," I said. "Hey, Eddie?"

This time he met my eyes.

"I couldn't help but notice that the Claymores we set had South African markings."

"Yes?"

"Look, it's none of my business, but, how in the hell did you end up with a roomful of African armament?"

"I told you already. I have not always been an old man."

"You know, with respect, that's not much of an answer."

He gently placed the Beretta on the table and eyed me with a look of minor irritation.

"You've got to tell me *something*, man," I said. "I mean, look what we're doing here."

"I once fought in the Congo. I fought beside Irish mercenaries during the revolution there."

"Mercenaries?" I must have looked incredulous.

"I have surprised you."

"A little."

"The Simbas had risen against the Congolese government. They captured the capital and set up a rebel government. They executed thousands of their own countrymen. It was very bad."

"Irish mercenaries?"

"The Congolese government army was very weak and disorganized. They paid mercenaries from all over the world. I was younger. My father was dead. I had no family and the money was good."

"Why have you never told me about this?"

"Why would I?"

"Because we're friends. We talk."

"I do not believe in revisiting memories too often. They fade away the more they are repeated. The best ones, I try not to revisit at all. I may need them one day."

"Okay," I said, and decided to press in a different direction. "So, what's in the safe?"

Eddie smiled at my persistence and resumed his work on the Beretta again.

# CHAPTER 34

Eddie was standing in the kitchen with a knife in his hand.

I watched with interest as he painstakingly chopped a sprig of green onion. He had already sliced a pair of limes, diced a number of yellow and orange peppers, and was preparing to marinate and braise a fine-looking cut of beef.

"No need to get too fancy," I told him. "It's only the two of us."

"Life is too short to eat ugly food."

He used the dull side of his blade to scrape the diced vegetables into a bowl, then turned to place the utensils in the sink. When he looked out the window, his face went blank.

"Are you expecting anyone?" he asked.

"I wasn't expecting *me* to be here."

"Then we may have trouble."

I had laid the Claymore triggers out in an orderly row behind the rail at the front of Eddie's house, one for each concentric arc we had placed earlier that morning. I tucked the .45 into the back of my jeans, picked up an M16 I had selected from Eddie's playroom, and left the house to get ready to set off the explosives, if it came to that.

As I passed through the doorway, I saw what had inspired Eddie's concern. A car was moving at a high rate of speed down the road from Miguel's Rancho Tronada and onto the long, narrow drive that led to Eddie's house. It was kicking up a trail of brown dust, and marking its passage more efficiently than if it had been flying a big red flag. If the driver was trying to be stealthy, he was doing a shitty job of it.

"Civilian vehicle," Eddie said as he came up behind me. He had a pair of hunting binoculars pressed to his eyes.

"How many passengers?"

"Difficult to tell. Too much glare on the windshield."

I flipped the selector switch on the M16 to auto, which would allow for three-round bursts of fire. I brought the rifle to my shoulder and sighted on the driver's side windshield. "You recognize the car?"

"No."

"Fuck."

I waited.

"You're going to have to make the call, here, Eddie. It's about a hundred and seventy-five yards to our first line of mines."

Eddie didn't respond.

"A hundred and fifty yards."

"I cannot see," he said, frustrated.

"A hundred and twenty."

"Stop that!"

"Make the call, Eddie."

"It is a civilian vehicle."

"You already said that. What's it going to be, man?"

"A few more seconds . . ."

"Time's up," I said. I two-tapped the trigger and sprayed a pair of bursts across the road just in front of the moving car. It braked abruptly, fishtailing the rear end and slowing significantly, but didn't stop. "Still coming," I said, giving voice to the obvious.

Eddie remained mute.

I sighted down the barrel again and stitched another burst across the grill of the car. I knew the muzzle velocity of the weapon was unlikely to penetrate the engine block and harm the occupants, but it definitely had enough balls to destroy the radiator or electrical system. It was the most conservative play, under the circumstances, and I'd still get a shot at taking out the driver and any passengers when they climbed out, if that became necessary.

Eddie's face was still pressed to his field glasses. "The driver's door is coming open," he narrated, which, of course, I could see for myself.

I watched a slim *gringo* unfold slowly from the car and raise his hands to the air. He was trying to shout something from across the distance, but I couldn't make it out.

Eddie lowered the binoculars and emitted a deep breath that he must have been holding inside as this whole scene had evolved. "I know this man."

"Who is it?"

"An American, like you," he answered, and stepped through the kitchen door and out to the patio beside me. "Put down the gun."

I levered the M16 into safe mode and propped it against the railing, but I still had the .45 tucked into the back of my jeans. My heart had already settled back into its normal rhythm, and I stretched myself out of the crouch I had been in and stood beside Eddie. We watched together as the driver stepped tentatively toward the house, his hands still raised to shoulder level. I could hear his voice more clearly now.

"Don Eduardo!" he called. "It's me. Sonny Limon!"

Eddie and I marched from the patio and approached the man until all three of us came to a halt about twenty yards apart. This Limon cat looked pretty shook.

"Senor Limon," Eddie said. "You may put your hands down."

He lowered his hands as though he had forgotten how they had gotten there, then he looked at me. "You killed the car."

"Came *that* close to killing you, dude," I told him. "Not real cool tearing into Eddie's ranch like a bat out of hell unannounced."

Limon eyed me for a couple of wordless seconds and turned his attention to Eddie. Those two seconds were all I needed to make the guy. I mean, I know cops, and I'm thinking that if this cat isn't a cop, then I'm Rod Stewart, right? While he didn't have the uptight, squinty demeanor of a Fed, I was sure I caught a distinct whiff of bacon coming off the guy. The next thing I'm doing is wondering whether Eddie is also aware that Limon is heat. I was about to say something, but Limon beat me to it.

"Don Eduardo, Yolanda Zamora is in the car. She needs help."

If Eddie was surprised, he didn't show it.

"She is injured?"

Limon nodded. "She's been beaten pretty bad."

"Let's get her inside," Eddie said.

I walked with the cop to the passenger side of the steaming, dying automobile, and helped him extract the woman and carry her into the house.

∘═╾═∘

I DIDN'T HAVE to be told that the woman lying on Eddie's sofa was the wife of 'El Rey' Miguel Zamora, but I didn't have to like it either.

In all my visits to this part of Mexico, I had made it a point to keep my distance from anything having to do with cocaine, El Rey Miguel, Rancho Tronada, or anything else that orbited too close to Zamora's world. Whether it had been purely my imagination or not, I had always felt that my affiliation with Eddie Chacon somehow insulated me from whatever else went on down here, a little bubble of El Brujo's protection. I minded my own business, bought or sold a little smoke—depending on the season—and did my best to stay the hell out of matters that didn't concern me.

The present situation, however, had b-a-d written all over it.

I was trying to figure out how an American cop had come into possession of the *padron's* woman in the first place, let alone how he spirited her away from Miguel's hacienda and dropped her into the lap of Don Eduardo Chacon. Oh yeah, and equally importantly, *why?*

"Tell me everything," Eddie said.

The cop named Limon eyeballed me again before he answered Eddie. "Who is this guy?"

"This man is a friend of mine," Eddie answered.

"I'm not real comfortable with this."

"This man is a friend of mine," he repeated in a tone that invited no discussion. "He is now a friend of yours."

"I have enough friends," Limon told him.

"It is my strong feeling that you will need one more."

Limon considered Eduardo's words, and I saw acquiescence creep into his expression. "I've spent the past few days at Rancho Tronada."

"Yes," Eddie said. "I remember."

– 262 –

"I told you that things have become increasingly . . ." he sized me up again as he selected his next words, ". . . unpredictable."

"I understand."

Limon gestured toward the unconscious form of the woman we had placed on the couch. Her face had been badly beaten, her nose and lips crusted with dried blood. Her breathing was shallow and ragged, and it was as likely as not that she had suffered some fractures to her ribs. "She's been a prisoner in her own home, and has been repeatedly abused at the hands of her husband. You said you once knew her father."

Eddie looked at Yolanda and something went out of his expression. "Miguel did this to her?"

"And worse. I think this kind of shit's been going on for a while."

I remained silent, piecing together the story that was apparently familiar to both Eddie and Limon. Despite the severity of her injuries, it was clear that Yolanda was both a woman of substance and elegance. I had seen my share of beautiful, rainy-eyed women, but this one would probably take the prize. It was equally clear that both of these men cared for her implicitly since they had just taken on enormous personal risk.

"How did you get her out?" Eddie asked.

"I went into town this morning with Miguel and one of his men. I had a phone call to make. When I was finished, Miguel stayed behind in El Salto, and sent me back to the ranch with his driver."

"Go on."

"I was in the kitchen getting something to eat when she finally came out of her room. It was the first time she had been out in days. I hadn't seen her myself since I've been at the ranch, but could hear the nightly violence being done to her. Nobody should have to deal with that."

"Again, how did you get her out?"

For a moment, Limon appeared unsure of himself and cast a glance out the window. Shadows were beginning to deepen inside the folds of the distant mountains with the arrival of afternoon. "I used the Valium you gave me, Don Eduardo. I ground several of the pills and slipped them into a drink she had asked me to make for her."

"And she passed out."

"Yes," Limon said. He was looking at Eddie again. "When she lost consciousness, I loaded her into the car they keep for the kitchen staff to use for shopping trips. I put her in the passenger seat and drove to the front gates. At first, the guards would not let me pass. But I told them that the Senora was extremely ill and needed immediate medical help."

"I am surprised they let you go."

"I can understand your skepticism."

"I merely said I was surprised," Eddie told him. "Please continue."

"The guards weren't going to let us go, but I asked them whether they would prefer to explain to Miguel that I had taken her to the doctor—and let me accept the penalty—or that they had allowed her to die because they failed to exercise good judgment. She is, after all, the wife of El Rey Miguel."

"So they relented."

"And I brought her here."

"His brother Marco? Does he know the Senora is gone?"

"I'm sure he does by now."

"They will be in a panic," Eddie said. "That will not be good."

"All due respect," I said, breaking my silence. "But we should probably do something for the lady. She needs to get that crap out of her system before she goes into respiratory arrest."

I had been around more than my share of overdoses of one kind or another. For this kind, the best thing to do was to empty her stomach the best we could, and flush her with fluids. She needed to regain her faculties if she stood any chance of assisting in her own escape.

"Do you know what needs to be done?" Eddie asked me.

"Pretty much," I said. "There're a couple of things that might make it easier, though. Mind if I take a look in your medicine chest?" I was hoping to find some activated charcoal and something I could use to pump her stomach. If not, we were going to have to deal with it the hard way.

"I will show you where it is," he said. "Take care with her."

NIGHT HAD FALLEN in full by the time we had finished pumping Yolanda's stomach, purging the drugs from her system, and hiding the car I had killed.

Yolanda was back on her feet, albeit gingerly, and more than a little groggy. Eddie prepared a fine traditional meal of chile verde, refried beans and fresh corn tortillas, which left us all satiated and quiet. We kept Yolanda awake for as long as possible, practically force-feeding her cool water and fruit juice, which seemed to help bring her back to life, though it was painful for her to move too much and she didn't have much desire for conversation, no matter how banal. The threat of impending violence was a nearly palpable thing, and there was no sense in pretending it wasn't there.

Eddie and Limon finally tucked Yolanda into a comfortable bed near the back of the house, between the room occupied by Eddie and the one he had given over for Limon's use. When they returned to the living room, where I sat nursing a beer I had taken from Eddie's refrigerator, Limon's expression was one of sheer exhaustion. I briefly considered making inquiries as to the reasons for his presence in Mexico, more particularly at the ranch belonging to Miguel Zamora, but common sense won out. I saw no advantage in sharing personal information with a man I was certain was an American cop, and an apparently dirty one at that. I had set aside the notion that the man was the spearhead of a full-scale sting, if only for the fact that he was not only well outside of his jurisdiction, but seemed to have somehow earned some modicum of Eddie's trust, a commodity one did not easily come by. Which left Dirty Cop as the only logical explanation for his presence.

I finally got a couple of minutes alone with Eddie when Limon went to his bathroom to wash up.

"How well do you know this guy?" I asked.

"I met him only recently, but I believe he is a man of character."

"He's a cop."

"How can you know such a thing?"

"It's a gift, Eddie. I can smell them."

Something flashed inside his eyes. "He has shown himself to be a man of courage, wouldn't you agree?"

"What, by kidnapping the *padron's* wife?"

"By *protecting* the *padron's* wife. From the *padron* himself."

"Which puts the woman in a very dangerous position."

"Perhaps." He took a deep breath and gathered himself. "Miguel Zamora once punished two men that he believed to be his enemies. He buried them up to their necks in the open desert not far from Rancho Tronada. In the night, you could hear the sound of predatory animals having their way with the exposed faces of those men."

"Christ."

"But *that* man," Eddie said, waving a hand toward the back of his house, "has acted upon his conscience. There are times when sides must be chosen."

Our conversation was cut short by the sound of Limon's approaching footsteps. Though he had to have sensed that Eddie and I had been talking about him, I had to give him credit for keeping it to himself.

Eddie removed three fresh beers from the refrigerator, and we followed him out the door. The three of us took seats outside under the stars, at the table that only a few hours earlier had been strewn with the working elements of a half-dozen handguns and automatic weapons. It still smelled of gun oil and spent rounds, but no one mentioned it. Nor did we discuss the likely fallout from Limon's kidnapping of Miguel Zamora's wife, and the repercussions that were sure to follow.

⚓

AS TIRED AS I had been, I woke early the next morning, unable to shut down my mind. I had tried to roll over and go back to sleep, but the thoughts kept coming like I had three TVs in my head, each broadcasting a different channel. It was still dark, without even the first faint traces of false dawn, and I was certain I was the only one awake. So I decided—screw it—to get up, and padded barefooted to the kitchen to brew some coffee.

I had taken only a few steps down the hallway when I heard a strange noise coming from the rear of the house. I hesitated,

– 266 –

unconsciously holding my breath as I listened. I stepped lightly as I followed the sound down the hall in the opposite direction from the kitchen, back toward the room where Eddie slept. I stopped in the deep shadow and listened again. It sounded like radio static, and the murmur of voices, though I couldn't make out the words. I took another few steps until I saw the faint glow of radio dials lighting the contours of Eddie's face. He was hunched over his desk, deep in concentration, and hadn't heard my approach. I was about to whisper something so as not to startle him, when I saw him key the microphone he held in his hand and speak into it.

"Brujo to Tronada," he said softly, then repeated the words twice more.

A muffled voice came back a moment later, and I had to listen carefully to catch the message. "Tronada back."

"Tronada, this is Brujo. Who is speaking, please?"

"This is Marco. Go ahead, Brujo."

"Marco, listen carefully. I have something you want. Something very important to Miguel. Do you understand?"

Whether it was my own fatigue, the early hour, or the outright shock at the betrayal that arced and snapped through the synapses of my brain, I don't know. But my reaction was visceral, and I couldn't hold my tongue. Eddie's head whipped in my direction at the sound of my voice, his eyes thrown wide when he saw me there.

"Jesus Christ, Eddie," I said. "What in the hell have you just done?"

# CHAPTER 35

The expression of shock at having been discovered melted quickly from Eddie's face.

"You are up early," he said. "Good."

"Eddie . . . Jesus," I said. The tape in my head was stuck on a continuous loop of *what the fuck?*

"You should make us some coffee," he replied.

"Who was that on the radio? What have you done?"

His expression was peaceful, solemn. "As I told you last night, sooner or later one must choose sides."

"And whose side are you on, Eddie?"

"Does it matter?"

My pulse was pounding and I felt like I had lighter fluid in my veins. "Of course it fucking matters."

"Good. That is what I thought you would say." He pushed back his desk chair and straightened himself. "Now, please go and make some coffee. I will wake the others. We do not have much time."

YOLANDA ZAMORA was clearly still in pain from her injuries, but the aftereffects of her encounter with Valium were mercifully minimal. Apparently, we had been successful at flushing her system, and Sonny Limon hadn't inadvertently OD'd her. Regardless, I had to admire the woman's grit. Most people I know would have emerged from the situation of the night before with an attitude of both fear and humiliation. This woman, however, comported herself with dignity, strength and obvious affection for Eduardo Chacon. Something in that indefinable relationship gave me hope that my friend had not, in fact, betrayed her.

Eddie had provided her with some clean clothes from his own closet, so she entered the kitchen wearing a pair of men's trousers belted tight at the waist to keep them in place, and a loose-fitting cotton shirt.

I admired the woman even more when I considered the horror show she'd been through with El Rey Miguel, and hoped like hell I wasn't selling my soul by casting my lot with Eddie and a dirty cop. I had no idea what was happening, and my mind was in tatters. I would have truly enjoyed toking a fattie right about then, but my better angels were in charge. I'm plenty smart most of the time, but I have to admit that I've come up short from time to time where common sense was required. Still, I wasn't about to let other people pay the price for my own choices. God only knew what was coming next.

⚬━━◆━━⚬

"WHAT ARE YOU doing?" Eddie asked me.

"Getting the det cords on the triggers squared away."

"I do not want you to detonate the Claymores unless it is absolutely necessary. It is important that I speak with Miguel."

"It wouldn't take much backup for him to outgun us here, Eddie."

"I believe that is unlikely. This is the sort of matter that El Rey Miguel would prefer to deal with more privately."

"And if you're wrong?"

"I am not wrong," he said. "Even a man as impetuous as Miguel Zamora will behave predictably more often than not. He stands to lose a great deal of face with his organization if he does not retrieve his wife quickly and quietly. What he needs most at this moment is to regain control."

"So you're just going to give her back." I was having a difficult time keeping the disgust from my voice.

"There is more at stake here than the well-being of Yolanda Zamora." I watched Eddie's eyes scan the empty arroyo and the first gray whisper of approaching dawn. "I need to speak with Miguel,

and I need to do so on my terms, on my—how do you say it?—
'turf.' Yolanda's arrival yesterday evening has just made that possible."

"You knew this was going to happen?" I was incredulous.

"I knew it would be something." Eddie waved my suggestion
away. "I told you as much yesterday. You act on the opportunities
you are given."

"How much time do we have?"

"Not long, I think." Eddie studied the sky again. "Shortly after
sunrise, I would guess. It would be to Miguel's disadvantage to arrive
here in the dark."

"What now?"

"You arm yourself, and see to it that Senor Limon is armed as
well," he said simply. "Then we wait."

◦━━◆━━◦

AS EDDIE HAD predicted, two pairs of headlights appeared on the
*caliche* road just as the sun began to show itself behind the craggy
peaks that marked the eastern horizon.

I had been waiting outside in the cool morning, leaning on a
post and recalling how much I hated waiting. Ask anybody who
has ever been in a combat situation and they'll say the same. Too
much time to think was not a good thing when you were psyched
and ready to rock, and I had often seen deals like this go from
squirrelly to full-blown batshit back when I was in-country. I had
been thumbing the safety on the .45 in my hand, listening to the
metallic click and trying my best to keep my mind calm and clear,
when I first caught sight of the approaching vehicles.

"Somebody's coming," I called into the house.

A moment later, Sonny Limon and Eddie joined me on the front
patio.

"Looks like a Range Rover and a Jeep," I said. "Those belong to
Miguel?"

Both Eddie and I looked at Limon, who was nodding his head.
"Yeah. They're Miguel's."

"Please be sure Yolanda stays in her room until I come to get her," Eddie told Limon.

"She knows," he said.

We watched them come, much like I had done only a few hours earlier when it had been Sonny Limon, only this time I didn't have my fingers on the trigger of a daisy chain of Claymores to give me the warm fuzzies. All I had was the pistol tucked into the back of my pants and an M16 an arm's reach away, propped up behind a potted palm. Eddie had been clear that he didn't want to start things off with an overt display of artillery in the hope that this might all go peaceably. I could only hope he knew what the fuck he was doing.

The cars skidded to a halt not far from where Limon's car had expelled its last breath, side-by-side in the middle of the driveway that fronted Eddie's house.

The two from the Jeep exited first. The driver was roughly the size of a refrigerator, and wore a wide leather holster with a revolver on one side and a bone-handled hunting knife affixed to the other. His hands were empty, but I had no doubt that he would show no hesitation in bringing either weapon to bear if it became necessary. The other guy was a wild-eyed cat who I estimated to be in his mid-twenties. He wore pointy Elvis sideburns and looked like he'd spent plenty of time with his face pressed into the powder. He held a nasty looking AK-47, and a pair of ammo-belts slung across his chest, Pancho Villa-style. I could see that it made him feel like a badass, but it was a colossally stupid thing to do. One stray piece of shrapnel hits that belt and the whole thing can go off like a string of Chinese firecrackers. Very ugly business that I had also witnessed before.

The two that emerged from the Range Rover were obviously Marco and Miguel Zamora. I had never seen either one up close, but could practically feel the electric energy that hummed around El Rey Miguel like a storm cloud. His arms hung casually at his sides, but his fingers tapped his thighs like he was jamming on piano with Coltrane and Miles. His brother, Marco, seemed wired up tight too, and eyeballed Limon, Eddie and me like he was skinning us alive.

"Don Eduardo," Miguel said pleasantly.

"Miguel," Eddie answered.

"And Senor Limon," Zamora's voice was freighted with sarcasm. "So good of you to take such an interest in my wife's health. *Muchas gracias.*"

Limon was standing off to my right, and slightly behind me. It was easy to see he was not digging this scene at all. Neither was I, and it felt like something was about to explode.

Zamora's eyes skimmed over my face, but he made no comment. Instead he made a show of studying his watch, then turned his gaze on Eddie. "Well," he said. "I need to be getting back. I would appreciate it if you would bring Yolanda to me."

"La Plaza has asked that I speak with you, Miguel."

Miguel's studied calm deserted him, if only for a moment. The muscles of his jaws tensed involuntarily. "I don't know what you are referring to."

"Let us not be obtuse," Eddie said.

It was clear to me that both Miguel and Marco had been completely unaware of any direct connection between Eduardo Chacon and La Plaza, and the revelation had them seriously rattled.

"Why would La Plaza speak with you?"

"They have expressed serious concerns regarding the Colombian matter."

"It has been taken care of."

"I believe they wish to do things differently," Eddie said slowly. "Your contact from Bogota is due in soon, is he not?"

Miguel licked his lips, and cast a sideways glance toward his brother.

"La Plaza agrees with me that you and Marco should accompany this man back to Colombia and straighten the situation out in person," Eddie finished.

Miguel made a dry sound in his throat that was meant to be a laugh. "That is not for La Plaza to decide."

"I believe," Eddie said, "that they have already made some decisions of their own."

"They would do no such thing without consulting me."

Eddie shook his head. "The man who controls the diamonds, controls the Colombians, no?"

If I thought I didn't understand what the hell was happening before, this mention of diamonds had me completely baffled. My eyes flicked from Miguel to Eddie and back again.

"You can't," Miguel said. "It is impossible."

Without warning, the revolver appeared in the big man's hand, and was leveled across the short distance and directly at the face of Eduardo Chacon. A half-second later, I had my .45 leveled on the big man, and Limon was locked onto the young Pancho Villa with his. The metal-on-metal rasp of hammers being thumbed broke the silence.

Eddie, Marco and Miguel remained empty-handed, staring at one another at the periphery of the sudden standoff. I felt a distinct premonition that this was about to bust out, and bust out fast.

"Listen carefully, Miguel," Eddie said evenly. "What do you hear?"

Surprisingly, Miguel did as Eddie had suggested and cocked an ear to the sky. "Nothing."

"In a few moments you will hear the sound of a helicopter," Eddie said. "It will be directing the actions of a cadre of General Acosta's troops."

"That makes no sense," Miguel stammered.

"They will be seizing control of Rancho Tronada."

The color drained from Miguel's face and he looked as though he might fall to the ground like a puppet whose strings had been severed. "You're lying."

Eddie shrugged. "It is as I said: the man who controls the diamonds controls the Colombians. And La Plaza as well."

Miguel did not hesitate.

"Shoot him," Miguel spat.

I hadn't moved my sights from the big bodyguard's forehead during the entire exchange, knowing that when the shit came down, it wasn't going to last long.

I was right.

I feinted to my left for the meager cover of the patio's railing and tapped twice on the .45 without hesitation, without a second thought, and opened a hole in the big Mexican's forehead just above his right eye. If he had been using an automatic, his reflex shot might have taken Eddie out. Instead, he fell backward with his unfired revolver still tucked into his fist.

I spun to my left and drew down on the wild-eyed kid, who had been caught completely off-guard. My first shot went wide, and sent him skittering on his hands and knees to a defensive position behind the Range Rover.

I crouched behind the railing, dropped my pistol and took up the M16. I thumbed the selector to auto.

Even before I heard the sound, I watched the side of Miguel's face explode in pink mist. A pair of shots from somewhere behind me had taken him in the hollow below his cheek, exiting through his ear and taking a chunk of his jaw with them. He lay writhing on the ground, clutching his head as the morning erupted in gunfire.

I brought the rifle to my shoulder and tapped three shots into Miguel's brother as he made a reach for the pistol in his waistband. He was fast, but I was faster. I couldn't tell where I had hit him, but saw him spin sideways as he dropped. To my right, I saw the muzzle flashes of Limon's .45 unload again in the direction of Miguel as he squirmed in the dirt.

I ducked back behind the railing and waited for the smoke to clear. It was difficult to see who was moving and who wasn't, which was when these things could really turn into an ass-puckering slice of anarchy. I leaned my head around the corner and caught a glimpse of young Pancho Villa attempting to drag Marco behind the Range Rover. He took a one-handed shot at Eddie, but it went high and ricocheted off the roof tiles. Eddie dropped to the deck and inched his way toward the doorway.

Still on my haunches, I crab-crawled sideways to where I had laid out the Claymore triggers, and waited until Marco and the kid were in range.

There was an unnerving second of nothingness as I triggered the Claymore, and I thought the fucking thing had malfunctioned. I was rewarded a moment later with a superheated *whump* followed by three explosions in rapid succession. The shrapnel drilled through Marco and blasted the Rover with a pattern of holes, but at least one piece had done what I'd expected and caught wild-eyed Elvis square in the ammo-belts. By the time the shells had cooked off, all that was left were a pair of smoking boots and a viscous red puddle of meat and blood.

By comparison, Marco had gone out easy, but there wouldn't be an open casket for him, either.

Then it went quiet, except for the sound of Miguel's agonized mewling.

Gray smoke floated in the air, and in the distance, the throp of a chopper's rotor blades came into my sphere of awareness.

Yolanda Zamora stepped across the threshold and onto the patio. She looked at Sonny Limon, gently took the pistol from his hand and walked in the direction of her fallen husband. Her face held no expression as she stood over him, though her eyes were lit from within like tiny flames. Miguel tried to speak, but his jaw was unhinged and hung at an ugly angle. She watched him for several seconds before, without a word, she leveled the barrel at his manhood and fired until the clip was spent and the hammer landed with the dull click of an empty chamber. Yolanda Zamora dropped the gun on his chest, turned and walked back into the house.

# CHAPTER 36

Miguel Zamora died slowly.

The sound that filled his ears as he bled out into the dust and gravel was that of small arms fire that pocked and rattled across the distance that separated Rancho Tronada and that which belonged to Eduardo Chacon.

It didn't last long.

All faded into silence within half an hour when the last of El Rey Miguel's men had either been killed in his service or laid down his weapon and surrendered to the soldiers controlled by La Plaza.

Eddie had curled himself into a safe place behind a heavy stone planter during the final seconds of our shootout. He was breathing heavily as I knelt beside him and placed a hand on his shoulder. I could read the signs of exertion in his face.

"I know that you had your moments of doubt," he told me. "But I appreciate that you chose to stand beside me."

I had nothing to say, only nodded my assent.

"They are dead?" he asked. Eddie's eyes roved the bloody scene.

"Yeah, Eddie," I answered this time. "They're dead."

We turned our heads and watched Sonny Limon walk slowly back into the house.

"I owe you an apology," Eddie said as he looked back to me. "This did not have to happen."

"You don't owe me anything."

"There are those who believe that inside every man lies a killer. I do not. I have seen them, and you are not a killer."

"You needed help and I'm glad I was here to do it."

I took hold of Eddie's arm and helped him to his feet. He wasn't disturbed or shaken as I might have expected. Instead he simply seemed . . . sad. He gazed past my shoulder then, and I followed the object of his attention as he took in the sight of the broken bodies strewn across his driveway.

"Should we expect any more of Miguel's men?" I asked.

"I do not think so. There is no more gunfire coming from his ranch. He is finished."

The air was still and heavy with the burnt chemical smell of a firefight. I stepped down the stairs and into the pale morning sun, intending to collect the dead men's weapons and cover their bodies.

"Leave it," Eddie said. "I am sure we are due for a visit from the men of La Plaza. Let them deal with this."

I was reminded yet again that the gap between winning and losing is the widest gap there is.

○━━◆━━○

YOLANDA ZAMORA was nearly catatonic.

She had drawn herself into a ball, wrapped her arms tightly about her knees and tucked her feet securely into the corner of Eddie's couch. Yolanda's face was void of emotion, and her eyes seemed focused on something in a distance that no one else could see. Sonny Limon was seated beside her, his arms around her, holding her gently. Sonny looked at us as Eddie and I came into the house, but said nothing. The room grew smaller every moment we stood there.

"It is probably best that we leave them alone, for now." Eddie took my arm and guided me to the back of the house. He unlocked the dead bolts to his gun room, and we passed inside. He left the door open as we took our places in two small chairs in a corner of the room. "Besides, you deserve some answers."

○━━◆━━○

"THIS IS NOT finished yet," Eddie began. "There is business with Bogota that remains to be settled, but it is not your fight."

"I'm here to back you up."

He shook his head. "This is a matter that can only be settled by the men of La Plaza and myself."

I waited for more, but his eyes had drifted away. "I don't under-stand," I said.

"You heard me mention diamonds earlier?"

I told him I had.

"And we spoke about my having once fought in the Belgian Congo."

"Eddie, I—"

"Please give me a moment." Eddie held up his hand. "From the outset of Miguel's relationship with the Colombians, he discovered that one of the most difficult and complicated aspects of their business together involved the transfer of large amounts of cash."

I was familiar with the problem, but likely never in the volumes that Eddie was talking about. I nodded, but kept my mouth shut.

"It is very bulky, and quite heavy," he continued.

I knew from my own business dealings that brand new currency weighs considerably less than used bills, and can be packed a hell of a lot more efficiently.

"Skin oils, soot and grime add much more weight and bulk than you might imagine. A quarter of a million dollars in used fifties weighs almost thirteen pounds."

I kept my mouth shut as he stood and began pacing the room.

"Yolanda's father—my friend, Francisco—is a banker," Eddie said. "Miguel went to him with this problem and asked that he help pro-vide Miguel with clean bills. Francisco wanted no part of it, and Miguel immediately responded by threatening Yolanda with harm if he did not comply."

"A hostage."

"Exactly," Eddie sighed. "So I took it upon myself to develop an alternative that I had hoped would extract both Francisco and Yolanda from the process. And, if I am going to be completely truthful, I intended to make a profit in the transaction and leverage my position with the members of La Plaza."

"Diamonds."

"Yes," he said. "Raw diamonds."

"The safe," I said, apropos of nothing.

He ignored my interruption. "The Irish mercenaries I fought beside in Africa were also very active in the revolution taking place in their own country. They developed a pipeline to smuggle illicit, uncut and unregistered stones out of the Congo to finance the IRA's activities."

"They needed a way to convert the diamonds back into currency," I observed.

"It was a perfect match," Eddie agreed. "I would travel to Mexico City with Miguel's cash and exchange it for uncut diamonds. I would take a small percentage, and Miguel had a new medium of transfer. Much simpler to transport, and much more difficult to trace."

And easier to skim, I thought to myself. No wonder everybody involved was so fond of the deal.

"The Colombians appreciated it," he said. "And so did La Plaza."

I bet they did. "So, what went wrong?"

"Miguel got greedy and, we believe, stole a load of Colombian cocaine."

"How the hell do you do that?"

"We are not exactly certain, which is why La Plaza raided Miguel's *rancho*. We are hoping that someone among his men will know where it is hidden."

"Then what?"

"I will advocate that we return it and dissolve La Plaza."

It was my turn to lose myself in thought. It was a lot to process. "Why would La Plaza ever agree to disband? They're making a fucking fortune," I said.

"It is as I tried to explain to Miguel." Eddie showed me a tired smile that seemed to accentuate his age. "The man who controls the flow of diamonds controls both the Colombians and La Plaza."

"But they can just continue on as before, using currency instead."

"And they probably will," Eddie agreed. "But they will have to do so without me."

"They'll kill you."

"Never. I am 'El Brujo' and the people of El Salto would never stand for it. Besides, I am old, and time is on their side. I am sure the Colombians would much prefer to set up a new *padrino* in some other part of Mexico and begin again. Their trust here has been broken."

"You're going to need somebody to have your back."

"No," he said, as he crossed the room and opened the safe. I watched as he knelt and examined the contents, then came back to me with a parcel in his hand. It was about the size of a shoebox, and wrapped with brown paper and twine. "This is for you," he said, and placed it in my hands.

"What is it?" I asked dumbly.

If I had to guess, I'd say it weighed about thirteen pounds.

"Freedom," he smiled. "You have always been a friend to me, but I must insist that you go now and never come back."

"You gotta be—"

"You need to go *now*," he repeated firmly. "Before La Plaza comes to see what has happened here. No one knows you here, and there is no need that they should. Please, take my truck and leave immediately."

I was about to say something more, but I saw Eddie's ears perk as the radio in the adjacent room squealed to life. He moved quickly to answer the call.

I remained in my chair, eavesdropping on a brief conversation in rapid Spanish. I caught only snippets that made no sense to me.

He returned a few moments later, and urged me to follow him outside to the front of his house.

⚓

"WATCH," HE SAID, and pointed across the weed-strewn arroyo.

The words had barely crossed his lips when I heard the distinctive sound of rotor blades rising out of the silence.

"This can't be good," I said. My most recent encounter with government choppers was still fresh in my mind.

"Do not worry," Eddie said.

The driveway before us was still littered with bodies, and I couldn't see where the arrival of a helicopter could yield anything other than a king-hell bummer. My line of work wasn't one of those things where you take a bullet and a couple of guys with suits and neat haircuts show up at your door and apologize to your family.

The chopper came into view, and I could see it was painted military green, but had been stripped of door guns or other weaponry. Back in 'Nam we would have referred to it as a "slick." It began to make slow circles over the general location of my trailer. I looked at Eddie with grave concern, which he studiously ignored. The slick hovered for a few seconds more, then touched down behind a rise that obscured our view.

For nearly a full minute, my eyes remained fixed on the empty sky when the relative stillness was suddenly cleaved by the *crump* of an explosion, followed by an enormous blossom of fire and black smoke.

"Holy shit," I said. "What the fuck was that?"

"Dario Cruz, the First Assistant to the Regional Governor," Eddie answered. "I am sorry for the damage to your trailer. It was wrong of me to destroy it without your consent, but there was no time."

"Seriously, Eddie," I said. "What the hell?"

"That was Senor Cruz on the radio just now. I suggested that he may want to search a trailer that had recently appeared on my property; that perhaps Miguel was using it to hide his cocaine."

"You sent this Cruz guy in on purpose?"

"He was a petty and devious little man. La Plaza will be better off without him," he said. "I will likely stand a better chance of survival without him, as well." He wrapped me in a strong *embrazo*. "Now, go, and do not come back."

"Eddie, listen—"

"I will always be grateful for having known you. Now, give me your promise you will never come back."

I looked at his face, and his expression left no room for me to doubt either his sincerity or seriousness. And I gave him my promise.

Los Endos:

# Pensamiento

Present Day

# CHAPTER 37

True to my word to Eddie, I never returned to Mexico, nor did I ever again deal weed or anything else of a mind-altering nature.

I took the cash and uncut stones he had given me and flew from Mexico City to Tahiti, then on to Rarotonga in the Cook Islands, a tiny cluster of palm-blanketed rocks in a forgotten backwater of the south Pacific. Two great things about Rarotonga in the mid-seventies: no extradition, and one of the world's most progressive and imaginative havens for the protection of one's assets. Not to mention, it's one of the most laid-back and spectacularly beautiful islands on the planet.

When you're on the run, what you don't want to be is in a hurry. If you're not in a hurry, a lot of good things can happen. Investments grow, memories fade, past indiscretions are forgotten. And people die. Another good thing happens, too. You can forge a completely new identity. But this takes time, and most people who find themselves on the run don't have the luxury of time.

I did.

I celebrated New Year's 1977 in a Rarotonga beachfront bar looking out across a tropical lagoon the color of turquoise and jade, and water so clear you could count the sea turtles from your barstool. I spent the next ten years watching the clock and waiting for the statutes of limitations to run out on my U.S. offenses.

So I used my time to catch up on my reading, and I watched the world change through my perusal of a New Zealand newspaper that arrived in my mailbox like clockwork, about two weeks after the date on the masthead. And change it did.

I read with interest as the cocaine business and the terror and violence that are its constant companions redefined the American lifestyle. I could have told you it was coming.

I had bugged-out of Mexico at the end of America's bicentennial. That same year, the city of Miami, Florida, investigated 104 murders.

At 2:28 P.M. Eastern Time on July 11, 1979, the first shots were fired in what would later become known as the Cocaine Wars. Two men were gunned down in an indiscriminate spray of automatic rifle fire inside a liquor store at the Dadeland Mall in Miami.

Two short years later, in 1981, there were 621 murders in that city alone. At one point in the early '80s, an entire Miami police academy class either went to jail or died due to their involvement with the Colombian cartels.

By 1984, yuppies from coast to coast were rushing home from work to catch the newest episode of *Miami Vice*, so they could vicariously participate in the whole fucking scene.

But the fun didn't stop there. Even the long-awaited—by me at least—death of disco did nothing to blunt the world's demand for blow. On the Mexican side of the border, business went on and on and on. So successfully, in fact, that in 2009 a major American business magazine included the fugitive *padrino* of Mexico's largest coke syndicate in its annual list of billionaires. In a turf war that claimed 6,000 Mexican lives in one year alone, the *padrino* had amassed a fortune estimated to exceed $12 billion. That's billion with a 'b.'

Colt Freeland and I, like a lot of other folks, had carved out a peaceful little enterprise in the forests of northern California, and it broke my heart every time I read another installment of the havoc that was being wreaked on the streets of both of the countries I had fled. I'd be lying if I told you that I didn't suffer intense bouts of homesickness as I waited out my self-imposed exile.

I knew that my patience was not only necessary for my survival, but that it would eventually garner its own rewards. I spent my time slowly and systematically converting my diamonds to cash, then placing the money into an Asset Protection Trust that would ensure the security of a retirement fund for both my mom and me. I consoled myself with the knowledge that by the time I was ready to leave these islands, I would have built myself a nifty little nest egg.

My other occupation involved the development of that spanking new identity I mentioned before. I have to admit it was easier back in those days. But still, I give myself a little credit for patience and ingenuity. It all paid off. My new handle is Snyder, a name I've grown attached to. The last one I hope to ever need.

In the off hours between managing my funds and self-reinvention, I engaged in another hobby that always brought a smile to my face. Once a month, I sent a postcard to that shitweasel Ricky Montrose, in care of Chino State Prison. The photo on the front would always depict a peaceful tropical sunset, an uninhabited, white sandy beach lined with coco palms, or the slender and graceful bodies of topless Polynesian girls. I had learned that Montrose was working off a twenty-year jolt, and I enjoyed messing with his head for ratting me out. Asshole.

I never signed the cards, and only wrote six words on the back, no return address, of course: *Pensamiento, chingadera. Tiene un dia buena.* Thinking of you, motherfucker. Have a nice day.

I never did like that guy.

His little girlfriend, Skye Dayton, made it to L.A. by the way.

She even ended up in the film industry, though probably not the end of the industry she originally had in mind. She died in 1994 from an unidentified infection she acquired in the practice of her craft. Acting can be a tough profession.

⊙═══╳═══⊙

AS FOR THAT poor sonofabitch who got himself murdered back in Bahia de los Mestengos. Turns out he really had been a drug-runner. The two sleazebags who rolled me had been sent down to kill him. Which, apparently, they did. I suppose I got off lucky only having my cash ripped off, but there's a distinct possibility that it owed to the fact that I had fought back hard—even as drunk as I was—leaving one with a busted arm and a nasty concussion, and the other with the use of only one eye. I'm not a big believer in coincidence, but there is such a thing as very, very bad timing.

⊙═══╳═══⊙

ONE OF MIGUEL Zamora's *pistoleros* caved in to the ministrations of La Plaza and copped to the whereabouts of the Colombian cocaine. Eddie "El Brujo" Chacon oversaw its return, then took his own advice, dismantled La Plaza, and retired from the business. He used the remaining diamonds and cash to finance the cattle business that Sonny Limon ran for him on the property that had once been known as Rancho Tronada. He proved to be both an adept businessman and a loyal protector of Yolanda Zamora. Five years later, Yolanda's father, Francisco, gave his blessing for her marriage to Sonny Limon and moved into the *casita* formerly occupied by Marco Zamora, where he spent his final contented years.

Eddie Chacon still enjoys his weekly trips into town for Market Day, though he requires a driver due to his failing eyesight. But a man such as Eddie doesn't need to see in order to understand the nature and value of his life. Nor do the citizens of El Salto. I suspect he will live for as long as he chooses.

Following the breakup of La Plaza, the Peacock—Comandante Rivera—was arrested. He was assassinated in prison within a month. General Diego "The Pig" Acosta, on the other hand, saw the writing on the wall and took his retirement. He spent the next dozen years holding court in his private club before dying at home in bed, after a particularly vigorous encounter with a very expensive dominatrix.

The disappearance of Steve Devlin and Sonny Limon was vigorously investigated, though no evidence of violence or foul play—beyond the unsolved break-in at Devlin's home—was ever uncovered. No charges were brought and the case was dropped. A year later, the Border Area Patrol Group was officially scrubbed.

◦━✦━◦

COLT FREELAND spent a few years up in Canada, laying low.

Once back in the States, he sold his aircraft business in Humboldt and returned home to Texas. He has a wife and two beautiful kids, and used his half of the money we made to purchase a chain of auto dealerships with his newly acquired name emblazoned in lights up there on the sign. He joined the Elks and the Rotary, coached three championship seasons of Little League, and proudly sat through two graduations at the University of Texas in Austin. He is awaiting the birth of his first grandchild.

❦

THESE DAYS, I spend my time in the small, respectable saloon I own in Hawaii where I tend bar, have a handful of trusted friends, and mind my own business. And, as far as I know, not one of them knows my past. Not one. *Nada*. And to tell you the truth, I don't think any one of them would ever dream of asking me about it. That's the way it is in the islands. That's the way I like it.

❦

SO MAYBE IT wasn't the war *on* drugs that so significantly changed our lives. Rather, it was the war *over* drugs. Either way, I'm not sure it matters. I only know that we skipped out in the nick of time, and that Colt and I were among the few who didn't go down as casualties.

I still have the lucky rabbit Colt whittled for me all those years ago. It sits beside my cash register, encased in a little glass box. I think of those days every time I lay eyes on it. We keep in touch through the Christmas cards we swap every year and keep promising to visit each other when we get some free time.

One of these days we'll make it happen.

CPSIA information can be obtained
at www.ICGtesting.com
Printed in the USA
FSHW010018011020
74337FS